THE RUMBLE MURDERS

Tom Knapp's house

Randall Road.

Ed's barn.

The Green

Ed's house.

Randall · Road

Dancey's house

Randall Green
and
"Hangman's Hill"

THE RUMBLE MURDERS

Henry Ware Eliot, Jr.

writing as

Mason Deal

COACHWHIP PUBLICATIONS
Greenville, Ohio

TO
T. G. E.
ACCESSORY
BEFORE THE FACT

The Rumble Murders, by Mason Deal (pseud., Henry Ware Eliot, Jr.)
© 2017 Coachwhip Publications
Introduction © 2017 Curtis Evans
Afterword © 2017 David Chinitz

Title published 1932
No claims made on public domain material.
Cover image: Chrysler Royal Rumble Seat Coupe (from advertisement)

CoachwhipBooks.com

ISBN 1-61646-405-4
ISBN-13 978-1-61646-405-9

CONTENTS

INTRODUCTION

Henry Ware Eliot, Jr. and Theresa Garrett Eliot

INTRODUCTION

Curtis Evans

THE ADVENTURES OF
THOMAS ELIOT'S OLDER BROTHER

Henry Ware Eliot, Jr. and The Rumble Murders (1932)

American entrepreneur and philanthropist Henry Ware Eliot, Sr. and his wife, Charlotte Champe Stearns, a former teacher as well as an amateur poet and volunteer social worker, both of old New England stock, had seven children, five daughters and two sons. One son, Thomas Stearns Eliot (1888-1965), achieved literary immortality as T. S. Eliot, distinguished author of essays, plays, and works of poetry, such as *The Waste Land* (1922), one of the landmark poems of the twentieth century. Less noted by literary critics is the fact that the great writer was also an immense fan of detective fiction, not only omnivorously reading it but going so far, during his years as editor of the lofty English literary journal *The Criterion* (1922-1939), as to craft his own set of rules for the composition of a unique, though not always intellectually respected, literary form.[1] It was, however, T. S. Eliot's older brother, Henry Ware Eliot, Jr. (1879-1947), who actually wrote a published detective novel: *The Rumble Murders* (1932). In a letter to his brother, Tom once self-effacingly admitted, "I am simply amazed

---

[1] For more on T. S. Eliot and his wide-ranging interest in detective fiction see Curtis Evans, "Murder in *The Criterion*: T. S. Eliot on Detective Fiction," in *Mysteries Unlocked: Essays in Honor of Douglas G. Greene* (Jefferson, NC: McFarland, 2014), 171-182 and David E. Chinitz, *T. S. Eliot and the Cultural Divide* (Chicago and London: The University of Chicago Press, 2003).

at any human mind being able to think out all those details. I am quite sure I could never write a detective story myself. . . ."[2] As Tom freely allowed, it was Henry who had the true mind for murder.

Henry Ware Eliot graduated from Harvard in 1902, a year after producing his first book, a collection of humorous light verse entitled *Harvard Celebrities*. After a year at Harvard Law School he left to pursue a career in printing, publishing, and advertising. From 1917 to 1929 he held a partnership in a Chicago advertising agency, but in the 1930s he found what has been called "his true calling" when he became a Research Fellow in Near Eastern Archaeology at the Peabody Museum, Harvard, where his principal work, published posthumously, was *Excavations in Mesopotamia and Western Iran: Sites of 4000-500 B. C.: Graphic Analysis* (1950). The book was deemed "a labor of love, of such magnitude as to be practically unique in the annals of archaeology. . . . a monument to [Eliot's] scholarship and devotion."[3] In its own more modest yet undeniably brainteasing way, Henry's *The Rumble Murders* is indicative of this same devotion to detail, as his impressed younger brother observed.

Like a popular contemporary American mystery writer, Carolyn Wells (1862-1942), Henry—physically slighter than Tom, who referred to his elder brother's "Fred Astaire figure"—suffered from deafness on account of his having been infected with scarlet fever as a child. "He acquired one of the earliest hearing aids," scholar William Harmon has noted, "a large ungainly box worn around the neck on a strap . . . but it permitted him to hear better and function socially." In 1926 Henry married Theresa Anne Garrett, an artist and illustrator from a socially prominent Louisville, Kentucky family. Having been devoted from his adolescent years to his brilliant younger brother, Henry as an adult gave Tom financial assistance after Tom settled in England, in addition

---

[2] Valerie Eliot and John Haffenden, eds., *The Letters of T. S. Eliot, Vol. 6: 1932-1933* (New Haven and London: Yale University Press, 2016), 230.

[3] Information on Henry Ware Eliot, Jr. in this paragraph and subsequent ones is partially drawn from the note on him accompanying the volumes in the ongoing series of volumes entitled *The Letters of T. S. Eliot,* (New Haven and London: Yale University Press), edited by Valerie Eliot and John Haffenden. See also Clyde F. Crews, "Scholar Finds Louisville Links of T. S. Eliot in Cave Hill Cemetery, *Louisville Courier-Journal*, 26 August 1984.

to advising him on investments. Henry accompanied his and Tom's mother on a trip to England to visit Tom in 1921, marking the first time that Henry left the United States, and with Theresa he honeymooned in Europe in 1926. A year later Tom declared that Henry's spirited native Kentuckian spouse had enlivened their "Puritanical New England family." People like Theresa "warmed us up," he chuckled, before repeating the phrase, which patently appealed to him, for emphasis.[4] Henry's vivacious wife may have inspired the winsome character of Jeanie Marsh, wife of one of the members of the moonlighting "homicide squad" in *The Rumble Murders* (and one of only two women characters of true significance in the novel).

The Rumble Murders won praise from American reviewers upon its 1932 publication by Houghton, Mifflin, with some of them indicating their awareness that the pseudonymous author, Mason Deal, was the brother of "one of the most top-hat literary figures in England," as bookshop owner and *Chicago Tribune* literary editor Fanny Butcher broadly hinted in her brightly written notice of the novel. An admirer and promoter of modern poetry, Fanny Butcher rarely reviewed detective fiction in her *Tribune* column, leaving such dross, in her view, to the *Tribune*'s mystery fiction critic; but she made an exception of *The Rumble Murders*, on account of the book having been written by T. S. Eliot's brother.[5]

In her review of *The Rumble Murders*, published under the heading "Critic Reads Just One Book for Pleasure," Butcher declared that Mason Deal's mystery was the first book that she had "read wantonly for pleasure for months." She amusingly expanded on this point, in

---

4 Crews, "Louisville Links"; William Harmon, "Eliots, Keatses and 'Keats' in Louisville, KY," *Time Present: The Newsletter of the T. S. Eliot Society* 62 (Summer 2007): 1-2; Valerie Eliot and John Haffenden, eds., *The Letters of T. S. Eliot, Vol. 3 1926-1927* (New Haven and London: Yale University Press, 2012), 246.

5 Celia Hiliard, "'Lady Midwest': Fanny Butcher—Books," in Huw Osborne, ed., *The Rise of the Modernist Bookshop: Books and the Commerce of Culture in the Twentieth Century* (Ashgate Studies in Publishing History: Manuscript, Print, Digital) (London and New York: Routledge, 2015), 96-97. After admitting her general lack of interest in mystery fiction, Butcher wryly explained, "I realize that the great are proverbial mystery fans, but I have never made any pretenses of greatness."

words that will surely strike a chord of recognition with any salaried book reviewer:

> It never occurs to most of you, I suppose, that a literary editor almost never can read a book with that lavish gesture of just being entertained.
>
> The galley slaves of old haven't much on us so far as keeping our knuckles tightened round the oars [of reading] is concerned. . . . We have to keep rowing, always conscious of the fact that no matter how hard we flex our muscles, or how fast we make the galley go on its way, we can never really do more than keep going. We can never really get ahead of the current.
>
> Books attack us in great waves, almost submerge us, and all we can is to cling bravely to our oars. With something over 5000 books published each year (in lean years) the poor literary editor—you can plainly see—never dares to read a book just because he wants to.

Happily, Butcher had finally been able to elude the scourge of the lash, so to speak, with *The Rumble Murders*, a novel that ordinarily would have gone to the *Tribune*'s mystery reviewer, Mortimer Quick, who "was all prepared to include it in his next charming and eupeptic discussion of the recent thrillers." "I snatched it from his fingers," Butcher triumphantly declared; and, having finished the book, she was glad that she had made the snatch, though she had no interest in detective fiction per se. Butcher had always suspected that the author, a "former Chicagoan" with "a very delicate and interesting sense of humor," was afflicted with shyness concerning "his own literary possibilities because Brother Tom had grown such a halo internationally"; but *The Rumble Murders* showed that the shyness of "Brother Henry" was manifestly unjustified, for the novel made clear that "if he wants to write, Brother Henry can do it without bringing anything but réclame to the family name."[6]

---

[6] Fanny Butcher, "Critic Reads Just One Book for Pleasure: She Is Curious About the Writing," *Chicago Daily Tribune*, 19 April 1932, 19.

Fanny Butcher aside, notices of *The Rumble Murders* tended to come from reviewers who actually read and enjoyed mystery novels *as mysteries*. The reviewer for the *Salt Lake Tribune*, though evidently unaware of the identity of "Mason Deal," found much of interest in the tale, which in the reviewer's judgment would earn the author a place within the charmed circle of mystery fan favorites:

> What with footsteps going up a concrete wall; a burglarized silo; a missing Colt 45; a barrel of excelsior; a lost family cemetery rediscovered; the queer cryptogram "Chain 10 join, 18 s. c. in ring, 2d row, 2 d. c. in each s. c.," and the baboon shooting the babyroussa [babirusa, or deer-pig, native to Indonesia], not to mention the two bodies crammed into the rumble seats of two cars, one driven into the lake—[The author] provides all the elements needful for a neat little puzzle.
>
> At least they supply plenty of thrills and excitement, and several "scoops" for the enterprising city editor of the Mirror and his associates, who term themselves the "homicide squad," the other three being a wealthy suburban resident and his guests, a writer of detective stories and a real detective, come "out of the west" for a vacation. The writer, George Gaynleigh, with his zest in the search for clues and his audacious intuitional deductions, and Hubert, of the sounder, unspectacular detective instincts, prove an able team, competent to solve such puzzlers as who dropped the gun in the "zoo," who drove the café-au-lait cabriolet, which left-handed lady owned the compact left in the ravine, and what about the canceled note signed by Abel and Jonas Beeson in 1867?[7]

As a detective novelist Henry Ware Eliot did indeed have a marvelous eye for material detail, something which, as we have seen, his brother, like the *Salt Lake Tribune* reviewer, had appreciatively observed.

---

[7] *The Salt Lake Tribune*, 29 May 1932, 31.

In his May 5, 1932 letter thanking Henry for sending him a copy of the novel, Tom lauded *The Rumble Murders*, though the now thoroughly Anglicized literary giant admitted that the novel's title had puzzled him until he discovered "that the rumble is the same thing as a dickey." (For those reading this introduction who are likewise puzzled, rumbles—or, to be more precise, rumble seats—were upholstered exterior seats which folded into the rear decks of two-seater, pre-World War II cars, making them excellent receptacles, as murderously enterprising Twenties and Thirties gangsters were well aware, for dead bodies.) Eliot went on to give his brother a short but insightful analysis of *The Rumble Murders*, the strengths of which he believed lay not only in its plotting but its social documentation:

> I read any detective story with enjoyment, but I think yours is a very good one; I am simply amazed at any human mind being able to think out all those details. I am quite sure that I could never write a detective story myself; my only possible resource for adding to my income would be to write children's verses or stories. . . . But apart from my astonishment at your skill in plot, I was especially interested by the book as a social document—I guessed that it was probably Winnetka [an affluent "village" sixteen miles north of downtown Chicago]. The picture of that society is extremely interesting to me; there is nothing like it in England. For one thing, you would never get that combination of wealth, crudity, and intellectual activity. "Country people," who form the stupidest, most intolerant, and most intolerable part of society in England, would never collect incunabula or mention Proust; intellectual activity, and interest in arts and letters, is found in isolated individuals all over the country, but otherwise is confined to a limited society, drawn from various natural classes, and most of the individuals composing which, I probably know. [8]

---

[8] Tom Eliot to Henry Eliot, 5 May 1932, in *Letters of T. S. Eliot, Vol. 6*, 230-31.

Henry was most grateful for his brother's encouraging words, parts of which he allowed Houghton, Mifflin to quote in publicity for *The Rumble Murders*. On May 15 he wrote his younger brother an appreciative reply:

> Your letter . . . with its praise of the Rumble Murders has cheered and heartened me immensely. . . . Houghton Mifflin were and seem still convinced that it is a good story, and a certain Unitarian minister in Brooklyn . . . wrote me an enthusiastic letter telling me how he kept his whole family up in the evening until he had finished reading it aloud. . . . I am writing another [detective] story . . . without this activity I should become melancholic. The writing of detective stories is a better "escape" than the reading of them.[9]

As in the case of some other promising neophyte mystery writers, however, Henry Ware Eliot's second detective novel seems never to

---

On real life uses of rumble seats for the dumping of the inconvenient bodies of murder victims, see, for example, these contemporary reports in the *New York Times*: "Two Gunmen Slain, Left In Parked Car: Blood Stains on Mudguard Lead to Finding of the Bodies Jammed in the Rumble Seat" (20 February 1932, 9) and "Ride Victim's Body Found in Parked Car: Man's Corpse Bound and Stuffed Into Rumble Seat of Auto Abandoned in Jersey," (11 December 1933, 29). Seven years after his letter to his brother T. S. Eliot in fact indeed produced a rather notable collection of children's verse, *Old Possum's Book of Practical Cats* (1939), which served as the basis for the hugely successful musical *Cats*, the fourth-longest-running Broadway show in history. Eliot's barbed assessment of English country people ("the stupidest, most intolerant, and most intolerable part of society in England") is interesting in light of Paul Grimstad's recent linkage, in an article in the *New Yorker*, of Eliot's love of "classic" detective fiction with "his sharp turn to the right politically" (see "What Makes Great Detective Fiction, According to T. S. Eliot," 2 February 2016). The distinctly unromantic view of the English countryside expressed by Eliot in those words written to his brother in 1932 seems at odds with the attitude embodied in fellow poet W. H. Auden's famous essay on detective fiction, "The Guilty Vicarage" (1948), wherein Auden avows, "I find it very difficult . . . to read [a detective story] that is not set in rural England."

[9] Henry Eliot to Tom Eliot, 5 May 1932, in *Letters of T. S. Eliot, Vol. 6*, 232.

have been published (possibly it was never actually completed), making the elder Eliot brother a one-hit wonder of sorts in mystery fiction, and one who sadly was long forgotten in that capacity. This new edition of *The Rumble Murders* not only pays due to an Eliot of accomplishment in his own right, but it gives modern readers a chance to enjoy a once almost hopelessly hard-to-find mystery from the Golden Age of detective fiction—one that is brimming with brio and humorous asides, such as that made after the detective novelist character, George Palmerston Gaynleigh ("The 'Palmerston' was silent, in so far as George could preserve silence on that painful infliction"), exhausted after a busy morning of amateur murder investigation, settles down "in a big chair to rest brain as well as body" with another staple of escapist genre fiction, the Western.

George clearly finds that the Western story makes rather fewer demands than the detective novel on the reader's reasoning capacity:

> The story was about Dick Warner. Dick was riding alone though a desert garnished sparingly with yucca, cholla, mesquite, chaparral, and like vegetation. He was talking to his horse, as all cowboys do, the horse having almost human intelligence as well as marvelous speed; from which conversation the reader might gather that Dick was going from somewhere to somewhere, because he was "wanted" (unjustly, it seemed) somewhere else. Dick hired himself out to a wealthy ranchman who needed a foreman in a hurry and got the impression that Dick was a bad hombre. The ranchman had a beautiful daughter, and as Dick could talk pure schoolbook English as well as cowboy, he made her acquaintance. She snubbed him terrifically on every possible occasion, however, especially after he had saved her from a grizzly bear, a prairie fire, and bandits in rapid succession. (The bandits, it appeared, were hired by a neighboring ranch-owner who had the most fell designs on the heroine, but whose conscience for some reason demanded a forced marriage ceremony.) The heroine's father, too, was mixed up in some kind of dirty work which George

could not fathom, including rustling his own cattle and sneaking about cutting his own fences at night. George reached a point where there was so much smoke, dust, shooting, and running about that he could not make out what was happening, and had about decided to pass it up, when the telephone bell rang.[10]

Join the book's high-spirited "homicide squad" of George Gaynleigh and his inquisitive friends Ed Marsh, Gil Hubert and Mike Macy as they attempt to solve the baffling mystery of the rumble murders. Can you beat these bright boys around the track?

---

[10] George has published two detective novels, *The Sheaghan Shillelah* and *The Murder at the Microphone*, but at his friend Ed Marsh's converted barn guest house he is currently working, during spare moments from the murder investigation, on a "highbrow" novel: "a curious medley of influences, chiefly Sinclair Lewis, Aldous Huxley, and Wyndham Lewis (the polemical one)," in which rather than "satirizing the babbittry or the booboisie" he has "undertaken the far more difficult task of satirizing the intelligentsia." George yearns to emancipate the world from "mass psychology," which he deems "as potent (and as patent) among the admirers of Cezanne and Satie as the devotees of Amos and Andy." In these reflections of the author on elite and mass culture, one hears echoes of his famous brother. (See the afterword by David Chinitz.)

THE RUMBLE MURDERS

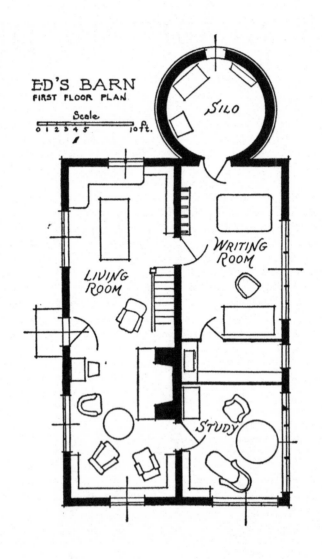

ED'S BARN
FIRST FLOOR PLAN

Scale
0 1 2 3 4 5   10 ft.

SILO

WRITING
ROOM

LIVING
ROOM

STUDY

I

ED'S BARN

About four o'clock on the afternoon of Wednesday, October 31, might have been, and in truth was, seen, alighting from the train at a flourishing suburb, a slight, deceptively boyish figure staggering under two bags. It was seen by three taxicab-drivers, simultaneously, the most active of whom leapt quickly from his car and attempted to wrest the bags from their owner's grasp.

The larger bag, a huge cheap suitcase, contained a portable typewriter, a large quantity of unpublished manuscript, and an odd miscellany of cherished books indicating a catholic and inquiring taste with no conceivable objective. The smaller bag, of the inconvenient but once popular type known as a kitbag, contained clothing. Both bags were pied with foreign hotel labels, the gay colors much dimmed with age and use. The initials, still visible on one bag, were G. P. G., standing, if anyone should ask, for George Palmerston Gaynleigh. The 'Palmerston' was silent, in so far as George could preserve silence on that painful infliction.

"Wait a minute, now," expostulated George, who had intended to escape. "How far is it to Mr. Ed Marsh's house?"

"Randall Green?" asked the driver. "Fifty cents. It's up the hill."

"Up the hill," sighed George. "All right. Fifty cents. No tip. Ten cents is only a tip to you, but it has bought me many a meal."

"'S all right with me," said the taxi-driver. "If you're a friend of Ed's, and broke, it won't cost you nothing. How's that?" He made the horrible explosive noises with his car which to taxi-drivers mean "Let's go!"

"Not so bad as that," said George, thumping heavily into the seat. "You a friend of Ed's?"

"Oh, everybody calls him Ed," said the driver, sensing George's skepticism. "He was president of the village for God knows how long. He started this town; o' course there was a town here before he come, but it wasn't no suburb then. Him and Knapp and Dobert and others that live in the Green formed a syndicate and bought the old Beeson place, the whole hill. Used to be called Beesonville, 'stead o' Westwood. Mostly woods then. Wait till you see the Green!"

"I know all about the syndicate," replied George, who was more intent on his course than the conversation. "You passed a red light just then."

"That's only a caution light," said the driver, making a swift left turn which took them at once out of the region of drugstores and cash-and-carry groceries onto a new concrete road. Two more turns, right and left, and the car shot up a short hill and turned, right, between two stone cairns or rustic pillars into what appeared to George at first to be a fine old campus of some small but historic college. Around a green-sward from which sprang stately elms the road made an irregular oval. Around the oval at discreet intervals stood prosperous-looking houses in the best Colonial tradition. The taxi entered a private drive, passed a fine old house of yellowed granite, and stopped at a barn built of the same material.

"Hot dog!" exclaimed George. "Is this Ed's house?"

"You goin' to the barn, ain't you?" asked the chauffeur.

"Might as well," said George, "and dump my bags. All right. Fifty cents. About twenty cents' worth, New York rates."

"Oh, yeah," replied the driver loftily. "But the trip 'ud take you five times as long in that burg." He spun his car around dexterously with a great snort and was off in a cloud of blue smoke.

George carefully counted his remaining cash. Three dollars and fifteen cents. Ed's invitation had come in the nick of time. George had been living with a devoted sister and an amiable brother-in-law who lived an hour's ride from the Grand Central Station, New York; but they were moving into their city apartment for the winter. Ed's offer was unlimited. Ed had spent a lot of money fixing up his barn. What for? everybody asked. For guests; Ed was in dire need of guests; the barn was his hobby, and he had to justify it. Would George accept a position as guest? That, reflected George, was the best trick he knew.

Why, continued George, as he looked at his surroundings, had it never occurred to him to pick out a wooded hill, borrow ten thousand dollars, induce a few friends to put in the same, and start a suburb? Why could he never pick an idea out of the air that was profitable instead of merely provocative, as most of his ideas were?

George lit a cigarette, and surveyed the scene. The rear of Ed's lot was bounded by an old stone wall; stone must have been cheap when this house was built, thought George; quarried near by, no doubt. Abruptly, beyond the stone wall, the ground descended into a gully or ravine, a wild thicket of brush and second-growth timber. Across the ravine was a small hill, partly bare cliff, partly thickly wooded. To right and left of it the view extended to the far horizon; the hills sprang from a flat and fertile plain of good farmland. To the extreme right—to the south must be the topless towers of Dynamopolis, twenty miles away, under a low pall of smoke; but a neighbor's house intercepted that view. George walked to the stone wall.

As he did so he observed two men apparently similarly enjoying the view. One was seated on the wall, facing George; the other, standing with his back to George, quickly turned around. Guests of Ed's, George surmised. He approached them as became one having the same status.

"Gaynleigh is my name," said George directly. "I'm a guest of Ed Marsh, just arrived. You are, too, I suppose?"

The seated man rose and extended his hand pleasantly. "Klarsen's mine," he said. "But I'm a guest of Mr. Crivington, here."

"I live across the Green," said Crivington stiffly, having made no motion to shake hands. George took in both men like a flash. Who says thought is not faster than speech? George's Proustian appraisal, which took no longer than a decent pause in the conversation, was somewhat as follows.

Crivington, thought George, is a young man on the make—what were the words of W. S. Gilbert?

> "A commonplace type young man,
>   A stick and a pipe young man—"

Slim, brisk, good-looking, slightly domineering, successful—no doubt about that. About George's age—the middle thirties; George had known others of the type, in college and in clubs; they always knew the right people, married the right girl, skillfully interwove business and social opportunity.

The other chap, though! What a man! Clean-shaven, straight-haired, aquiline, Nordic; a big fellow, but lithe as a panther. As pretty a lad, a recruiting sergeant or football scout would have said, as he ever clapped eye on. A natural athlete, judging by the clean set of his shoulders and his easy, lounging stride; and, by his steady blue eye and winning smile, a born handler of men. A man's man, all over; the sort who would be baffled by the simplest woman. If any college had ever set its impress on him, it was obliterated in the larger personality of the man.

George was wondering whether Klarsen was a polar explorer or a captain of Marines, when Crivington put in his word.

"How do you like Westwood?" he asked.

"Beautiful!" exclaimed George enthusiastically, turning to the view. "It's fascinating. This fine old campus in front here, with all you extremely urban people living around it, and then this wild mountain fastness right in your back yard, so to speak. Delightfully incongruous. Nature is the only artist nowadays who dares to be romantic and bombastic."

George, I must explain, appreciates as a writer that conversation which sounds clever usually falls flat in print; but he has never fully realized the converse truth that ideas which may be admired in a book will hardly be suffered in conversation. Crivington looked as horrified as if George had uttered some abominable bolshevistic heresy.

"Did Mr. Marsh come with you?" asked Crivington. George noted the careful avoidance of mutual intimacy in the use of the 'Mr.'

"I haven't seen him yet," said George. "I was just going to see whether Jeanie was home."

"You're not a detective, I take it?" asked Crivington.

George's glance mingled surprise and amusement. "Do I look like a detective?" he asked.

"Pardon the question," said Crivington, smiling. "I believe Ed is bringing out a detective as guest—some chap he met out West. You don't know anything about that?"

"All Ed wrote me," said George, "was that I would share the barn with a Mr. Gil Hubert. He seemed to think that would be a unique and edifying experience. I suppose there's some catch in it."

"Well, Harold," said Crivington to his friend, "let's ramble on. I've just been showing Mr. Klarsen around the neighborhood," he explained to George. "Hope we'll see you again."

"Slight thaw," commented George to himself. "I take it that Mr. Crivington has a complex against detectives. Now, how do you get into this barn?"

George walked around to the west side of the barn, which presented more nearly the aspect of a house, having two large windows with geranium boxes, and a simple but pleasing doorway. He picked up his bags and carried them to the door, which he unlocked with a key that Ed had sent him.

George dumped his bags on the floor and looked around at a very comfortable living-room, extending the length of the barn. At one end was a big oak table and window-seats; at the other, a flock of hospitable easy-chairs; facing him a great stone fireplace. At the left of the fireplace stairs led up to bedrooms; to the left of the stairs and the right of the fireplace were doors into other rooms, one having the appearance of an office, the other of a study.

"A nifty den," was George's mental comment. "Ed must have cleaned up nicely on his real-estate venture."

George put his head into the doorway of the room at the left of the stairs. A flat-top desk, swivel chair, and table. This was the room in which Ed had said George could do his writing. Perfect! At the north end of the room was a door which appeared to lead outdoors. George tried the knob; the door was locked. As he did so, he heard a faint scraping sound which seemed to come from the other side. He paused and listened. But the next sounds he heard were from a different direction. He looked out of the window and saw that Ed had arrived in his car.

II

THE SILO

George stepped out on the drive and saw Ed just closing the doors of his garage, which occupied a sort of half-basement under the farther side of the stone barn—a place, as Ed told him later, formerly occupied by pigs and chickens. Ed was a six-footer, one of those men who appear, in street clothes, to be lean as a rail, but in the swimming-pool as full-muscled as a young prize-fighter. Competitive sports, for the most part, bored him; but Ed was a hardy sportsman and a genial camping companion.

With Ed was an elderly stranger, who might have been Buffalo Bill, George reflected, if his silvery hair had been longer; or William H. Taft, if his figure had been stouter. A man of about sixty-five, perhaps older, but sound as a dollar and seemingly equally nimble. Solidly built; a life of ease might have made him corpulent, but he was evidently a man who lived much in the open. A ruddy, genial face; mustache and slight imperial. A nice old chap, thought George; but a detective? No!

"Hey, George!" cried Ed, leaping to shake his hand. He snatched off George's hat. "Still got your hair, old-timer? Not so thick, not so thick; still you don't have to let your back hair grow long and use it for a toupee. George, this is my young friend Gil Hubert; Gil, this is my old friend George Gaynleigh. Gil, George, is the greatest detective in the world outside of pure fiction. George, Gil, is a writer—"

"Wait a minute!" cried George. "Why dig that up?"

"A writer of detective stories," continued Ed ruthlessly.

"Only spasmodically," pleaded George. "Very spasmodically, I might admit. I'm sure you've never read any of them, Mr. Hubert. Ed won't read them."

Hubert chuckled silently. "I read sea stories," he said. "Never detective stories, or Western stories. I suppose every one likes best what is remote from his own experience."

"Are you really a detective, Mr. Hubert?" asked George. "Or is that one of Ed's feeble jests?"

"I was one, at least," said Hubert. "I avoid it now as much as possible. It's a discouraging profession. Cleverness counts for little. The greatest detective, as one of my fellow detectives once remarked, is Mademoiselle Bonne Chance—'Lady Luck.'"

"Ah," said George, whose ear had caught a certain inflection. "You've been in France, perhaps?"

The detective shot a quick, keen glance at George.

"You have a good ear," he said. "I've been in France, yes; and other places; but only on business."

That little shrug was French, too, thought George; slight but unmistakable.

"Gil has come a long way over the alkali desert," said Ed to George, "and I know you always have an honest thirst, George. If you'll come inside I'll see what can be done about it."

Ed herded them into the barn and they sat down, at the big oak table. Ed produced a bottle of Bourbon and spun the glasses on the table like an old-time bartender. Hubert took very little, but took it straight without a wink. He looked around the room with interest.

"Nice place you've got, Ed," he said. "About the size of my hut. You've got steam heat, though. I depend on wood fires, but I have all the wood I want for the cutting, and that's good exercise."

"Where is your place?" asked George.

"Amelia, South Dakota," said Hubert, with a twinkle in his eye. "I built most of the house myself, so you can judge."

"How do you like my fireplace?" asked Ed. "Needs a good pair of moose antlers over it. I'm counting on you to help me get them sometime."

"That's easy," said Hubert. "The hard part is to get you out there."

"I asked you here first," retorted Ed.

"Tell me about this place," said Hubert. "Is this the barn that burned down?"

"Yes," said Ed. "I bought this house nearly ten years ago, with all its contents; it dates back to 1820 or so. I saved all the good stuff; got a few good antiques; put the rest in the barn. You never saw such a mess of old beds, bureaus, chairs, buggies, stoves, agricultural implements, and what not, as I had there. Well, while the house was being remodeled—Jeanie and I were away—the barn caught fire and all the stuff burned up. Saved me a lot of trouble getting rid of it. The walls stood, and I rebuilt it as you see. Couldn't waste a good stone building; it makes a good garage, and a hang-out to work in, or play in."

"I suppose this is local stone," ventured George. "From the hill across the ravine, maybe."

"No," said Ed. "The granite quarries were farther south. That across the ravine is a mica quarry. Thar's mica in them thar hills."

"Let's go out and look around," suggested Hubert. They strolled out on the drive.

"Mica," pondered George. "What is mica? What is it good for? I don't seem ever to have felt the need for it."

"I think they use it in telephones," said Ed. "It used to be used in stoves, to peek through and see how the fire's getting on. Isinglass, they called it. But I guess the mica business is flat. The quarry is very much abandoned. I wish the syndicate had bought that hill, though. I doubt if anyone could build on it, but at least we could keep the picnickers off. You see that dead tree there, sticking out of the cliff?"

"That one that looks like a hand?" asked George.

"Like a hand?" asked Ed. "How does it look like a hand?"

"Very like a hand," insisted George. "See that stump for a thumb? And the other bough, with four fingers? A hand, clutching at the air."

"Well, well," observed Ed. "That shows what a romantic imagination can do. What I was going to say was that I did have an old tin tray hung there once and we used the ravine as a rifle range. But we had to stop on account of the picnickers coming there Sundays."

"I think I see an old road going up the hill," said George.

"You do," said Ed, "and you can go up there if you like. And to tickle your Gothic fancy I'll inform you that that used to be called hereabouts 'Hangman's Rock.' But you'll get yourself very unpopular in Westwood if you call it that."

"'Hangman's Rock'!" exclaimed George. "How perfectly swell! Any town can have a Soldier's Monument, but few can boast a Hangman's Rock!"

Hubert had turned and was studying the barn.

"Is that a silo, Ed?" he asked.

Ed laughed. "It's a silo for books," he replied. "I just built that. It's got two stories and two windows—you can't see them from here, one faces north, one west. It's fireproof and thief-proof. I keep my rare books in it, manuscripts, autograph letters, and such."

"Ah, yes," said Hubert. "I remember your telling me about your collection. I want to see it."

"The silo looks rough now," said Ed, "but I shall have it stuccoed. Completes the rural effect; a white lie, so to speak, but a plausible one."

"How do you get into this silo?" asked Hubert.

"From what I call the office, inside," said Ed. "I'll show you when we go in again."

George had been peeking in the lower window of the silo and now appeared to be inspecting the wall closely.

"You don't see any cracks in the concrete, do you, George?" asked Ed anxiously.

"I was just wondering," said George, "how a man could walk up the side of a concrete wall."

"Hey?" asked Ed, peering over George's shoulder. George pointed to two spots on the wall, one at about the level of his eye, the other a couple of feet higher. Ed and Hubert stared at them. They had unmistakably the form of the human foot.

"Footprints on a perpendicular wall!" exclaimed Ed. "Swan to Guinea! I'd like to see the man that made them!"

"There are four footprints," said Hubert, glancing upward, "and they lead up into that open window. Painters been at work here, Ed?"

"Not since August. Is that paint?"

"It's mud," said Hubert, rubbing one of the spots with his finger. "Black earth, and fresh."

They stared at the spots. The lowest one was a smudge; then two clear ones, then another smudge, near the window.

"I'll get a ladder," said Ed. He dodged into the barn and returned at once with a short ladder. He set it against the wall and mounted it.

"They're footprints all right. He slipped a little here, but there are two plain outlines of feet." Ed climbed up two more rungs and peeked inside the window. Then he slammed the windows shut and descended the ladder.

"Any of your incunabula and encheiridia missing, Ed?" asked George.

"They're all missing," said Ed, "but for a very good reason. They're all at the Art Museum, in storage. I shall have to take them off their hands pretty soon, too. But I don't want to put them in the silo until it's jolly well dried out. That's why I left the upper window open."

"There's Ed for luck," said George. "But how the deuce did the man get up?"

"Where did you get that ladder, Ed?" asked Hubert.

"From inside the silo. The silo is always locked up. I keep this ladder inside the silo to get from the lower to the upper story temporarily. I'm having stairs made."

Hubert walked back a little way and stared at the top of the silo. Then he stepped to the driveway and scrutinized the ground closely.

"No chance for footprints on this gravel," he said. "But it's evident that someone has been here recently, bringing a rope, with which he scaled your silo. Is the ravine boggy?"

"At the bottom, yes," said Ed, "though it's been a fairly dry summer. You think he came from the ravine?"

"Well, there's no water hereabouts. And he was wearing moccasins, which were wet purposely, probably. Indian moccasins; not the store kind."

"Moccasins!" exclaimed George. "Shades of Fenimore Cooper!"

"I don't believe he was an Indian," said Hubert, smiling. "But these are moccasins; can't be anything else. I've followed many an Indian trail as a lad."

"What would he attach the rope to?" asked Ed.

"Well, you've got a nice round knob on top of your silo. In fact, I never saw a wall better adapted to scaling."

"Why the rope?" asked George. "Just to be bizarre?"

"No," said Hubert. "A ladder would be a rather conspicuous object to carry around and harder to remove quickly. This man is evidently one to whom scaling a wall is a simple trick. Looks as if he was raised west of the Mississippi. That rope-throwing lets out your local talent, I should think."

"That narrows the field down, I should say, to Fred Stone," suggested George. "Or Harold Lloyd, maybe."

"I suppose the fellow lassoed the knob," said Ed, "but how did he get it off again?"

"That's easy," said Hubert. "If I had a rope I could show you."

"Get a rope, Ed, for the love of Mike!" said George. "This is a real show!"

Ed dodged into the barn and came back with a coil of rope.

"I don't believe this is long enough," said Hubert, "to reach to the top of the silo. But I can demonstrate on something else."

"You don't get off that easy," said Ed. "I'll get you a rope if I have to drive to the village for it."

He ran into the house and returned with a clothesline. "If this isn't long enough, you can tie the two together," he suggested.

Hubert tied, not a noose, but a large bowline with a bight about six feet in diameter. He spun it around in the air like a fancy roper at a rodeo.

"Ed!" cried George excitedly, "I have here three dollars and fifteen cents, the same being my total assets, exclusive of uncollectible debts. This sum expresses my conviction that Mr. Hubert, rope champion of two continents, will have the rope around the knob on the first throw. Even money. Are you a sport?"

"You're on," said Ed. "I think you've got the soft end of the bet, but I'll not suffer your taunts."

Hubert whirled the rope, threw it, and it dropped gently over the knob like a living thing that obeys its master. The rope hung from the knob.

"Now, gentlemen," said Hubert, "if you wish to scale the wall, you may. I admit that I have no desire to do so, though there was a time when I could. It's not difficult."

Ed attempted it, but got no farther than the second footprint, while George derided him.

Hubert shook the rope, it flew off the knob, and to carry out the drama he stepped into the brush and flicked the end after him.

"My word!" said George. "It didn't take you long to prove yourself a sleuth."

"What's downstairs in the silo?" asked Hubert, peering in the lower window. "Looks like some steel cabinets."

"My correspondence files," said Ed, "and my modest but precious supplies of liquor."

"Did he get any of that?" asked Hubert.

"The cabinets are locked," said Ed complacently.

"Nothing in there of value?" asked Hubert.

Ed's jaw dropped suddenly.

"My God!" he exclaimed. "My guns!"

III

THE COLT AUTOMATIC

Ed ran around to the front door of the barn, George and Hubert following him. Ed strode through the living-room and entered the small back room which he called his office. He took out his keys and opened the door at the north end of the room.

The three crowded into a circular room ten or twelve feet in diameter. At the right of the steel casement window facing the door was an improvised rack supporting rifles and shotguns, four in all. The room contained nothing else but a four-drawer steel filing cabinet and a larger steel cabinet with shelves, such as is used in offices. In the ceiling was a square hole, cut for the stairs, whose temporary absence Ed had explained. The door of the room was of steel, stamped in panels and painted white to match the woodwork of the building.

"Well, gentlemen," said Ed, scowling, "I guess he got it."

"Got your gun?" asked Hubert.

"My automatic," said Ed. "I left it in here the other day, meaning to put it in the cabinet later. It was a Colt, forty-five, 1917 Army model."

"Where was the automatic?" asked Hubert. "On top of this cabinet?"

"No," said Ed. "It was lying on the floor, under the window."

"Ah," said Hubert, as if that made a difference. "Well, Ed, I guess you'd better report it to the local police. You're sure the cabinets were locked?"

Ed rattled the doors and drawers by way of proof. He unlocked the larger cabinet. On its shelves were bottles of Scotch, Bourbon, gin, vermouth, sirups, and also some home-made wine; two upper shelves were empty. Ed made a hasty inventory and declared that nothing was missing.

35

"What's in the filing cabinet?" asked Hubert.

"My correspondence, in the top two," said Ed, unlocking that also. "A few old prints, autograph letters, of no value, in the third one. The bottom drawer's empty; I just cleared it for a transfer file."

"You looked around upstairs, didn't you?"

"Yes, when I was on the ladder, outside. I also locked the windows then; they have a spring catch. There's nothing whatever upstairs."

"Well, the man couldn't have seen the guns through the window, so that's not what he broke in for. And I don't suppose he could guess there was liquor in the cabinet. He may be a bibliomaniac who has heard of your collection, but that seems rather fantastic. I can't make the fellow out. But we ought to find some finger-prints, on the case-ments or cabinets. And the police can be on the lookout for strangers in the neighborhood."

"You say," continued Hubert, looking around the room curiously, "that you're having stairs made to get up to the second floor?"

"Yes. Steel stairs, that will fold up against the ceiling. They'll be jointed, and have a counterweight, like a fire escape, and there'll be a trapdoor to cover the hole. I'm also having steel shelving made and boxes for manuscripts and letters. I'll have the room plastered inside and tinted. And I'll have burglarproof glass put in those windows."

There were sounds of a car arriving outside. "Here comes Jeanie," said Ed, locking the door. "Don't say anything about the gun, anybody."

Jeanie was fair, tall, and athletic in type, though not particularly so in fact. She had a tendency, for outdoor wear, toward mannish over-coats and flat heels, in the Boston manner—the *imprimatur* of Eastern schooldays; nevertheless, she managed to wear the filmiest evening gowns with *chic*.

"Will you put my car in, Ed? Oh, hel-lo, George! Why didn't you wire us to meet you at Union Station? How do you do, Mr. Hubert? Delighted that you've come. And if you're not comfortable out here, do remember that we've got perfectly good guest-rooms in the house. It was Ed's idea putting you out here, not mine."

"It's luxurious," said Hubert, "but if I have any complaints, I'll re-port to you."

Jeanie approved of Hubert at sight. Having expected something in a two-gallon hat and bearskin chaps, she was relieved to see a well-tai-lored old gentleman who might have been a retired army officer, and bore not the least resemblance to the fanciful word picture Ed had given her of his Western friend.

"We'll be in shortly," said Ed. "Take a look at your trinkets and the spoons when you go in, Jeanie. A sneak-thief has been around here—a trick burglar."

"A burglar! Did he get anything?"

"I think not," said Ed. "I'll tell you about it at dinner."

"Well," remarked Jeanie when they had gathered in the big living-room of the house—a room effected by throwing two original rooms together —"I think you're all awfully smart at detecting, but I'll bet you've forgotten one thing."

"What's that?" asked Ed, pausing in his exercises with the cock-tail-shaker.

"It's Hallowe'en!" said Jeanie triumphantly.

"Hallowe'en!" exclaimed Ed, resuming operations. "If that's the younger set's taste in Hallowe'en jokes, they're headed for state's prison, is all I can say."

"I'm afraid," said George, "that you credit the young idea with more subtlety and imagination than it's wont to show. In my youth the perfect jest was to ring the doorbell and to hit people over the head with a stuffed stocking when they came to the door."

"Oh, children are much cleverer now," said Jeanie. "The movies have broadened their minds. I'll give ours an alibi, though. They were parked over at Dobert's all afternoon. By the way, Ed, Laura's left us."

"Laura? The flawless jewel? The paragon of nurses?"

"She got a telegram from her father in Chattanooga. Her sister's dying and Laura has got to take care of her father."

"That sounds final. You'll never get a combination nurse and governess to beat her. A very superior person. Much too superior, in fact; her only fault. People used sometimes to think she was a needy cousin of ours."

"Oh, she knew her place," said Jeanie. "But I think I'll worry along without anyone now. The children are pretty big."

Ed poured the drinks and sat down.

"Apparently that thief didn't get into the house," he said. "You didn't miss anything?"

"No," said Jeanie. "And Solveig was in the house all afternoon."

"Solveig," said Ed to the maid as they sat down to dinner, "did you see anyone around the place this afternoon?"

"The photographer," said the maid.

"Oh, yes. Well, he's no thief. Did he take those pictures of the house and barn?"

"Yes, sir. I watched him. He was through by four o'clock. He said he'd have pictures tomorrow."

"No one else?"

Solveig shook her head.

"I met two gentlemen by the wall behind the barn," said George. "One of them was named Curvington or something like that."

"Hugh Crivington," said Ed. "I have a few mental reservations about him, but I'd hardly accuse him of shinning up a wall with a rope. Who was the other party?"

"A man named Klarsen—a beaut! The kind who could ride a company of leathernecks and they'd love him to death."

"I never heard of him," said Ed.

"I think I have," said Jeanie. "Doesn't he work for the Electric Company?"

"What electric company?" asked George.

"The Dynamopolis Electric Company," said Ed. "They have a big plant about two miles east of here. Hugh's a vice-president."

"Is that so?" asked George. "Crivington is quite a smart chap, then?"

"He was smart to marry Borg's daughter," replied Ed. "Borg is president of the Company. But at that I don't think Borg would have Hugh around if he didn't have some stuff. He'd settle a million or two on him and ship him off to the Riviera if Hugh was no good."

"I suppose Klarsen is an electrical engineer, then," said George.

"Let's get Hugh and Ann to bring him over tonight," said Ed. "This valiant Viking sounds good."

"Now, wait, Ed," said Jeanie. "How many people are already coming over?"

"Tom and Frances Knapp," said Ed. "And Arthur Dancey. That's all—no, wait a minute. Mike Macy said something about dropping over. Nat Flint might come. To tell the truth, I was telling some of the boys about Gil, and they want to meet him."

"That's crowding Mr. Hubert pretty hard," protested Jeanie. "I'm sure he wants to turn in early and get a rest."

"I should be delighted to meet your friends," said Hubert. "But I'd like a little account of them beforehand, so's to know who's who."

"Well," said Ed, "Tom Knapp is a real-estater; he was one of the syndicate; the Knapps live next door, to the north. Arthur Dancey lives next door to the south; he's a nice fellow, very quiet; lives with his mother, who's an invalid. Arthur came here two years ago; bought the house off of some other people who moved East. He'd just married then; his wife died six months later, and he got his mother to come here. Mike Macy is city editor of the *Mirror*; not bad, for a chap thirty years old. Nat Flint lives over in Merivale Park, six miles east of here, on Putnam Lake Road, that runs north and south through all the older suburban towns. He's in the grain business, or hay and feed, or something. He's a minor musical genius; he may bring over a saxophone or a concertina, but let's hope not. Did you ever know Nat, George?"

"No," said George. "I know Tom Knapp, and I remember Mike Macy as a kid in short pants when I was home from college."

"Well," said Ed, "I guess we'd better not lug in the Crivingtons. I'd like to meet that chap, though."

"What else do you know about him, Jeanie?" asked George.

"Mr. Klarsen? Oh, I don't know. He was in the war, I know—got a lot of medals and decorations. I think Ann Crivington used to speak of him."

"Oh," said George.

"What are you oh-ing about, George?" asked Jeanie, amused.

"Nothing," said George innocently. "I never heard of either of them till today."

IV

THE PARTY

After coffee Ed telephoned the local police station at Hubert's suggestion, going out to the barn for this purpose, in order that Jeanie might
not overhear him.

"I don't think it would add to the good cheer of our guests," Ed said
to Hubert, "to know there was a burglar prowling in the ravine with a
gun. He's got plenty of ammunition, too; the son-of-a-gun took two
extra magazines of cartridges that were with it."

The Knapps came over, and with George and Jeanie came out to the
barn. Dancey came later, also Mike Macy, and finally Nat Flint, bringing nothing more formidable than a piccolo, his latest ambition, with
which he improvised *obbligati* to whatever feasible material he could
extract from the radio.

The telephone bell rang, and Ed answered it.

"Who?" asked Ed. "Lay off, Nat, lay off. Somebody turn off that radio. Hullo, Hugh. Sure. Come on over. Fine! Bring him along. Glad to
meet the feller. Sounds interesting. Right-o!"

"Ed!" protested Jeanie. "The place just won't hold any more people!"

"Hommes 40, chevaux 8," said Ed, sizing up the room. "I hope
Klarsen isn't a fat man."

"Who's Klarsen?" asked Nat.

"Engineer of the Electric Company, I think Hugh said."

"Get him to fix this radio," said Nat. "It's one of their make. It back-
fires."

"He wouldn't bother with a radio," said Ed. "He sells turbines and
generators and installs them. He's also sales manager. I don't know
what he does in his spare time."

A few moments later Hugh's party arrived. First, Ann Crivington, framing herself in the doorway, as if the room were a box at the opera, and dressed accordingly. Blonde hair and a faultless complexion produced the effect commonly considered 'dazzling'; one of those women, not definitely a beauty, who somehow get that reputation by the simple process of expecting it. Of a type so successful in her heyday that she had never risked altering it to meet the taste of the hard-boiled decade; a type, however, thought George, that still launches an occasional ship. A roving eye, veiled by an affectation of languor; a woman almost totally unable to converse with men without flirtatious implication. The occasion not being propitious for that, Ann pillowed herself effectively in a corner window-seat under a wall light and chattered to Jeanie and Frances Knapp.

Ed introduced Hugh and Klarsen to Hubert, gave them highballs and showed them around the barn, which Klarsen admired generously. After Ed had explained the silo to them, Hugh turned to him and asked, with what seemed almost like asperity, "What the devil have you got a detective here for, Ed?"

Ed was irritated. "Look here, Hugh," he said, taking his pipe out of his mouth, "I invite anybody I please to my house, and this man is a friend of mine. If detectives aren't in your class, it's too bad, that's all."

"Now, Ed," said Hugh, instantly conciliatory, "you've got me wrong. I'm not knocking your friend. I thought perhaps you had hired the chap."

"I should say not," said Ed, mollified. "I'm not trailing anybody, and it would have to be big stuff to interest this fellow. He's been with the International Police, and he's done jobs for Uncle Sam."

The medley of guests coagulated into groups, Hubert in particular drawing an audience of inquisitive but respectful admirers.

Nat Flint tried to razz Hugh a little, Hugh being just the kind of person that a person like Nat loves to razz.

"What are you doing in the market, Hugo?" asked Nat. "Are you insiders buying or selling Dynamopolis Electric?"

"I'm holding on to all I've got," said Hugh stiffly.

"That's what you told me about a year and a half ago," said Nat. "I had thirty points profit, and hung on, and lost fifteen of it. And I was lucky at that; it went to twenty below where I bought it."

"Disregard fluctuations," said Hugh. "Pick up all you can get on recessions."

"You talk like a blooming broker's sheet. I suppose fifty points is just a fluctuation, eh?"

"They're dusting off that old yarn," continued Nat, "about a flaw in the Company's land title. Is there anything in that?"

"That's nonsense. We can't spend our time denying all the fool rumors that speculators want to spread around."

"It may be nonsense," said Nat, "but it seems to be good meat for the bears once in a while. I've got a notion that the birds who spread the rumor are picking up the stock. How about it?"

But Nat got no further change out of Hugh. He went and joined Ed and the ladies in a discussion of local school problems. Klarsen seemed to prefer male company in the other room, where, perched sidewise on a disk, he was in his turn holding the rapt attention of Hubert and Mike Macy.

Suddenly there was a knock at the door. Ed answered it, stepped outside, and closed the door. George peeked out of the window.

"Who's that at the door?" asked Frances Knapp.

"I think it's a dick," said George uneasily.

"Who's Dick?" asked Frances, who did not read detective stories.

"A dick? Oh, it's the same as a bull—a harness bull."

"A bull!" exclaimed Frances.

"Not a four-footed bull," said George. "A flattie, or flatfoot. A 'busy.' Excuse me, I've got to go out."

"Go on," said Frances. "Tom, what's a harness bull?"

"A harness bull?" said Tom. "A harness bull's a cop."

"A cop?" asked Frances. "What's a cop doing here?"

"What's that?" asked Hugh excitedly. "A cop at the door?" He opened the door a little way and slammed it shut quickly. "What's all this with the police about?"

"Rest easy, Hugh, rest easy," said Jeanie. "It's nothing at all. We thought there was a sneak-thief here this afternoon, and reported, but we didn't know they were going to send a cop over."

"A sneak-thief?"—"Did he get anything?"—"Did you see him?"—and so on and so forth from everyone present. Jeanie gave them the briefest possible account of it, leaving out the most interesting details. Hubert stepped outside, and found George and Ed, with the policeman, around the corner staring at the silo. The upper window was open.

"Look at that, Gil," said Ed. "Our friend's been back again."

"Humph," said Hubert grimly. "Didn't you lock those windows, Ed?"

"I'll take my oath on it," said Ed. "And they're jimmy-proof, positively."

"And the fellow's erased his footprints," said Hubert, stepping to the wall.

"You don't say!" said George. "How could he do that? He couldn't reach them without a ladder."

"He had a ladder," said Hubert, flashing a light on the ground. "The ladder from the silo. You can see fresh marks on the gravel where it rested."

"That doesn't make sense," said George. "He'd have to get in first, to get the ladder."

"Then he put the ladder back inside, and jumped out of the upper window," said Hubert. "Here's a plain mark where he landed."

"I'll say it doesn't make sense," said Ed.

"That's news!" said Mike Macy, who had joined them. "'Fly Burglar Scales Silo.' Top inside, with a pic; good for the light touch, maybe."

"Confound it, Mike!" said Ed, "do you think I want a pic of my house in your sheet, with dotted lines and crosses?"

"Well," said the policeman, "it's kids done it, if you ask me. They've got us jumping all over town tonight. But we'll keep a lookout for strangers, and for that gun."

They went inside again, where everyone was busy swapping burglar stories. Hugh and Ann Crivington had on their wraps and were making adieux.

"Hugh, you're not rushing off!" protested Ed. "And taking Mr. Klarsen too?"

"Harold has to get into town," said Hugh. "Much business, much business. We must run along too."

"Well, you must bring him again. Has he gone already?"

"Just went out to look at his car, I think," said Hugh. "Good-night, Ed. Good-night, Jeanie."

"But where is Mr. Klarsen?" asked Jeanie. "He hasn't said good-night to me yet."

"Hugh!" exclaimed Ann suddenly, "his car's gone!"

"So it has," said Hugh irritably. "Well, we'll walk over. He needn't have been in such a hurry."

Gradually the other guests drifted away. George and Hubert turned in upstairs. Ed and Jeanie walked to the house.

"Ed," asked Jeanie, "do you think that was Hallowe'en kids?"

"Might have been," said Ed hopefully.

"But what on earth became of Mr. Klarsen?"

"He went in town, I suppose. He lives at a hotel when he's in town. He's single, you know."

"I don't think he said good-bye to a single person. He was putting on his coat, and I was just going to shake hands with him, when he stuck his hands in his overcoat pockets, said 'By Jove!' and dashed out of the door."

"Bashful guy, maybe."

"Bashful, nothing," declared Jeanie emphatically. "I'm positive that he meant to come back—and he didn't!"

V

THE FIRST RUMBLE MURDER

George arose heroically next morning at seven, and discovered at once that Hubert was already up and gone. George cast a glance around Hubert's room. On a chair were a pair of corduroy trousers and by it a pair of high boots, damp with dew.

"My word!" he exclaimed to himself. "If the old gentleman isn't on the job already! Up and dressed him in outing garb, took a stroll across country, came back and changed to d.b. sack, and I suppose is having his breakfast now."

Arriving at seven-thirty at the house, George found Ed and Hubert on their second cups of coffee and morning cigars.

"Good-afternoon, George," said Ed. "Expect to get any breakfast at this hour? Gil has already been up nearly two hours."

"Yes," said George. "And you?"

"Not a chance," said Ed. "I found Gil downstairs reading the paper, and we put breakfast forward a little."

"That's not so early out where I come from," said Hubert.

"Out where they get up a little earlier," said George, spooning a mouthful of cantaloupe. "Out where the dawn is a little pearlier. *That's* where the West begins."

"Gil's been doing some of his celebrated stuff," said Ed. "Found some tire tracks on the old road to the quarry, some cracker boxes, and banana peels."

"Nothing important, probably," said Hubert cautiously. "But it's an interesting place over there."

"I hope," said George, "that you can now tell us the man's height and weight, brand of tobacco he smokes, and whether he has a glass eye and served in the 89th Punjaub Rifles."

45

"He smokes Bull Durham," said Hubert, "and I can guess at his weight and height. I'll poke around this morning and see what else I can find. The incident may be trivial, but it is puzzling, and puzzles have an attraction for me."

"Good-morning, gentlemen," said Jeanie, entering at that moment. "What's that about puzzles? I hope they catch that burglar. I had a mighty poor sleep, I can tell you, wondering whether he'd come back. I suppose he didn't?"

"He didn't bother me any," said George. "I slept like a top. It's a great life if you don't waken."

"Don't get nerves, Jeanie," said Ed. "You'll have two sturdy male protectors while I'm away all day."

"I should think I might have nerves. Burglars that come back when there's nothing to burgle, and guests that disappear without notice."

"Who else disappeared without notice?"

"Well, there was Arthur Dancey. He'd hardly got here before he said he must skip off. Said his mother was sick."

"Which everybody knows is true," said Ed. "Well, I must be off with the old dinner pail. I hope you'll have it all solved and the burglar in custody when I return."

George unlimbered his writing apparatus and his unfinished manuscript after breakfast, and set up shop in the writing-room of the barn, which Ed had told him was his for the purpose. But the unaccustomed surroundings, particularly the pleasant view across the ravine from his desk, played havoc with concentration.

After an hour's ineffectual effort, George strolled into the living-room to stretch his legs. Hubert was settled in a big easy-chair, with a pipe and 'Moby Dick.'

"I dare say you've read that a good many times," said George.

"I don't know how often I've read it through," said Hubert, "but I've picked it up a hundred times. For some reason I never have fathomed, it stimulates thinking for me to pretend I'm reading this book."

"I know how that is. I read Croce when I get stalled. My subconsciousness goes on with my own problems."

"If you're not busy," said Hubert, laying down his book, "I wish you'd help me just a minute. I'd like to move those cabinets in the silo."

"Glad to," said George. Together they moved both cabinets away from the wall. Hubert stooped and picked up something which appeared to George to be very small. Hubert took it to the window of the other room and examined it.

"A clue?" asked George, enraptured.

"It fits in," said Hubert thoughtfully. "You see what it is? A shaving cut from a piece of twig. It bears out my belief that the fellow wedged the window catch when he entered the first time. I looked for a wedge outside, but he may have thrown it away some distance."

"He wedged the lower window catch, so that he could get in again from the outside?"

"Yes. Now, then, it's evident that he was inside the silo when he whittled this wedge. Well, Ed swears that he, Ed, tried the lower window before we went to dinner, and it was securely locked. I think he's right about that. Now, what do you know?"

"Nothing," said George, after reflection. "I think you'll find me an ideal Watson, Mr. Hubert."

"Well, I think that proves that the man was in the silo when Ed locked up."

"What! Why, Ed looked into the silo, upstairs and down, before we went in to dinner."

"True. But he looked into the upper window from outside, on the ladder. When he looked upstairs, the man was downstairs; when he looked downstairs, the man was upstairs. There's no other conclusion possible."

"By golly!" exclaimed George. "That'll give Ed a jolt. The man could have blown Ed's head off."

"The ladder was outside then. But an active man could easily scramble up through that hole in the ceiling. While we were at dinner the fellow may have looked through the cabinets—Ed left them unlocked—and then wedged the window. Then he took the ladder and erased his footprints, and put the ladder back in the silo. Now, whether he went away and came back we don't know; but we know that he was here while the party was going on."

"That's right," said George. "Because he leapt out of the upper window. The guests blocked his way through the lower one. But now, why on earth did he come back? To spy on us?"

"That," said Hubert, shaking his head, "is the mystery. At any rate, he must be a very nervy chap, and not a professional, if I know anything about criminals."

"Well, well. He must have left finger-prints, though."

"We'll not find any finger-prints," said Hubert gloomily. "Unfortunately I gave the man some excellent advice on that point, while he was over my head and I didn't know it. You see that he has removed his footprints. It was gross carelessness on my part."

"Humph," said George, scratching his head, "I guess it's just as well. There might have been a little fireworks if we'd discovered him."

"I think," said Hubert, "that we won't tell our hostess about this at lunch."

After lunch Jeanie was going in town to do some shopping and go to a tea, and Hubert said he would ride in with her and look up an old friend of his at Police Headquarters. Jeanie was to pick him up at the University Club again at five-thirty.

George went at his work again in the afternoon, quit about five o'clock, and came into the house to forage for refreshments. He got a couple of cookies and a bottle of ginger ale from the maid, and sat down in the living-room of the house.

As he seated himself, he noticed a large manila envelope on the table by him, and setting down his glass, he picked the envelope up and peeked inside of it. He saw at a glance that it contained photographs of the house, and since it was unsealed, he had no hesitation in looking at them.

The photographs were about eight by ten, glossy, and microscopically clear. In spite of their literalness, the lights and shadows of the wooded scene gave them a natural beauty.

George looked them all over indolently, and then began to arrange them, grouping those of the house and those of the barn, when his eye was arrested by a human figure in one of them. This picture was one of the barn, showing the west and south sides, from the direction of the house. A bit of the quarry hill was visible in the background, but the silo, from that viewpoint, did not show. The figure which George noticed was standing at the left of the picture, at the corner of the barn, and near the silo. It was somewhat camouflaged by the background of bushes, and the head was blurred, as if the person had moved while the picture was being taken. From the neck down, however, the figure was perfectly clear.

George looked through all the other pictures again, but found no other with any human object in it. He put the pictures back in the envelope and took them out to the barn.

Ed got back about six and rolled up to the barn in his shiny black and nickel coupe. George met him outside, with the envelope in his hand.

"Here are your photographs, Ed," he said. "I want to show you something."

Ed took the photograph that George handed him and examined it. George pointed to the man's figure.

"Looks like a boy scout," said Ed. "Sweater, khaki trousers, and puttees. Kind of stuff that you buy at these so-called army and navy stores. Do you suppose that's our man?"

"You ought to be able to get a fair enlargement of that," said George. "Then maybe we can tell more about it."

When Jeanie and Hubert arrived, they, too, were shown the photograph. It seemed evident that the man, whoever he was, had for the moment at least been unaware of the presence of the photographer. In order to get exactly that view, the photographer must have had his camera stationed in a little grove between the house and the barn where he would have been more or less hidden. And no doubt the photographer himself had been unaware of the presence of the figure, while timing the picture.

The subject afforded material for speculation during dinner. Hubert agreed that enlargements should be made and given the police, but observed that the costume was a favorite one with country hikers. After dinner Jeanie got a magnifying-glass, and looked closely at the photograph.

"Do you know what I think?" she said. "I think that's a woman. Look at it, Mr. Hubert. Look at the hand that's on her hip, all spread out. And look how she's standing. You never saw a man stand like that."

Hubert gave the picture a careful scrutiny with the glass, then took a smaller one of his own and looked at it. "I shouldn't go so far as to say that," he said, "though I think women's perceptions are more acute than men's about women. But no man from the cow country ever dressed like that. And this person has not got on moccasins."

All turned in early and were up betimes.

Ed was reading the morning paper with a grim smile when George joined the others at breakfast. "Here's a real mystery for you to unravel, Watson," he said to George, handing him the paper.

"Nude Body Found in Millionaire's Car," read George.

> "'Almost nude, the body of an unidentified man, who had apparently died of gunshot wounds, was found early this morning in the closed rumble of the car of Mr. J. Clopendyke Clifford, financier and wealthy resident of Petunkawoc. Mr. Clifford made the discovery shortly after midnight on arriving at his home in Petunkawoc whither he had driven his automobile from the city.
>
> "'Mr. Clifford reported the matter to the Petunkawoc police at once, but was unable to conjecture how or when the body was placed in his car. He stated positively that he had never seen the man before and that he only discovered the body when opening the rumble to take out a suitcase he had placed there yesterday. The suitcase was missing, evidently having been removed by the murderer.
>
> "'Mr. Clifford told the police that his car had been parked all day yesterday and last evening under the south approach to the Monument Avenue Bridge, he having spent the evening in the city at the theater with friends.'"

"What's that got to do with us?" asked George, puzzled. "Petunkawoc is six or eight miles east of here."

"Nothing to do with us," said Ed. "I only thought you liked mysteries, that's all."

"Oh, I never read about murders in the papers," said George. "A murder isn't necessarily news; they happen every day. Usually it's just a story, and a bum one at that. The only thing duller than a murder is a trans-oceanic flight."

"You'd call this news," said Ed, "if you knew J. Clopendyke Clifford."

"And who, if anybody, is Mr. J. Clopendyke Clifford?" asked George.

"Clopendyke Clifford," said Ed, "is known as a capitalist, chiefly because nobody knows exactly what he does. He's mixed up in everything and connected with nothing definitely; he's apt to pop up in any big deal. He has an office in the Spindler Building Tower, near the Monument Avenue Bridge—the same building that I'm in. Not even his name on the door, and you have to be a Houdini to get in to see him. I've had good letters of introduction to him twice, and been bounced out by his secretary both times. You have to have something he wants or he won't do business with you."

"What is he? A big speculator?"

"He's a speculator in controlling interests. Ordinary speculators buy shares. Clifford buys controls."

"A monstrous parasite," said George.

"Some people call him that," said Ed. "Others call him a financial wizard."

"Sounds unpleasant to me," said George.

"His wife is worse," said Jeanie. "She got a lot of space in the papers about a year ago because she tried to get her jewels past the customs officers, and I haven't a doubt that she did it just to let the world know how much the jewels cost. You ought to see her at the opera, all draped up with them like a chandelier."

"Well," said Ed, "me for town. Maybe the noon papers will have it that Mr. Clifford is being detained by the police."

VI

THE CAFÉ-AU-LAIT CABRIOLET

Ed Marsh walked to the round table by the oriel window, that being the popular designation of the table in the main dining-room of the University Club where Ed and a number of others, a more or less changing personnel, customarily had lunch. Under his arm he carried a bunch of newspapers which he had picked off the table in the hall where they were laid out for the use of members at meals.

"Don't bring any more papers, Ed," said Gerry Barclay, shooing him away. "We've got three of every afternoon paper here now."

"All right," said Ed. "Here," he said to a waiter, "put these back on the table, will you?"

"Now, then," said Ed, sitting down and picking up a paper, "have they discovered any bloody shirts in Mr. Clopendyke Clifford's ashbin or anything like that?"

"No such luck," said Toomey Potter. "The murderer is still at large. The police are combing the countryside. The net is being spread far and wide and Police Commissioner Kleehorn is confident that the criminal will shortly be apprehended. All that sort of thing. The *Spy Glass* is even worse than usual. There's only one afternoon paper in this hick town. Let's see what Mike Macy's got. Gimme the *Mirror*." Toomey jarred the table in reaching for it.

"Have a heart, Toomey!" cried Gerry. "Look at my soup now!"

"'Rumble Slayers Flee North?'" read Toomey. "Wonder what papers would do without slay, flee, rap, probe, oust, quiz, flay, and the rest of those strange monosyllables.

"'A report received at Murray Street Station of a mystery car which sped at a high rate of speed through Glen Lomond early Thursday morning, nearly running down Patrolman F. X. Ryan of the Glen Lomond force, may offer a possible clue to the slayers of the unknown man found this morning in the rumble of the car of Mr. J. Clopendyke Clifford, well-known financier and resident of Petunkawoc.

"'Patrolman Ryan was unable to give a description of the car other than that it was a cabriolet of café-au-lait color.'"

"I'll bet Patrolman Ryan never said that," said Gerry, "unless he's a good yodeler."

"Well, I call that a pretty bum clue," said Ed. "The body is found in Clifford's car early this morning, Friday, and the so-called mystery car was seen early yesterday morning, Thursday. That's either a perfect alibi or a misprint."

"Ed's right," said Gerry. "The body was put in Clifford's car Thursday night, under the bridge. The police are all wet."

"Did you read what the coroner's physician says?" asked Charley Bullivant, lean, grave, whose least utterances had the air of finality and precision becoming to a member of the legal fraternity.

"No," said Gerry, "what does he say?"

"He says," said Charley, "that the murdered man had been dead thirty hours. That means the man was murdered about midnight Wednesday. This car was seen about an hour and a half after that."

"I'll bet the coroner's physician can't tell within fifteen of those thirty hours," said Ed aggressively, "how long the man was dead."

"Within one hour," said Bullivant flatly.

"How do you know, Ed," asked Toomey, "whether that mutton chop of yours is two hours old or a week old?"

"Damn you, Toomey!" said Ed, regarding his chop unfavorably. "Waiter, change this chop for eggs Benedict, will you?"

"Well, anyway," said Gerry, "if this mystery car was seen in Glen Lomond, which is twenty miles north of the bridge, at twelve-thirty

Thursday morning, those fellows couldn't have put the body in Clifford's car at 9 A.M. Thursday, which is the earliest that his car could
have been under the bridge. Einstein himself couldn't do it."

"Might have turned back and done it," said Bullivant. "Doubling on
their tracks—an old trick."

"Act your age, Charley," said Ed. "Those birds were in a hurry. If
they had a body in their car, do you think they'd come strolling back to
town with it?"

"Here comes Sam Winkler," said Toomey, "with an extra. What you
got, Sam?"

"'Trace Mystery Car to Dugan's Grove,'" read Sam, seating himself.

> "'The so-called mystery car for which the police are
> searching, and which is suspected of having some con-
> nection with the body discovered in the rumble of Mr.
> J. Clopendyke Clifford's car, is reported by the Clayton-
> ville police as having been seen at 2 A.M. Thursday at
> Dugan's Grove. A man giving the name of B. F. Ost stat-
> ed to the police that he collided with a tan or light brown
> Packard cabriolet parked at that hour near the entrance
> to Belloduomo's roadhouse, the car having its tail-light
> dark. The driver of the car was nowhere to be seen, but
> while Mr. Ost was looking for a policeman someone en-
> tered the car from the roadside, which is thickly shaded,
> and drove sway at a high rate of speed. Mr. Ost, howev-
> er, obtained the license number of the car. The number
> is that of a resident of Merivale Park, who stated that his
> license plates were stolen from his car last night while it
> was parked on Putnam Lake Road.'"

"That sounds like Hallowe'en stuff," said Gerry. "A bunch of
drunks. Apparently they drove due north on Putnam Lake Road, passing Petunkawoc, Glen Lomond, and Dugan's Grove. The state troopers
ought to catch 'em."

"What's the argument?" asked Sam. "Whether these fellows could
have put the body in Clifford's rumble?"

"That's it," said Ed. "Put your eagle eye and legal brain to work, Sam."

"What makes you children think," asked Sam, "that the body was put in Clifford's car under the Monument Avenue Bridge?"

"The morning papers said so," said Gerry.

"And whose theory was that?" asked Sam.

"It was Clifford's theory, by golly!" said Toomey.

"And he might be wrong, yes?"

"I see no reason," said Sam importantly, "why they couldn't have done it in Petunkawoc Wednesday night. Clifford's car might have been parked out on the road there."

A chorus of skepticism greeted this.

"Stick to the evidence, Sam," said Bullivant. "There's nothing in the record to the effect that Clifford's car was parked on the road in Petunkawoc at that time."

"I move that that be stricken from the record," said Toomey, "as irrelevant, incompetent, inconsequent, and immaterial!"

"Motion overruled! Objection sustained!" cried Gerry, banging on the table with a spoon.

"According to that," said Ed, chuckling, "Clifford has been toting this body around in his rumble about twenty-four hours. Some Hallowe'en prank, what?"

"Why don't you read the papers, Sam?" asked Gerry. "Didn't you see in the morning papers that Clifford put a bag in his rumble Thursday morning and presumably didn't see any body?"

"You're also overlooking something else," said Bullivant. "'Dr. Heinz, coroner's physician,'" he read from his paper, "'gave it as his opinion that the body was placed in the rumble not less than twelve hours after the man was shot, basing his conclusions on the small amount of blood found in the rumble.'"

"What the coroner's physician says," replied Sam, "about the length of time the man was dead is no doubt correct. But when he says the body was put in the car twelve hours afterwards, he's just guessing."

"Don't you suppose he knows how long a man bleeds?" asked Bullivant.

"As for what Clifford says," continued Sam, "that's not conclusive either. There's nothing to support his statement about the bag."

"You believe, then," said Bullivant, peering over his glasses at Sam in his best cross-examining manner, "that Clifford found a body in his car Thursday morning, toted it to town, left it in his car all day and evening under the bridge, and then lugged it back to his house again. What was his motive for that?"

"Listen, Charley," said Sam with the air of elaborate patience affected by people whose patience is exhausted, "I didn't say Clifford found the body in his rumble Thursday morning. I said he didn't put his bag in his rumble. He could be mistaken, couldn't he?"

"Here's the dope about the bag," said Ed, folding his paper the more easily to read it. "Clifford put a bag into his rumble Thursday morning when he left his house; the bag contained papers and stuff he'd been working on at home. He took out the bag when he parked under the bridge, took the bag up to his office, took out the papers, and when his secretary went out to lunch about noon, the secretary took the empty bag and put it back in the rumble. Clifford couldn't be mistaken about all that."

"Let me see that item," said Bullivant sharply. Ed handed him the paper.

"What merger is that, Charley?" asked Gerry facetiously. Bullivant ignored the query.

"When Clifford gets busy with a lot of papers," said Toomey Potter cynically, "it means there's money in it for Clifford and a short deal for somebody else."

"Do you know him?" asked Bullivant severely.

"I'll say I know him," said Toomey. "The big stiff. He put the kibosh on one of the sweetest pieces of business we ever had all set. Took it over to the Fifth Nash, and the bonds were a flop, too. Wanted too damn much for 'em."

"He looks like a Turk, to me," said Gerry. "He must have some stuff, though. He's got all the big shots eating out of his hand."

"Well," said Bullivant, pushing away, "I'll leave the dirt to you scavengers. I must get back to the office."

"Ha, ha!" said Toomey, as Bullivant's long figure threaded its way among the tables. "Wily old Charley's got something on his chest. Did you see him glaring at that item Ed showed him?"

"Why?" asked Ed. "Charley isn't Clifford's lawyer, is he?"

"No," said Sam Winkler. "Charley's representing opposite interests from Clifford right now, I think. And I'll bet that keeps Charley guessing."

"Well," said Gerry, "who is this murdered man? Nobody seems to take any interest in him."

"I've got a swell hunch," said Toomey, "that Clifford knows who he is."

"Some under-cover worker of Clifford's?" asked Gerry.

"It looks to me," said Toomey, "as if Clifford didn't want it known how that body got into his rumble. The coroner's physician is just a cheap machine henchman, and you know as well as I do that Clifford is their big meal-ticket. I'd say the coroner's physician tried to put over a fast one, and the police muffed it. Willoughby failed to play ball once before, you remember, and the City Hall has it in for him. Maybe we'll have a new Chief of Detectives soon."

"Dirty work at the crossroads, Toomey," said Ed. "Maybe we'll have a new Police Commissioner, if Willoughby catches that car."

VII

MIKE ASKS A QUESTION

Mike Macy stopped in at Ed's barn on his way home that evening.

"Hello, Mike," said Ed. "Glad to see you. You had some good stuff today; you had more than any of the other papers. Any extras out tonight? Any stuff that's too raw to print?"

"There's a good bit more in the last edition," said Mike. "We're skinning the morning papers nicely on this case. The police are turning Tony Belloduomo's place upside down now. I don't know whose orders that was. Kleehorn won't talk, and is sore about something. This mystery car looks like a red herring to me. Tony doesn't know anything about it; says his place was full of people, coming and going; big night there, some kind of Hallowe'en whoopee. There's no doubt in my mind that the body was put in Clifford's car under the bridge, between noon and midnight Thursday; and this brown Packard that they're chasing couldn't have been there then. Somebody is bugs."

"I wish you'd tell me, Mike," said George, "why it doesn't occur to somebody to ask Clifford a few questions. Instead of grilling this honest Sicilian and turning his speakeasy upside down, why don't they give Clifford what they call 'the works,' and tell him to 'come clean'?"

"Clifford is hardly a suspect," said Mike. "A man as busy as he is can account for every minute of his time. He spent an hour Thursday morning at his office, then made some calls on various people, had lunch at the Upstairs Club, then to the bank, back to his office, taxi to the Dynamopolis Club at four; met two men there for a conference, had dinner with them—in a private room—then went to the theater with them. Clifford won't say who they were, and he's within his rights. The

58

part-time ticket girl at the club said Clifford bought three tickets to 'Coffee, Rolls and Honey,' at the Princess."

"They might inquire whether he actually used them," suggested George. "Well, that's all right for Thursday. Now, where was Clifford between the hours of six Wednesday night and six Thursday morning?"

"I thought you affected to be bored by newspaper stories this morning, George," said Ed. "If I remember rightly, you said they were just bum stories."

"Well, this one has the makings," said George. "I'm doing the best I can with it."

"Wednesday night," said Mike, "Clifford was working at home with his secretary."

"Is that a man, woman, or piece of furniture?"

"A man," said Mike. "He was very busy this morning, telling reporters nothing. His name is Peace."

"And how long did this Peace conference last into the night?"

"Peace was out there all night. He rode in with Clifford in the morning."

"Was Clifford's car locked up in his garage all night, as he said it was?"

"As a matter of fact, it wasn't. At least our reporter, who got out to Clifford's house on the jump this morning, got hold of Clifford's chauffeur, who's new on the job, and the chauffeur told him the car was outside the garage all night, because Clifford told him he was to take Peace to the station after they got through their work. But Clifford never called him."

"Then these fellows in the mystery car could have put the body in Clifford's car Wednesday night?" said George. "That's a fair enough reason for chasing them."

"Why didn't Clifford see the body, then?" asked Mike. "He put a bag into his rumble, took it out again, and Peace put the empty bag back into his rumble Thursday noon. And saw no body."

"The Greeks had a word for that," said George. "Boloney."

"Look, George," said Mike, "Clifford's place covers a lot of ground. It's the old William Wellington Hurry place; Clifford bought it ten years ago when he was first beginning to be heard of. The garage is well inside the grounds; you can't see it from the road. And anybody who wanted to dump a body into Clifford's car would have to drive well into the grounds to do it. It's not likely the car would have been standing outside or near the gates."

"And anybody who dumped a body in Clifford's car would have had to have a special reason for choosing his car and no other," suggested Ed.

"Maybe they did," said George. "Or maybe the man was shot on Clifford's place. The police ought to question his *ménage*."

"And his menagerie," added Mike, with a grin. "Maybe the baboon did it."

"Who, Clifford?" asked George.

"No," said Mike, as soon as order was restored. "Haven't you ever heard of Mrs. Clifford's private zoo?"

"Everybody who lives in Dynamopolis has heard of Mrs. Clifford's zoo," said Ed.

"Even Peace has to crack a faint smile when he's handing out flimsy about the latest zoo news," said Mike. "Believe me, Mrs. Clopendyke Clifford has the most efficient news service of any of our social leaders. Every time the coati-mundis have twins, or the ichneumon gets its tail chewed off by the aardvark, the world knows it."

"You don't say!" said George. "I should think that hobby would be a bit smelly. Got any lierns or taggers?"

"Nothing bigger than the baboon," said Mike. "Unless it's the baby-roussa."

"Who takes care of these animals?"

"Oh, they have a professional."

"I like this fellow Clifford," said George enthusiastically. "He's got a swell background. If I were a detective, I'd just love to snoop around that place. Did anyone interview Mrs. Clifford?"

"She was much indisposed," said Mike. "Her famous press service was out of commission."

"What do you think, Mr. Hubert?" asked George. "Don't you think the local police are overlooking a bet?"

"It would hardly become me to criticize your police," said Hubert, who had been listening in his easy-chair with amusement; "especially without any first-hand knowledge of the case. I have some good friends on your detective force, whom I know to be competent."

"What did the dead man look like?" asked Ed.

"I'd hate to tell you," said Mike. "He was shot square in the top of the head, at pretty close range. No powder marks or singeing of his hair, though. Well, the coroner's physician then discovered that he had another bullet in his abdomen—both from the same gun. The abdominal wound was a light one, not fatal; it's evident that that was the first shot fired; that dropped the man, and the second shot finished him off. That shows deliberate intent to kill, all right; killed a helpless man. But the man's head was cleverly bound up with strips of the man's own shirt and undershirt; a neat job of first aid; might almost have been done by a doctor. Looks as if friends had attempted to rescue the man."

"What kind of bullets were they?" asked Hubert.

"From a Colt automatic, forty-five."

"Have they tried to identify the man?"

"Oh, yes. But the B.C.I. has no photographs or finger-prints of him. They've made a lot of photographs of him to broadcast. I don't think the papers will use them, though," Mike added.

"What kind of a man is he?" asked Ed.

"I didn't see him," said Mike. "But they say he is lean and wiry, intelligent-looking, not of foreign extraction, slightly gray hair, close-cropped. The doctor says he's fifty years old, but the boys say he didn't look over forty. Kind of man who might be a skilled mechanic or foreman; not a crook type; but then I've seen lots of crooks that didn't look like crooks."

"Don't you think, Mr. Hubert," asked George, "that a rumble is an unusual place to choose for concealing a body?"

"If the body were put there under the bridge," said Hubert, "it might be the only available place for hiding it."

"But if it wasn't put there under the bridge," said George, "the rumble of a car would be a most unlikely place to dump a corpse. It wouldn't necessarily delay the finding of the body, for the owner of the car as likely as not might open the rumble as soon as he returned to his car. Petunkawoc is full of thick hedges and has quite a lot of forest land available for the dumping of corpses, with much greater dispatch and privacy and less danger of being caught red-handed than when putting it into the rumble of a car."

"There's sense to that, George," said Mike approvingly. "I see what you're coming to."

"The only good reason for putting a body into a rumble," said George, "is to transport it somewhere else."

"Right-o!" said Mike. "To throw the police off the track."

"That ought to let Clifford out, then," said Ed. "If he had put the body into his rumble, he'd hardly be likely to cart it out to his own house again."

"That's exactly what he would do," said George emphatically. "And then give the alarm. It would save him the messy and rather dangerous job of secretly disposing of the body himself."

"Let's see," said Mike, rubbing his brow thoughtfully. "Did that ticket girl say yes, Clifford ordered those tickets in person, Thursday afternoon. Yes, sir, it could be that Clifford left his car under the bridge Thursday evening purposely to make it appear as if the body had been put in it there, by somebody else."

"But the coroner's physician," said Ed, "said there was practically no blood in the rumble."

"The coroner's physician," said George, "may know his business as a doctor, but as a detective he may be a boob."

"You're right there, Mr. Gaynleigh," said Hubert. "That's rather out of a doctor's province."

"I don't see that," contended Mike. "The way in which the blood dried on the body showed clearly that it had lain on the other side for at least twelve hours before it was put into Clifford's rumble. The physician explained that to the reporters."

"I'm no physician," said George, "but how did they get the body into the rumble after twelve hours? *Rigor mortis*, you know."

"The physician's notion," replied Mike, "was that the body was brought there in some other car, packed the same way, perhaps in a rumble. Clifford's car, you know, has a side door to the rumble. That's why they picked his car, probably."

"Suppose," said George, "the body was wrapped in a rug, or piece of tarpaulin, when it was put into Clifford's rumble—in Petunkawoc. That could be removed later."

"It could," capitulated Mike. "That would take the blood, and in removing it the body might be turned over. Nobody was with Clifford when he arrived home that night."

"And this bag business is pure fiction," said Ed. "The boy's clever. I mean Clifford, not you, George."

"Ah, there are keener minds than Clifford's working on this case," said George complacently. "Now let the search of Clifford's place begin! And I suggest that the discreet Mr. Peace be shadowed to see that he doesn't buy any tickets to South America for a vacation."

"What do you think of George's spiel, Gil?" asked Ed. "Does it click?"

"Mr. Gaynleigh's method is erratic," said Hubert, "but stimulating and useful. The use of imagination in solving murders sometimes provokes sarcasm in police circles, but I myself regard it as a great help at times. It's sanctioned in scientific research, and is quite as well suited to detective work."

"Well, it's hot dope," said Mike. "Now, I want to ask you a favor, Ed, before I go, which has nothing to do with the subject under discussion."

"Sure, I'll get you a drink," said Ed, getting up, "and the rest of us, too."

"Thanks," said Mike. "I accept. But this is something else. I've heard, from one of our sources of information, that the Dynamopolis Electric people are looking for their man Klarsen. I've heard he hasn't turned up at the office yet. Now, the party from whom we have our information wouldn't be in a position to know much. There's no use asking the top kicks at Dynamopolis Electric; they never talk to reporters. Now, I don't know Crivington well enough to ask him about it casually, but I thought you might, Ed, without making him sore."

All listened to Mike with close attention.

"You don't think, do you," asked Ed, "that Klarsen is mixed up in this murder business?"

"Don't get that idea," said Mike, smiling. "Just forget about the murder for the moment."

"Well," said Ed, "I'll call up Hugh, gladly." He took up the telephone.

"Westwood 5. Is Mr. Crivington there? This is Ed Marsh. Yes, I'd like to speak to him, please." Ed took a good puff on his cigar, his mind busy. "Hello, Hugh. How about bringing Klarsen over for a little chat tonight, Hugh? I didn't get much chance at him the other night. What? That's too bad. Maybe you can do it some other night. Klarsen's still in town, isn't he? Where is he? I see. A hard life. I don't envy him his job. Well, solong, Hugh. Sorry."

"Hugh doesn't know where Klarsen is," said Ed, "but he usually doesn't know. Klarsen reports to Schwenhauser or somebody. But Hugh says Klarsen is away most of the time, and often the office doesn't know where he is till they get a wire."

"Well, I guess that's official enough," said Mike. "I'm much obliged, Ed. Thanks for the drink."

"By the way," he added, as he pulled his battered felt hat over his eyes, at the doorstep, "did any of you happen to see what kind of a car Klarsen had when he was here?"

"Don't think any of us saw it," said Ed. "Klarsen was the last to arrive and the first to leave. Why?"

"Well," said Mike, "I heard that he drives a light brown Packard cabriolet. However, there are lots of those around. Solong, sleuths."

VIII

THE SECOND RUMBLE MURDER

The morning papers were certainly out of luck on the Rumble Case. They had very little that Mike had not told the others the evening before.

It was Saturday, and a football day, and Ed, knowing the crowd would be at lunch early, arrived at the round table by the oriel window at twelve-thirty. He found the table surrounded by more chairs and occupants than there was room for.

"Admission by card only!" cried Toomey Potter. "Here, Ed, I've been saving your seat for you, and having an awful battle to do it. We'll have to take a private room if this mob of murder fans is going to swarm over us like this."

"'Mystery Car in Lake Yields New Victim,'" read Ed, glimpsing the big headlines of Toomey's paper. "That must be hot off the press; I didn't see it on the streets. Get me a paper, waiter. No, that's old. Read it aloud, Toomey. Loud and clear."

"'Second Body Found in Rumble,'" read Toomey. "'Awaits Identification.'

> "'A second victim of the rumble murderers was found early today.
>
> "'The slain man, shot through the heart and stripped of clothing as in the first rumble murder, was discovered jammed into the closed rumble of a car submerged in Lake Putnam near the bathing beach.
>
> "'This death car was identified as the same mysterious automobile bearing the stolen license plates, for

which the police have been searching since Thursday morning following the discovery of the first rumble victim in the car of J. Clopendyke Clifford.

"'A resident of Claytonville driving early toward the city first saw what he thought to be the top of an automobile almost under the surface of Lake Putnam about two hundred yards from the bathing beach boathouse. He telephoned his observation to the Nash Corners Station of the State troopers without revealing his identity.

"'State Police Sergeant Nathan Woolsey led his squad to the scene and when they hauled the car ashore found the corpse in the rumble. It had been in the water for some time, probably since Thursday morning, according to the troopers.

"'The car, a tan-colored Packard cabriolet with canvas top, evidently was run into the lake shortly after leaving Dugan's Grove where it was seen early Thursday morning.'"

"The afternoon papers are certainly getting all the breaks," said Ed. "Is there any more about it?"

"The rest is warmed-over stuff from yesterday," said Toomey. "You can have the paper now."

"Those murders are connected," said Charley Bullivant sagely. "That's what they call a murder pattern. The murderer gets a certain technique, and follows it from habit."

"I wish I'd brought George Gaynleigh in," said Ed. "He had a theory about the other murder that was a peach."

"George Gaynleigh!" said Toomey. "Where'd you see him?"

"He's staying out at my house," said Ed. "I thought I'd told everybody that."

"For Heaven's sake!" exclaimed Toomey. "I want to see old Gameleg. I used to bunk alongside o' him in prep school. Bring him in here next time."

"I gave him a card to the club," said Ed. "But George came here to work. He's writing a big fat book."

"How's George making out with his writing?" asked Gerry.

"George had it all figured out," said Ed, ignoring the question, "that Clifford toted the body in town and back again to remove the apparent scene of the crime from his place, and then yanked out whatever he'd put into the rumble to catch the blood."

"Rubbish!" said Bullivant contemptuously. "Can you see a man of Clifford's caliber—no matter what you think of his business methods, and he is disagreeable—taking a chance like that? He may be hard-boiled, but he's anything but crude."

"He's crude enough in some of his methods," said Toomey. "That Singing River coal strike, for instance."

"Well," said Gerry dubiously, "you'll never pin this on him. Clifford is a smart old fox."

"You're putting Clifford in the beer baron class," said Sam Winkler. "Anyway, he wouldn't work so close to home."

"You're right," said Bill Cummings. "A couple of Polaks down-state is different from sticking somebody in your own car. I wonder who this second man is, anyway?"

"Well," said Gerry, "Skid and I are going to the Yale-Notre Dame game. Anybody else going? Got room for one more."

"I'm going with Mort Welby," said Cummings. "How about your rumble, Gerry?"

"You're welcome," said Gerry. "If there are no bodies in it. I haven't looked lately."

"Here comes Perry Humphrey back again," said Toomey. "Going to eat another lunch, Perry?"

"I just picked this paper off another table," said Humphrey, opening a newspaper. "Listen. Big scoop."

"'Extra. Three o'clock. The body of the murdered man found in Lake Putnam this morning has been positively identified by McIvor Macy, City Editor of the *Mirror*, who arrived on the scene by aeroplane. It is that of Harold M. Klarsen, Sales Manager and Assistant Chief Engineer of the Dynamopolis Electric Company.'"

Ed leaped up and seized the paper from Humphrey and stared at it. "God!" he exclaimed, "the valiant Viking!"

IX

THE MISSING SUITCASE

Ed drove home in a preoccupied and not at all cheerful mood, his teeth clamped on a cold pipe, his thoughts concentrated on the events of the party at which Klarsen had been his guest Wednesday evening. Ed's first emotion of sincere regret—though he had had less than five minutes' conversation with Klarsen that evening—was succeeded by increasing concern as to possible disagreeable consequences to himself, his family, and his friends.

Ed pictured the police crashing in, reporters swarming over the house and barn, taking photographs, inquiring who was at the party and what Klarsen did 'when last seen.' Well, Klarsen was Hugh's guest; let Hugh attend to that. A later edition of the *Mirror*, which Ed bought on the street, gave some account of Klarsen's life and war record, and mentioned him as Hugh's guest on that evening. Good for Mike, thought Ed.

The police commissioner, according to the *Mirror*, was still vigorously insisting that though the two victims had been dead approximately the same length of time, the mysterious driver of the Packard cabriolet had a perfect alibi for the 'bridge murder.' The 'bridge murder'! The police, accustomed to reliance on stool pigeons in routine gang murders, were plainly out of their element in this affair. Perhaps there were political angles to it. George had hit it pretty closely, thought Ed. Both murders might have been committed in Petunkawoc; that would tie them together. But another aspect of the case was worrying Ed, which he unconsciously thrust from his mind. This was the fact that an unknown man had entered his house Wednesday night, and that simultaneously Klarsen had silently disappeared.

68

George and Hubert were in the barn when Ed got home. They had not seen the later papers, but Hubert, it appeared, had been in town in the morning at Police Headquarters, where he had heard the news.

"Well, Gil," said Ed, "this is not so hot, is it? Shall we all have to go into court and testify as to everything we did Wednesday night? There's not much that we can tell them about Klarsen."

"You might have to testify at the inquest," said Hubert. "I'll go in with you. I don't think they'll want the guests. All you can testify is to when Klarsen left the house. About ten-thirty, wasn't it?"

"About that time," said Ed. "It was while we were out looking at the silo, with the policeman. And that puzzles me, too. Jeanie says that he left abruptly. He didn't say good-bye to her, but dashed off as if he'd suddenly remembered something. She thinks he went to look at his car; I believe Hugh said he had. But Hugh seemed surprised when he didn't come back. He and Ann evidently expected him to take them home."

"Is that so?" said Hubert attentively. "Did no one see Klarsen drive off?"

"No one saw, or *heard* him drive off," said Ed. "That's the funny part. I'm sure I'd have heard his car starting at that distance."

"Or noticed his lights," said Hubert, "if it was when we were outside. You're sure he was parked near by?"

"He drove the Crivingtons up to the barn," said Ed. "Naturally he'd park near by."

Hubert pondered this.

"What did they say about it at Headquarters, Gil? You were there when the report came in?"

"Yes," said Hubert, with seeming reticence. "I talked with Willoughby for about an hour. But Willoughby never theorizes—not aloud, anyway."

Ed picked up a large envelope that lay on the table. "What's this?" he asked.

"Photographs of the first rumble victim. Face and finger-prints. I got those at Headquarters this morning. But it's no one I ever saw."

Ed shoved them back in the envelope hastily.

"For goodness' sake," he said, "stick them away where no one will pull them out unexpectedly."

"I occupied myself when I got back here," said Hubert, "in dusting your cabinets for finger-prints. The cabinets were wiped. There are only my own and Mr. Gaynleigh's prints, which we made later."

"I'd almost forgotten that episode," said Ed. "It seems very trifling now."

"Have you seen anything of Crivington since the party?" asked George.

"No," said Ed. "I've got a notion to call him up. If Hugh's running to form, though, he won't be very communicative."

There was a rap at the door. Ed hopped up and opened it.

"Well, well, Mike," said Ed. "Off for the afternoon, eh? Atta boy. They ought to give you a week off for that scoop."

Mike tossed off his hat and coat and dropped wearily into an easy-chair.

"Weary but triumphant, eh?" said George. "Tell us about it. How did you identify the body?"

"Well," said Mike, "it was a hundred-to-one shot, and I felt like a fool playing it. I blew some of the paper's money having a plane ready at the Lowenthal Field and hopped to it when the news broke. Klarsen had a ring on that I remembered, a curious green knobbly stone, and a scar on his neck that he had told me was from a shell splinter. The tip of his little finger was gone, too; I'd noticed that. But there wasn't a bag or a scrap of paper of his in the car."

"Did you examine the car?" asked Hubert, with a keen professional look. He reminded George of an old dog who hears the baying of the hounds in the distance when he is tied at home.

"Superficially, I did. I wasn't there very long. I left Lowry there as soon as I'd identified the body, and made for a telephone to get the story in, and then flew back."

"What kind of tires did it have?" asked Hubert.

"Two U.S.," said Mike, thinking carefully, "on the front wheels; one Goodrich, left rear; one Goodyear, right rear. The U.S. were worn, but not smooth; the others fairly new. He'd driven over eighty thousand miles, by the speedometer. The car looked as if it had seen service."

"Any footprints around? Near the water?"

"Several. A man's footprints. And they showed plainly that the man shoved off in a canoe."

"Where did he get the canoe?"

"From a shed up on the shore. But the question is, where did he get a paddle? The boathouse was locked up, and there was no sign that anyone had broken in. Anyway, the trail stops there, because the lake is several miles long; in fact there's a chain of lakes, and he might have gone ten or twelve miles by water, and landed anywhere in the woods."

"Have they a pair of Klarsen's shoes?"

"They're hunting for baggage at the hotel where he generally stayed."

"Any sign of a scuffle by the lake?"

"Lowry didn't say so," said Mike. "But a bullet was found in the drip-pan of the car, under the engine; it had been mushroomed against the engine block. And there was a hole that it came through in the foot-board. But they figure, from the angle, that that couldn't have been the bullet that killed Klarsen. It looks to me as if it had been discharged during a grapple for possession of the gun, inside the car."

"What kind of a bullet?"

"A forty-five," said Mike, "from a Colt automatic. There was no sign or mark of the bullet that went through Klarsen. That was probably a forty-five, but that's all they can tell about it. No shells found."

"Do you suppose that was my gun, Gil?" asked Ed grimly.

"Your gun?" said Mike. "Why yours?"

"I guess I didn't tell you," said Ed, "that the thief who broke into the silo took my automatic?"

"Gad!" said Mike, sitting up. "That is interesting. Do you think that chap was the murderer?"

"I wish to thunder I hadn't told you about it now," said Ed. "I suppose you'll be putting that in your paper."

"Oh, you're all clear," said Mike. "You reported the theft as soon as it happened. But this idea that someone was gunning for Klarsen—or Klarsen gunning for someone—is certainly intriguing."

"I should say so!" said George. "That's bringing it close to home. Maybe you'd better take a look in your own rumble, Ed."

"Do that, Ed!" said Mike, edging forward in his chair. "By gosh, I think I feel a hunch coming on."

"Go to hell," said Ed disgustedly. "This is no subject for light kid-ding!"

"It wouldn't do any harm, Ed," suggested Hubert sagaciously.

Ed knocked out his pipe and got slowly up, muttering. Mike got up out of his chair and followed Ed out of the door. George caught the infection of curiosity, and Hubert followed along in the rear as Ed unlocked the garage doors. The rumble of Ed's car was presented to view.

Ed pulled up the lid and peered cautiously into the rumble. The expressions on the faces of the others suggested that they fully expected to see a body crumpled inside.

Ed reached in and tugged at something which stuck for a minute. Finally he extricated it and lifted it into view. It was a medium-sized leather suitcase. On the end of it was hot-stamped in neat capitals, 'J. C. C.'

All looked at one another with a wild surmise. Ed stared at Hubert helplessly. Mike was the first to break silence.

"Wow!" he howled. "Gosh, what a break! This is my lucky day! You see it, don't you?" he asked Hubert.

"Bring it indoors, Ed," said Hubert quietly. "And don't touch anything but the handle."

They all marched back. Mike was the only one who was vocal.

"Triple star night extra," he said, looking at his watch. "They can hold for it. And a Saturday afternoon! That's skinning 'em!"

Ed set the bag on the table. "Now, then," he said savagely, "how the hell did that get there?"

"Listen, Ed," said Mike. "You park under the bridge every day, don't you?"

"Yes," said Ed curtly, looking at Mike.

"You parked under the bridge all day Thursday, didn't you?"

"Yes."

"You came home at five-thirty Thursday?"

"Five P.M."

"O.K.," said Mike. "The body was put in Clifford's rumble between noon and five o'clock Thursday, *under the bridge!*"

All stared at Mike and considered the implications of this statement. Hubert opened the bag. It was empty.

"You've got two separate and distinct murder mysteries," declared Mike.

"And I'm mixed up in them both!" said Ed gloomily.

"Wait a minute, now, Mike," said George. "You figure that someone took Clifford's bag out of his rumble to make room for the body, and then chucked the bag into Ed's rumble to get rid of it, while both cars were parked under the bridge?"

"I do," said Mike.

George laughed. "That just shows how damnably clever this Clifford is," he said. "You'll print that, and the public will swallow it, hook, line, and sinker. And the joke of it is, you can't help it; you've got to print the facts, but you can't print inferences."

"What are your inferences?" asked Mike intently.

"That Clifford brought the body in and brought an empty bag in, and slipped the bag into Ed's rumble to create a false picture of the crime, to wit, that it happened under the bridge instead of in Petunkawoc."

"By George, George, you've got a busy little brain," said Mike.

"For the love of Mike, Mike, stir up your own!" said George, laughing.

"What do you think of that, Mr. Hubert?" asked Mike.

"George is right," said Hubert. "He's busted that alibi. But on the other hand, it's theory, not proof."

"Something tells me," said George, "that this Clifford person is one of the most ingenious liars ever born."

"May be," said Mike. "But the bag's a fact. And I'll have to telephone the desk toot sweet and get action!"

"Hold on, now, Mike!" said Ed sternly. "I've got enough publicity coming already, with an inquest that I'll have to attend!"

"What the hook, Ed? It's got to come out. You can't stick that bag away or burn it. Ask Mr. Hubert!"

"Gentlemen!" said Hubert importantly. He fished in his vest-pocket and produced a gold-plated shield which he held by its point. "I am an officer of the law." He put the shield back. "Moreover, I am authorized by your chief of detectives, Mr. Willoughby, of Dynamopolis, to conduct independent investigations of anything coming under my observation that seems to bear on either of these two crimes. Mr. Willoughby is an old friend of mine. I have been of assistance to him several times in my field, and he has done some great favors for me. He knows that I will cooperate with him punctiliously.

"Now, I will settle this argument by taking charge of this bag, and I will be responsible to Mr. Willoughby and to the law. And the first thing that I shall have to do will be to notify Willoughby by 'phone about this bag. This evidence is immediately vital. And Ed, I'm sorry to say that nothing that Mr. Macy or I can do will keep this out of the papers. But I don't think you'll find yourself an important feature of the news. Am I right, Mr. Macy?"

"You are, Mr. Hubert. You're a mere detail, Ed; the bag's the lead. Your name will appear just once, and you can brag about it to your grandchildren."

"And my name, Mr. Macy," said Hubert, "must not appear once. It's a matter of professional courtesy, but extremely important to me."

"I won't even mention it to the chief," said Mike. "I don't have to. I was on the spot myself."

"All right, then," said Hubert. "Now let me have that 'phone."

Hubert's telephone call was brief. Evidently Willoughby was a man of few words, who wanted nothing but facts.

"It's yours," said Hubert to Mike. Mike seized the telephone, and was almost equally brief.

"Now, Ed," said Hubert, "I'd like to lock this bag up. Isn't there a lock on your cabinet, in the silo? I guess you'll have to move some of your liquor out."

"I'll move it out now, and we'll have a drink," said Ed. "I need a jolt. This is the first time I've ever bust onto the front page in a murder story. Wonder how Jeanie'll like it?"

X

THE BARREL OF EXCELSIOR

The Sunday morning papers, having little that was new on the rumble murders, did not give them a streamer heading. They did, however, have one new item that provoked discussion. The footprints at the edge of the lake where Klarsen's car was found were compared with a pair of Klarsen's shoes found in a trunk at the hotel where he always stayed; and they were found to be Klarsen's own footprints.

It was admitted, however, that the shoes might have been on the murderer's, not Klarsen's, feet when the footprints were made, since it did not seem reasonable that Klarsen should have shoved off in a canoe, leaving his car on shore, and then have been shot and brought to land again. But, as Hubert observed, murder itself was not usually a reasonable business.

"It's sometimes harder to catch a stupid criminal," said Hubert, "than a clever one. A stupid criminal does illogical things; and the gaps in his logic are gaps in his trail. It's often easier to predict what a clever criminal will do."

"And an insane criminal," said George, "would be most difficult of all."

No sign of an abandoned canoe had been found in the lake or on the shores, nor any sign of the clothing of either of the two murdered men, nor of anything which Klarsen might have been carrying in the car. Hubert cautiously suggested that the footprints on the shore, and the marks of a canoe, might be a ruse.

Breakfast over, Hubert said that if Ed and George had no engagements, he would like to hold a conference in the barn. He also said that he wanted Mike Macy in on it. Ed called up Mike, who accepted with alacrity his appointment to the 'homicide squad,' as he called it, and promptly joined them.

"Gentlemen," said Hubert in a formal manner when they were all comfortably lounging in easy-chairs, "I want to enlist your help. We have as neat a little puzzle in these rumble murders as I have ever seen, and I have somewhat rashly offered my services to my friend Willough- by for what they may be worth. I get no credit for what I may accom- plish, it is true; but I get no public blame if I fail, though I should feel as badly, I think, to play the fool for Willoughby as if it were my own case. Willoughby will cooperate with me entirely, but I find it some- what of a handicap not to be able to cover the whole field. I wish very much that I could have seen the car in the lake and the footprints *in situ*, but I shall have to rely on information and photographs.

"I will begin by telling you what I have observed myself in this vicinity. I think we all know all the details of this little incident of the thief in the silo who obtained Ed's gun. Who or what manner of man this was puzzles me greatly; whether he came to steal, or to spy, or to commit murder, we don't know. I am pretty sure that he came from out West. Klarsen, as I learned in conversation with him Wednesday night, had also just come from the West, in his car; but whether the two knew one another is something for rather difficult investigation. It might help us to know more of the intimate history of Klarsen. But we'll take one thing at a time.

"I think we will also dismiss the subject of the first rumble murder from our present inquiry. There may be a connection, though it must be a singular one if so. But that matter is in the hands of Willoughby.

"Now, early on the morning after the episode of the silo thief, I made a little expedition into the ravine and over onto the hill opposite. One reason I did so was this: after I had gone to bed on the night of the party, I noticed a light from the headlights of a moving car flash faintly into my window and move along the wall. I got up and looked out of the window, but saw no car moving anywhere. I could not see much in the darkness, but my recollection was that no car moving in either direction along the highway could throw a light into my window at that angle.

"I didn't see anything particularly suspicious in the morning when I explored the hill, though I did see that someone had been eating there lately, and I saw the remains of a camp-fire. I looked into the quarry, which is an interesting place. I then followed the road which leads from the quarry down the hill into the ravine and out onto Buttermilk Road, the highway which runs east and west and also passes the entrance to the Green. I was looking for automobile tracks.

"This old road evidently hadn't been traveled much, and I was able to make out two sets of tracks that were comparatively fresh. One set of tires were Fisk—at least the ones that were not too worn to recognize were Fisk. And as nearly as I could judge—it isn't always easy—the car that wore these tires went up on the hill—and apparently didn't come down.

"The other set of tires more recent than the Fisk—made tracks both ways. I was pretty sure of the direction of the tracks because at one place, about fifty yards from the highway, this car had evidently slipped off the quarry road—which is eight or ten inches higher than the adjacent ground at this point—into the ditch. Then it had started again, got back on the road, and had driven to the foot of the quarry hill. At this point, however, the quarry road is loose fine rock and shows no tire tracks.

"This second set of tracks showed that the car had entered the ravine coming from west on the highway, and had left the ravine to continue east on the highway. Now, Mr. Macy told us last night that Klarsen's car wore two U.S., one Goodrich, and a Goodyear. Now that is a rather odd set of tires; most people stick to one make pretty much. And the tracks that I saw in the ravine were those of two U.S., one Goodrich, and a Goodyear."

The others stared at Hubert in silence. Mike reached for a match and relit his pipe, long since gone out.

"I certainly appreciate your calling me in this morning, Mr. Hubert," he said. "There's a good story in this."

"But not one for the papers yet, Mr. Macy," cautioned Hubert. "I am going to hold you *incommunicado* as to anything that comes out in our conferences, unless special exception is made. You will appreciate that I don't want publicity, and that also your good friends Ed and Jeanie don't want it, and that if you start it they will be overrun with your rivals coming out here. And if the story should end up with ourselves looking foolish, the less printed about it the better."

"I'll bet that's a reporter now!" said Ed as the telephone bell rang. "Let's get out of here."

"I was going to suggest that we take a stroll over to the hill," said Hubert. "It's a nice day."

All assented gladly.

"Now, Ed," said Hubert, when they had on their overcoats, "you told me that you used to go in for rifle practice here before they stopped you. Did you ever go in for pistol practice?"

"Why, yes," said Ed. "A little, at one time. I'm no crack shot, if that's what you want to know."

"I'm not asking about your marksmanship," said Hubert, with a smile. "But if there are any bullets from your automatic around here, I'd like to have them."

"I see," said Ed gravely. "Well, before I cleaned my pistol and put it in the silo a few days ago, I fired the last couple of shots off out here, at a tree."

"And did you hit the tree?" asked Hubert.

"To the best of my knowledge and belief, I did," said Ed. "I saw the bark fly."

"Do you think you could find the tree?"

"I might. It would take some shinning, though, to get the bullets. The tree was halfway down the ravine, and I hit it fairly high up. The holes will be hard to find."

"Well, suppose we try that later on, when the sun is in the West and lights up this side of the trees. Now let's look at those tire tracks in the ravine."

They climbed over the stone wall at a little distance from the barn and walked single file down a clear path which led diagonally down the side of the declivity.

"There used to be a gate in the wall there," explained Ed, "but I closed it up. We seldom walk down into the ravine."

The path led out of the ravine, and they shortly abandoned it to tramp through brush and thicket to where the old quarry road was visible.

"Here we are—" began Hubert, and suddenly stopped. He looked down at the road beneath his feet, then walked down it a short way in the direction of the highway, and returned. He took off his hat and scratched his head thoughtfully.

"Gentlemen," he said grimly, "the tracks have been obliterated."

"Since Thursday morning?" asked George.

"Since Thursday morning," said Hubert. "Someone has brushed them with boughs torn from the bushes. And left no footprints of his own."

Hubert stared at the ground perplexedly. The others waited for his explanation, but it was not forthcoming.

"Well," Hubert continued finally, "here is where the front and rear wheels, on the left side of the car, went off the road, and stopped. And you can still see where the rear wheels dug in in starting up again. There's no doubt about which way that car was headed. It went on toward the quarry. Well, let's proceed in that direction."

"Now," said Hubert, as they arrived at the point where the road began to ascend the hill, "do you think the car turned here, or went on up the hill to the quarry? The treads of the tires are lost on this crushed stone."

"By Jove," said George, "I take my hat off to anyone who'd drive up that road at night."

"You could do it," said Ed. "It's a good hard road. It's narrow and winding and dark and steep, and the bushes are badly grown over it, but it's well built. It's made of chaff from the quarry."

"Well," said Hubert, "do you see my bedroom window from here? Some car that night flashed its lights into my window for a moment. A car turning here would have done it, and the lights would have moved in just the direction that I saw them move."

"What time was that?" asked Mike.

"At eleven-thirty-one, by my watch. I made a note of it."

"And Klarsen left the house at ten-thirty," said Mike. "What was he doing out here for an hour?"

"You seem to have observed Klarsen more closely than any of us that evening, Mike," said George. "Did he eat any of those olives or nuts or any of that junk?"

"Come, now, George," said Ed. "Whether I poisoned Klarsen or not is immaterial. He was shot through the heart."

"I see you're thinking about the autopsy," said Hubert. "It's true that any such food in the stomach would fix the time of death pretty closely."

"Well, I don't think he ate anything," said Mike. "He smoked Ed's cigars most of the evening."

"The question is," said George, "was he shot and brought out here, or was he shot out here, or was he shot somewhere on the highroad to Lake Putnam?"

"You're going too fast, Mr. Gaynleigh," said Hubert. "Let's go on up the hill and see what we see."

"A tough little hill," commented George, as they paused for breath at a point where a view was opened through the trees. "Hullo!" he said, almost with a start. "There's that old tree. If you don't think it looks like a hand, Ed, take a look at it now!" He pointed to the dark silhouette against the open sky.

"A swell gibbet," said Ed. "Hangman's Hill! Maybe there's something in that name."

They proceeded on up the narrow road, which in places was almost a tunnel through the overarching bushes, and emerged into open ground, a flat area, white and glittering in the sun. This ground, evidently, was made of accumulated waste rock produced in quarrying. To their left, darkly in shadow and contrasting with the dazzling brilliance of the ground on which they stood, was the quarry, a large cut in the hilltop, not visible from Ed's house. The walls of the cut were twenty feet high, forming three sides, terraced by the working of the quarry, rough and menacing. They resembled in effect the ruins of some ancient Greek theater, in the pit of which was a large stagnant pool, the depth of which was not apparent to the eye. To the front and right of the explorers were tall woods, among which some pine and spruce still darkened the depths. At the far side of the small plateau of waste rock the road appeared to continue through the woods, but it was no more than a pair of ruts covered by fallen leaves.

"This is a 'dank tarn,'" said George. "A good place to wail for a 'lost Ulalume.' The murderer showed excellent taste if he chose this spot."

"Here are signs," said Hubert, "that people have been eating here. There's a cracker box that looks rather new. Here's a piece of oiled paper; that's more significant; looks as if it came from around bacon or butter. But this is what interests me most," he said, pointing to the ground. "The remains of a camp-fire. They've been kicked around, but it's plain that cooking has been done up here. Do your picnickers go in for hot meals much, Ed?"

"I've never observed them with a telescope," said Ed, "but I think they generally eat out on that bare rock to the south. It doesn't stand to reason that they'd eat here in this dismal place."

Mike began looking for tire tracks, and Hubert walked on down the rough road through the woods. Ed inspected a tumbledown shanty by the quarry. It had evidently been a tool-house, and contained nothing but a bench built along one wall, some old boxes, a rusty crowbar, pieces of heavy chain, and some much-rotted rope. There was also a rusty iron wheel which might have come from a portable pump or engine for drilling.

George struck into the woods in an easterly direction and soon came to an open clearing on the side of the hill toward the plain and away from Westwood. The field was overgrown with high grass, wild blackberry vines, and small underbrush. It looked as if it might originally have been cleared for a small house. It offered a scanty view of the plain below, obscured by trees; and below on the concrete highway George could hear the motor cars passing.

Hubert finally came back to the quarry. "Ed," he asked, "do people junk their cars up here?"

"I've never seen 'em in the act," said Ed. "But I shouldn't put it past them."

"This track through the woods leads to a steep cliff," said Hubert, "at the bottom of which are thick woods. Quite a drop. I daren't peep over any farther, but I think I saw the remains of a car down there."

The whole party walked in the direction from which Hubert had come, and halted at the brink of a steep declivity. All confirmed Hubert's report that there was a rusty and badly smashed car down below.

"Where there's one, there may be more," said Hubert. "I'd like to get down there, but I wouldn't risk my life or yours in doing it. Some of this loose rock that's been dumped over here might start to slide on us. I wonder whether we could get there from the foot of the hill?"

"I think so," said Ed. "But my advice is to change our clothes before we try it. Let's tackle that this afternoon."

"Well, I'm game to go down there," said Mike. "In fact, I'll do it myself if no one else goes."

"I'm shamed into volunteering too," said George, "though I'd much rather loll in an easy-chair with a book on the Lord's Day. But, Ed, you'll have to issue me a regulation O.D. outfit, shoes, shirt, and pants. I have only two suits of clothes, and I don't propose to sacrifice either."

"Well, let's go back," said Hubert. They descended the hill and came out into the ravine.

"I must say," said George, as they picked their way through the brush, "that the picture I get is very queer. I see Klarsen driving to the foot of the hill, then walking up to the quarry, spending the best part of an hour there, coming down, turning his car, and driving hell-bent through the north country. Do you suppose the other car was chasing him?"

"Your clairvoyant methods, George," said Ed, "are likely to gum up the solution of this mystery badly. I have a good deal of doubt about your Clifford reconstruction, though I do think Clifford's own story is no better."

"I don't believe Klarsen drove away from here," said Mike. "It's much more likely that he was killed here."

"Then why didn't they throw his body over the cliff?" asked George. "Why carry it thirty or forty miles away?"

"We may know more about that this afternoon," said Hubert.

"Now, boys," said Ed, as they came to the other side of the ravine, "I want you to help me look for something." He looked up at the barn to get his bearings, and then plunged into the thicket on the hillside.

"I'm looking for a barrel," he said. "It'll save me a lot of work if we can find it."

"Not another body, Ed?" asked George.

"No," said Ed. "A barrel stuffed with excelsior. Scatter, and hunt."

In a moment Mike hailed them. "Here you are, Ed!" he cried. "Will this do? Ha! I see! Clever boy, Ed. You ought to find a lot of bullets in that."

He hove the barrel on his broad shoulders and plodded up the hill with it. The end of the barrel showed plainly that it had been used as a target for pistol practice.

"Those bullets are a couple of years old," said Ed. "But they ought to do."

Mike dumped the barrel on the driveway, Ed got a hatchet, and cracked the barrel open. They pulled out the impacted excelsior and shook out, one by one, twenty-seven bullets.

"That ought to do you, Gil," said Ed.

"Fine," said Hubert, picking up the last one. "This is a good morning's work. Let's wash up now and eat."

XI

THE JUNKED CAR

"Well," said Jeanie as soup was being served, "what have you four discovered in your explorations?"

"Not very much," said Ed. "Our thieves seem to have been camping out on top of the hill over there, but there's no sign of their presence there now. I've got half a notion to buy that hill. I'll bet I could get it for very little. I think I might be able to find someone to build on it. Good lots in Westwood are scarce now, and that one's got some scenic advantages. It would take money to build there, though."

"Horace and Mary Potter drove over after you'd left," said Jeanie. "Especially to see you, George. I thought you'd be back any minute. I asked them to stay to dinner, but they couldn't. Horace wants you to call him up."

"Well, well," said George, pleased. "I'm sorry I missed them. I'd like to see Toomey. I'm quite fond of him. I'll buy him a lunch with the three dollars I got from the *New Yorker* yesterday."

"Come in with me to lunch tomorrow," said Ed. "I'll need your moral support, with all the razzing I'll get about that suitcase and everything."

"Well, I don't know," said George. "I have a sort of razz-berry complex myself. I have too much difficulty explaining to people what I've been doing with the years since I left the classic shades. I passed up the class reunion last year."

"Never you mind, George," said Jeanie. "By your next reunion you'll be the principal speaker, the well-known author, who will now explain his romantic rise to fame. Can't you hear them cheering?"

"I suppose Toomey and Mary wanted to know all about our own sudden rise to fame, didn't they?" asked Ed of Jeanie.

"Oh, yes," said Jeanie. "We'll have to get used to that. Toomey says he can't see why the whole bunch that was at the party isn't given the third degree. He says it isn't being handled right. It's not like any detective story that he ever read, he says."

"He's right about that," said George. "I suspect Mike Macy of having a hand in the crime. His fanatical journalistic enterprise might lead him to obtain a scoop in that way."

"I think all the guests of Wednesday night," said Hubert, amused, "will have little trouble proving that they weren't at Dugan's Grove at two o'clock Thursday morning."

"Well, I don't know," said George. "In any detective story we'd all have a devil of a time proving our innocence, and every one of us would have done something suspicious that evening that he or she refused, for personal reasons, to explain. Now I've got an alibi that is an alibi. I was right under the same roof with Mr. Hubert from Wednesday evening till Thursday morning."

"I suspect," said Ed, "that you'd like to see me beaten with a rubber hose to make me tell how that suitcase got into my rumble."

"Why not?" said George. "I should say the law is a bit of a snob if it treats the inhabitants of Westwood any different from the inhabitants of Paradise Alley."

"I don't know about the law," said Hubert, "but I don't think detectives as a rule are bothered with social distinctions. Of course they have to be more careful about false arrest in the upper strata. You can't beat a man like Clifford with a rubber hose. But I rather think the criminal statistics of Westwood would make a better showing than those of Paradise Alley."

"I'm glad you think so, Mr. Hubert," said Jeanie. "My opinion is that it was that woman in khaki that did it."

"Oh, if there's a woman in the case," said George enigmatically, "*tout le monde* is suspect."

After dinner Ed brought some old clothes out to the barn for George, and they dressed for the afternoon's work.

"Mr. Gaynleigh," said Hubert, as they tramped across the ravine, "I'm going to assign you to sentry duty on the top of the hill. While it's rather unlikely, we don't want anybody to junk another car over the cliff while we happen to be underneath, or to try any other monkey business."

"That's a pretty soft detail," said George. "Wish I'd brought a good book to read. That's better than looking for corpses under the cliff. Good hunting, boys!" he called to them as he started up the hill.

George decided to take up his post first on the highest point of the hill, which was the top of the rock forming the quarry walls. Here he could look down into the pool on one side, and facing the other way, across the ravine to Ed's house, and up and down the ravine to right and left. Looking down to the right, he saw the others disappearing into the thicket. Looking to the left, he could see the old quarry road leading out to Buttermilk Road.

To his surprise he saw, walking along this road toward the highway, the figure of a smartly dressed woman. She turned up Buttermilk Road in the direction of the Green, and on up the hill. She turned her face once toward him, and George made a guess at her identity. He thought, though he was not certain, that it was Ann Crivington.

Hubert, Ed, and Mike tramped along the ravine at the base of the great rock cliff on which George was perched, until Ed showed them a place where he thought they could penetrate the woods and get to the base of the cliff at the foot of which the junked car lay. It was bad going, full of great rocks, dead stumps, fallen and rotting trees, and dead leaves and deep moss that sunk half a foot under their heels. It was dusky even at that hour of the afternoon. Finally they rounded a corner of the cliff and saw before them half a dozen or more cars scattered about, in various strange positions and all in an extreme condition of wreckage.

All were old, beyond a doubt; rust proved it. The searchers walked on, casting an eye to one side or an other, and came to an old green touring car on which some nickel plate still shone. It was upside down.

Hubert looked at the chassis a moment. The car had landed nose first; the front wheels were sticks and the front tires shreds. Hubert poked the rear tires. "Fisk," he remarked.

"Time to re-tire," commented Ed.

"This car is old," said Hubert, "but in spite of the condition it's in now, it doesn't look to me as if it had been old enough to junk. I wonder if we could turn it over."

Ed looked at Mike grimly, but Mike did not bat an eye. They all took a grip on the car and managed to tumble it over, right side up. Ed peered in cautiously. There were no bodies in the car.

The engine was telescoped into the body of the car, the steering-wheel post stuck up through the top, and the front seat was smashed. Hubert pulled out the oil gauge and looked at it. He opened the cap of the gas tank; there was a short gush of gasoline, due to the slant of the car.

"The rear tires have air in them," said Hubert, "and there's a couple of gallons of gas, I should guess, in the tank. It may be that the car was in an accident before it came here, and was towed up; but I doubt that. The license plates are gone, but that's true of most of the cars here. I'll take the factory number and the motor number; we can perhaps trace the ownership through those, though I hope we don't have to write to all forty-nine states. I'll do one other thing." He took out a jackknife and scraped some of the accumulated tar and mud from under the fender. He put this in a red cotton handkerchief and put it in his pocket.

Then he took from his pocket a box containing a bright red powder, dipped a camel's-hair brush into it, and proceeded to dust the gas lever and the dashboard instruments. The light was none too good and at times he resorted to a big flashlight that he had brought. He also dusted the headlights. Changing to a silvery powder from another box, he dusted the ledges of the car doors. Finally he tried the back of the car, selecting the most likely spots. He put away his implements, looking much disgusted.

"The car has been carefully wiped," he declared. "Which is itself a fact in evidence, but not so satisfactory as finger-prints. But I'm pretty sure of one thing: the car was driven over on its own power, not pushed. The gears are in neutral, but that means nothing, after the smash they got."

He and Ed tore and pulled at the wreckage inside of the car, and found a few tools, but nothing offering a good surface for finger-prints.

Mike meanwhile had been tramping around, valiantly beating the high undergrowth with a stick, when suddenly he called to them. He was holding up a small gold object gingerly in his fingers.

"I found this where the car was before we turned it over," he said. "Here's the exact spot. Either this came out of the car or it was dropped there before the car came down."

Hubert took the object carefully from him. It was a cheap 'compact' for makeup, such as are sold in drugstores. Hubert looked at it inside and out. He laid it carefully on a large boulder and dusted it outside and inside.

"It's got finger-prints," he said. "Nice clear ones. And they are, of course, those of a woman. And a left-handed woman," he added, examining the box closely.

"Now, how the deuce can you tell that?" asked Ed.

Hubert looked surprised that Ed should ask. "Her right thumb-print is on the mirror," he said, "and her left thumb-print on the bottom of the box. Did you ever see a woman use a vanity case?"

"Every day for the last ten years, at least. But I never observed the operation closely."

"Well, she uses her left hand to hold the mirror, and her right hand to dab the stuff on her face. That is, if she's right-handed. This woman does the opposite."

"Can you tell her right thumb from her left on that?"

"I can, by its position; and by the opposing index finger on the other side of the cover of the box. If you'll hold both of your hands in front of you, as if you were holding an imaginary letter, you'll see what I mean. This woman seized the mirror with her right hand and closed the box with her left hand."

"Well, it's a long shot," continued Hubert. "Any picnicker might have thrown it over the cliff. But we'll keep it just the same. Have you got a clean handkerchief?" He sprayed the compact inside and out with a fixative, dried it, and then wrapped the thing gently and put it in his breast-pocket. "This car will probably stay here undisturbed. Now, Mr. Macy, that was all you found, wasn't it?"

"No bodies," said Mike cheerfully. "At least not within the zone where they would be if thrown from this cliff. Of course they might have been thrown from another part of the hill. Do you want to explore further?"

Hubert rubbed his chin. "It would be a good hard day's work to cover all the ground where a body might be, and we have no definite reason to suppose that there are any bodies here. There might be a gun, but I doubt if we'd ever find it. Let's get back to civilization."

Ed celebrated the return to civilization by shaking up cocktails for them in the barn, George having joined the others as soon as he saw them wave to him from below the hill.

"Could you swear in court, George," asked Ed, "that the lady you saw in the ravine was Ann Crivington?"

"I'm afraid not," admitted George. "I never saw her but once before, and that was in entirely different clothes. I'd have followed her up, but that I had my orders. But what puzzles me is where she came from. If she was on the hill when I was coming up, she must have hidden till I passed her. If not, she must have been approaching the hill until she saw me on top, and then turned back again. Either action would be queer."

"Oh, I don't know. She might be curious about the affair, like anybody else, and want to look around. No doubt she thought your actions were suspicious and her own perfectly natural."

"What sort of a person is Mrs. Crivington?" asked George.

"Wholly respectable. But a most unscrupulous flirt. Always was. I suspect she's got Art Dancey on the string now; anyway, I used to see Art teaching her golf strokes out on the Green about every evening before dinner. But her reputation's safe with him, Lord knows. Art is the soul of old Southern chivalry."

"Do you suppose, Ed," asked Hubert, "that Mr. Crivington would give us any information about Klarsen's activities and private life?"

"I don't know," said Ed. "Depends on what kind of a mood he's in. Sometimes Hugh is very close-mouthed and sometimes he forgets for a few minutes that he's a vice-president. I'd like to talk with him. Do you want to take him into our confidence?"

"Provided he'll take us into his," said Hubert.

"I'll call him up now and see if he'll come over," said Ed. He took the telephone.

"Westwood 5," he called. "Hello. Can I talk to Mr. Crivington? This is Ed Marsh. What about? Why, I'm his neighbor, across the Green. All right." Ed waited, his hand over the mouthpiece. "The maid seems to think she's his private secretary. I suppose they've been dodging reporters all day, and—hello! Yes, hello, Hugh. Come on over, Hugh, and have a cocktail. What? Naturally, I want to talk about Klarsen. Damned sorry. Fine chap. What? Yes, George and Hubert are here—" Ed paused, and his face reddened. "Look here, Hugh, I understand your troubles, but—" evidently Ed was interrupted again. "Listen, Hugh—what the hell's the matter with you, anyway? Well, by gosh!" Ed hung up.

"I'd like to crack him one on the ear," said Ed. "Something's eating Hugh. Never knew him so nasty. High-strung chap. I guess his nerves are pretty well shot over it, though."

"I gather," said Hubert, smiling, "that Mr. Crivington feels that we are a bunch of unlicensed amateurs who are butting into his company's affairs."

"That's about it. But I don't see why he should get so excited about it. Do you suppose he saw us out scouting today?"

"If he did, I don't see why he should object. I suppose I could show him my authority, but I'd rather work quietly if I can. He'll have to talk at the inquest, and we'll go and listen."

Jeanie was outspokenly skeptical about George's identification of Ann Crivington.

"What kind of a dress did she have on?" she asked.

"A tweed suit," said George unhesitatingly. "Light brown."

"Everybody's got a tweed suit," said Jeanie. "How was it cut?"

"With scissors, I guess."

"What kind of a hat did she have on?"

"A small hat. Dark brown."

"A turban? A tricorne? A beret?"

"Lord, I don't know," said George. "Why don't you ask me whether it was a Patou or a Reboux model? I'm no milliner."

"Well, if you're trying to convict Ann, I'll give her a complete alibi. If you think she'd ever touch, let alone carry, a compact like that thing you showed me, you don't know Ann, that's all."

"Is she left-handed?"

"Left-handed? Yes, she is. At least she plays tennis with her left hand. What have you got on your mind, George? You're just trying to make me think you're smart."

XII

GEORGE DONS RUBBER BOOTS

Monday morning Hubert rode in with Ed, taking along the suitcase, the twenty-seven bullets, and the sample of mud from the junked car. They went together to Headquarters, where Hubert introduced Ed to Inspector Willoughby, who questioned Ed closely. Willoughby was a big, chunky man with a scrubby mustache, who looked, thought Ed, as if he feared neither man nor the devil; a good fellow when friendly, but a bad one to have after you; and so thoroughly hard-boiled that Ed had the unfamiliar sensation of feeling like a fragile porcelain cup in close proximity to a large iron kettle. Willoughby shook hands cordially with Ed and thanked him, and Ed left Hubert there with him and drove to his office in the Spindler Building.

George had agreed—foolishly, he now thought—to a suggestion of Hubert's that George should explore the ravine for shells, guns, articles of clothing, or anything that might look like a clue. He was also to keep an eye out for broken or trampled bushes, footprints, or any signs of blood. George set about his task as soon as Hubert had left.

As he strolled down into the ravine, the Herculean magnitude of this assignment was apparent to him. By some remotely happy chance one might discover a shell or a bullet in such ground; but the only really efficient method would be to burn or uproot all the vegetation. However, George did spend about an hour in this search, selecting the spot where Hubert had shown them the marks made by Klarsen's car in slipping off the old road into the ditch, and examining the ground for a radius of about twenty feet from this spot. He found, however, no shells, guns, hats, buttons, or cigarette stubs; and if any signs of blood were to be discovered, it could only be by crawling about on one's hands and knees with a lens. George rebelled against reverting to the quadruped. He applied himself to mental work.

What caused Klarsen's car to slip off the road here? he asked himself. The road curved slightly, but it was level and plenty wide. And Klarsen was an expert driver on all kinds of roads. Either he was driving without lights, thought George; or he was attacked here; or someone else was driving the car.

George set out to retrace the probable course of the car after leaving Ed's place. He walked south on the old road until he came to Buttermilk Road, then up that to the two stone pillars at the entrance to the Green. To the right, as he turned in, was Dancey's house, a charming white building set well back among the trees. George walked past Dancey's gate, came to Ed's driveway, turned in, and ended his walk at the stone wall at the back of Ed's lot, on the edge of the ravine. This was where Ed's visitors parked their cars; the ground, theoretically, was grass-covered, but was nearly bald from such use.

George lit a cigarette, observed the view, then turned his back to it and sat on the wall, kicking his heels against it. He was out of breath, which annoyed him; too much sedentary work, too many cigarettes. To get out of breath in a five-minute walk! Still, it was uphill, all the way; he hadn't noticed that before.

Uphill all the way? That meant downhill the other way! George hopped off the wall and studied the ground. Yes, it could be done. Unlock the brakes, give the car a push, and it would roll down the lane, out into Randall Road, out the gates, and coast down Buttermilk Road with enough speed to carry it well into the ravine if one turned in there. There the thief could tinker with the ignition and start it, if he were something of a mechanic.

Klarsen's car would have had to be parked the right way, though. Ah! Klarsen drove the Crivingtons up to the barn; then he would have to back up, and would no doubt park with the rear of his car to the stone wall.

George examined the tire marks, and avoided stepping on them. He looked also for footprints. Footprints, in his opinion, were vastly overrated in detective work. All the guests must have left footprints, and mighty poor ones. But a glint suddenly caught his eye. Ha! a bullet? No, a triangular piece of steel. A broken knife blade, on the grass.

George picked it up carefully by the points and regarded it skeptically. This was the kind of thing that solutions hung on in detective stories. Detectives in detective stories, he reflected, always made fun of detective stories.

Not knowing what a real detective would do in such circumstances, George acted as much as possible like a fictional one. He put a ring of pebbles around the spot where he had found the blade. Then he carried the blade carefully into the barn, laid it on a clean piece of paper, put the blade and paper into an empty drawer of his dresser, closed the drawer, and locked it and pocketed the key.

He thought he would call that a morning's work. He lit a cigarette, looked over Ed's bookshelves, and picked out a detective story to read. It was entitled, 'The Clue of the Bent Toothpick.'

After luncheon George thought best not to take up the search for more clues until he had digested his excellent meal to some extent, so he continued awhile with his easy-chair and detective story. It was with a guilty start, therefore, that he put away his book hastily on hearing footsteps approaching. George looked at his watch. It was a quarter past three. He opened the door for Hubert.

"I'm afraid you find me slacking on the job," he said apologetically. "I covered a good deal of ground this morning, but I confess I'm no detective. It seems to me impossible to find anything in that kind of ground."

Hubert chuckled. "I'll bet you suspect me of putting up a practical joke on you," he said. "Unless we can localize the scene of the crime by other means, I dare say you are right. But I thought you might stumble on something."

"I did, as a matter of fact," said George, "but I'm not very sanguine about its value. A broken knife blade, by the stone wall."

Hubert looked surprised but hopeful. "That has possibilities," he said. "Well, I had pretty fair luck this morning. I have reports on the bullets and the mud sample."

"What about the bullets? They're Ed's, I suppose?"

"Fifteen out of the twenty-seven bullets," said Hubert, throwing his hat and coat on the window-seat, "are from one gun, and twelve from another. Both Colt automatic, forty-five. The imprints of the bore on the fifteen bullets are the same as those on the bullet found under the hood of Klarsen's car."

"Is that positive evidence, or surmise?"

"Positive. The comparascope superimposes the image of one bullet over that of the other. In this case the bullet from the car was somewhat mushroomed, but the marks of the bore are clear."

"Gosh!" said George. "That looks as if Ed's gun did the job, all right. And as if the silo climber fired the shot."

"Not quite—not until we know whether those fifteen bullets, or the other twelve, came from Ed's gun."

George considered this with acute concentration. "Perhaps Ed has two guns," he said.

"I don't think he has two forty-five Colt automatics. However, he ought to be able to tell us whose the other gun is."

"Do any of these bullets match up those in the first rumble victim?" asked George.

"No. We hardly expected that. That man was shot with a Colt forty-five, Schlogl, the expert, says, but they haven't the gun nor any other bullets for comparison.

"Finally," continued Hubert, "the scrapings of mud and tar from the fender of the junked car that we looked at yesterday contain the same kind of mud that was taken from the fender of Klarsen's car by the police. That's a type of colloidal soil found out West—we call it gumbo out there—and further analysis ought to localize it more specifically. I'm going to have a fender taken off of the junked car so they can compare the deposits stratum by stratum."

George sank back into his chair. "I shall live up to my role of Watson," he said, "by exclaiming, 'Marvelous, my dear Hubert, marvelous!'"

Hubert laughed. "It looks a little as if this trouble had its origin out in my part of the country," he said. "The police may be able to find, from state registration of motor cars, whom that junked car belonged to—unless it's a stolen car, which it may well be. Still, that would tell us something. And I think we can limit the field to perhaps eight or ten states.

"Well," continued Hubert, "now we'll look at your knife blade. I suppose you handled it carefully?"

"I haven't touched the surface of it," said George. "I'll get it. It's upstairs."

George went upstairs and came down again with the knife blade on the paper and set it on the table, feeling much like a schoolboy handing his parent a very bad monthly report. He lit a cigarette and tried to appear nonchalant.

Hubert got out his powders and brushes, pulled up a chair to the table, and pulled the paper with the blade on it toward him. He dusted the blade, looked at it, and then examined it with his microscope. A scraping noise from Hubert's chair caused George to look around.

Hubert got up, took out his keys, and went to the door of the silo, unlocked it, then unlocked the wardrobe cabinet, and took from it the gold-plated vanity box which Mike had found at the foot of the cliff. Carrying this carefully, he laid it on the table beside the knife blade. He sat down and examined both blade and vanity box with his pocket microscope.

After a few minutes' inspection, Hubert shifted his chair and looked around at George. "This is interesting," he said. "Both of these objects the knife blade and the vanity box bear the same fingerprints. And both are the finger-prints of a woman."

"The same woman?" asked George, elated.

"Positively. No two people have the same fingerprints, you know; not even twins. Take a look through the glass."

George squinted at the finger-prints. To his untrained vision they certainly seemed the same. He examined his own thumb by way of comparison. "These prints look eccentric to me," he said. "My own seem to be of a simpler pattern."

"These have what is called a lateral pocket loop," said Hubert. "If I had an enlargement of these prints, I could point out to you any number of minute ridge characteristics which establish them beyond doubt as the same. Of course, I don't claim to be an expert. But I'll bet my shoes and walk home barefooted if the experts don't agree with me. You couldn't ask for better impressions."

"What follows from that?"

"I'm sure I don't know. Where did you find the blade?"

"I can show you exactly if you'll come out a minute."

They walked to the stone wall by the parking place, and George pointed to the circle of pebbles with which he had conscientiously marked the spot.

"That's good work," said Hubert. "Very keen of you to mark the spot exactly. Now, I wonder how long the blade has been there, and how it got broken. It's not the kind of thing a woman carries; it's a man's-size hunting knife. It's possible that she merely picked the thing up, out of curiosity, and dropped it again."

"Or threw it there. From down in the ravine."

"If that's the case, she's ambidextrous. Because the prints on the blade are from the right hand."

"I thought someone might have been tampering with Klarsen's car," said George. "I noticed this morning that the ground slopes almost continuously from this spot down into the ravine, by way of the road. The car might have been stolen and coasted."

"A shrewd bit of observation," said Hubert, "and worthy of a professional. But there's some contradictory evidence farther along the road. If I'm not mistaken, the engine was started just beyond Ed's gate."

"Is that so?" asked George, surprised and disappointed. "It's true, the slope isn't great in the Green, but the car could easily be pushed to the main road."

"Your guess is as good as mine. The gravel shows no tire pattern. But outside Ed's gate are two depressions, and there's gravel all over the sidewalk still. Someone started a car there, and stepped on it hard. It may not have been Klarsen, but we mustn't shut our eyes to the possibility that Klarsen was driving that car.

"Well, now," continued Hubert, as they walked back to the barn, "it's four o'clock. Do you want to call it a day, or are you game for another little job—a rather mean one?"

"I'm with you," said George, though he would have been quite content to rest on his laurels. "What have you in mind?"

"Ever do any fishing in rapids?"

"Never. I know what you mean, though. Like the pictures that you see in summer resort and railroad ads, man standing in the seething waters with hip boots, a fly rod, a creel, and a landing net. Always has a pipe in his mouth, to show how easy it is. But where are the rapids?"

"I shall have to disappoint you as to that. Your fishing will be in still waters. You won't need a rod or creel, but you'll need a rake. I've got one of Ed's, and I've got his hip boots. I want you to wade in the quarry pond for me."

George's stomach suddenly registered a faint protest.

"Not looking for bodies, are you?" he asked.

"No, indeed," said Hubert, laughing. "I'm looking for whatever may be there. It may be a gun, it may be license plates, or it may be only cooking utensils. I'm ashamed to ask you to do it, really, but you're a better man than I am when it comes to nimble work."

"Oh, I'm not kicking. I'm rather curious about that, too. Where are the hip boots?"

"Up in my room. Don't put them on; carry them over there. I'll change my clothes in a jiffy."

Hubert was downstairs again in a few minutes, and they marched off, George carrying the boots and rake. They mounted the hill to the quarry, and sat down to get their breath.

"I don't think it's very deep," said Hubert, "but the bottom may be rough. Feel your way with the rake and look out for holes."

Wearing the hip boots, which were a trifle too large for him, and carrying his rake as a staff, like Saint Christopher, George waded into the pool. At once he got an indication of the character of the bottom, for he came within an inch of slipping and falling flat at the first step. He raked with his rake, and also, rolling up his sleeves to the shoulders, he felt the bottom with his hands.

"What we ought to do," said Hubert, "is to pump out this pond. But we'll see first what we get this way."

George fished out a number of tin cans, a small oil stove, and a heavy iron wheel, which, however, he dropped into the water again.

"Seems to be a lot of junk here," he said. "I don't think I've missed anything so far. If I'd stepped on a license plate I think I'd know it. There isn't a flat inch on the bottom."

George had covered about two thirds of the pond, when suddenly he stepped into a deep depression in the bottom, just as he was stooping. Something flew up, hit him between the eyes, and fell back into the pool. George sat down hard, up to his neck in water. Hubert hopped in and gave him a hand.

"Gosh!" said George, feeling his head. "That was quite a whack. Did you see what that was?"

"Some kind of a stick. Better wade out, and we'll run home and get you a stiff drink."

"Might as well see what that was," said George. He poked around, reached under the water, and brought out a stout-handled spade. With this and the rake as staffs, he made his way ashore.

"Sit down and let me get your boots off," said Hubert. He emptied the boots of water, slung them over his shoulder, took the spade, and made George hurry ahead of him.

On reaching the barn, George skipped upstairs, took a hot and cold shower, and Hubert came up with a glass of whiskey. George was soon downstairs in his own clothes.

"Well," he said to Hubert, filling himself another short drink and lighting a cigarette, "I'm afraid that's not much in the way of results. A broken knife blade and a spade. I should be a junk dealer, not a detective."

"I think you're entitled to the spade, as booty," said Hubert. "It's not a bad one, either. A little rusty, that's all."

"Here comes Ed," said George. "Maybe I can sell it to him."

"Well, gentlemen," said Ed. "Here are the evening papers. Not much in them; my fame is brief. I have to go to the inquest tomorrow, though. What news have you got? Where did you get that shiner, George. Been battling with ruffians?"

George recounted the episode of the spade, and also told Ed about the knife blade.

"Let's get this straight, now," said Ed. "As I understand it, Ann Crivington, dressed in khaki trousers and moccasins, scaled the silo, pushed a car over the cliff, threw a spade in the pond, and then went and played mumblety-peg by the stone wall out here. Is that your conclusion?"

"We've discarded the spade," said George. "The spade is mine. I'll let you have it for the absurd sum of one dollar, paid in hand. You can use a good spade."

"Let's see it," said Ed. He took it to the window, turned it over in his hands, rubbed it, and examined it carefully.

"You're a pair of crooks," he exclaimed. "This is my spade!"

"Your spade?" said George indignantly, leaping up.

"Look at that!" Ed pointed to some scratches on the shank, forming the initials 'E. M.'

"Ha!" exclaimed George. "Then kindly explain what you were doing with it before you threw it into the pond. Burying bodies?"

"Someone stole it out of the garage. What on earth did he want with it?"

They stared at one another in perplexity.

"I think, after all," said Hubert, "that we might put the spade with our other souvenirs. Now, Ed, I want to ask you another question." He told Ed about the ballistic report on the twenty-seven bullets from the barrel of excelsior.

"Who, besides yourself, Ed," he asked, "fired at your barrel target and left bullets in it?"

"It was Art Dancey," said Ed promptly. "We had a little shooting-match one time, and I lost. He's a crack shot, that boy."

XIII

SEVEN AND TWENTY BULLETS

The telephone bell rang at that moment, and Ed answered it. "Right-o," he answered cheerfully. "We'll be right in. Dinner," he announced to the others.

Jeanie insisted on getting the latest developments. "You can hide out in the barn all you like," she said. "I know you're all in earnest about this thing. But I want the news. You can trust me not to breathe a word to anyone. Nobody's more anxious to keep out of the papers than I am, and no one appreciates more than I, Mr. Hubert, what you're doing for us. I know that if it weren't for you we'd be plagued to death with reporters and detectives."

Hubert gave Jeanie a résumé of the day's happenings. Jeanie was interested in the idea that a woman might be implicated, and said that so far as she knew none of the maids, nor anyone in the Green, ever went over on the hill, as it was not regarded as a cheerful place for a ramble. Hubert suggested to Jeanie that she take around to her neighbors and neighbors' maids one of the enlarged photographs of the figure in khaki, to get a popular vote on its sex, and possibly even to identify the person. Jeanie was delighted with this idea.

Ed found difficulty in accepting George's theory that Klarsen's car had been stolen.

"Assuming that it was," he objected, "it still remains a mystery how Klarsen could become aware of the fact at that particular moment. He must have been telepathic."

"He didn't have to be telepathic," said George. "He had heard there was a thief around, he discovers that he's left his keys in his car, and rushes out, to find it gone."

100

"Not his keys, George," said Jeanie. "I hadn't thought of it till this minute, but he had just put on his coat, he pulled his keys out of his pocket, muttered some excuse, and dashed off."

"Well," experimented George, "something was stolen from his car and he was driving after the thief, then. Some valuable engineering plans or patents. Or some secret formula for the utilization of atomic energy. A scrap of paper that could blow up the world. You know what deviltry this electronic research is."

"We'll know more about that," said Ed, "when the world blows up. I agree with Gil that imagination has its uses in detective work, but I think it should be salted with a pinch of fact."

After coffee Hubert went out into the barn, and returned bringing six glossy prints of the khaki figure by the barn, enlarged from the photograph.

"Now, Mrs. Marsh," he said, looking at Jeanie mischievously, "I am going to train you in detective work. I have here six prints of this mysterious figure. I'd like you to take one to Mrs. Knapp, one to Mrs. Dobert, and so on around the Green, and ask each lady to hand the photograph to her servants and ask them whether they have seen any such person in the neighborhood lately. And then note in pencil on the backs of the photographs the names of the persons who looked at them."

"But why six photographs?" asked Jeanie.

"You'll see. You are to wipe the surfaces clean before presenting them—and you are not to wipe them afterward."

Jeanie threw back her head and laughed merrily. "Pretty cute, Mr. Hubert. Are you going to examine all the finger-prints?"

"It's the maids' prints that I'm interested in, not those of your friends; but you might as well get them all. I rather think this clue will be eliminated. But I'd like you to be present at each interview, if possible, and hear what is said."

Ed chuckled. "You may unearth some family skeletons, Jeanie. We'll find out who owns that bum vanity box."

Mike Macy dropped in after dinner, and the 'homicide squad' went into session in the barn. Mike listened with interest to the day's revelations.

"What I want to find out now," said Hubert, "is whose cars were parked outside here the night of the party. I have a memorandum"—he took out his notebook—"of the tire tracks I found there. Klarsen's we know. Some one had a Ford, with smooth tires."

"Guilty," said Mike. "Nobody would ever steal that car. I only use it in the village."

"Now, who has Firestone tires?"

"Nat Flint has a Lincoln," said Ed. "I guess that would be it."

"Probably," said Hubert. "Who has four Goodyears, somewhat worn?"

"Where were they?" asked Ed.

"Parked at the wall, just this side of Klarsen's."

"They're not Knapp's. Tom and Dora walked home; they live next door. They're not Hugh's; he came in Klarsen's car. Art Dancey lives next door; he wouldn't have driven in here; his own garage is only a few feet away."

"Dancey has a new car, anyway, hasn't he?"

"Well, no. It's the one he had when he came here. It's at least two years old. It's a Chrysler coupé, maroon."

"Are you sure?" asked Hubert. "The other morning—Friday, I think it was, as I walked in to breakfast I saw a maroon coupe outside of Dancey's garage, but it looked pretty new to me."

"Dancey keeps his car pretty clean. But if he did have a new one, it would be a Chrysler, I'm sure."

"Dancey," said George reflectively. "He was that quiet fellow, wasn't he, dark, neatly dressed, slight build? Rather a dim Mazda?"

"About five-watt," said Mike. "I don't think he's dumb, but I never got much out of him but a few polite phrases."

"Dancey's all right," said Ed. "Nice fellow. Not much pop, but a real Southern gentleman, yes, suh; grandfather was a Confederate general or something. Dancey hasn't a spark of humor, but he has an Old-World courtliness that the ladies think is pretty."

"What does he do?" asked Hubert.

"He's an architect, off and on," said Ed. "Mostly off, I guess. Has plenty of money; all he needs, anyway. He's also the best golf player and the best tennis player in Westwood, by a long shot."

"So he's that hyperthyroid?" said George. "I didn't get his name that night."

"What do you mean by hyperthyroid?" asked Ed. "I thought a hyperthyroid was a person with a goiter."

"Not necessarily," said George. "One of the symptoms is that deep-set, staring look in the eyes that Dancey has. Did you ever read Crile or Berman on the endocrine glands?"

"Ha," said Ed. "Gentlemen, we have with us tonight Mr. Philo Vance, who has done a little original work, in an amateur way, on the ductless glands, the results of which have been given to the world in a monograph in the Journal of Medical Research, in which Mr. Vance disputes some of the conclusions of Crile and Berman. See footnote."

"What I was going to say," said George, "may be more important. Mr. Dancey, I think, knew Mr. Klarsen."

"What!" exclaimed Ed. "You mean, before he met him here?"

"I do," said George. "I don't think Dancey was introduced to Klarsen at all the other night. You remember that Dancey left early; in fact, just after Klarsen and the Crivingtons blew in. Someone said his mother was sick. Well, I happened to see Dancey coming out of the writing-room, with his overcoat and his hat in his hand, and just that minute Klarsen spoke to him. I didn't hear what Klarsen said, but Dancey brushed right by. Then I heard Klarsen say, 'Oh, forget it, Art!' I remember that name clearly."

"Humph!" said Ed. Hubert looked interested and pulled at his pipe. Mike shifted in his chair, and lit a fresh cigarette.

"Have you seen Dancey since then?" Mike asked Ed.

"Dancey's gone to Richmond," said Ed. "His mother's brother and sister-in-law live down there, in their old family home. As soon as cold weather comes on, his mother gets a yen to go back to the old place, so Dancey takes her back. She spends most of the winter there."

"Did he drive there?"

"Oh, no, I don't believe so. His mother wouldn't make that trip by automobile. She's much too delicate."

"Is Dancey coming back?"

"Sure he's coming back. Unless his mother has a critical attack of some kind, he'll be back right away."

"Well," said Mike, "he's had time to be back by now."

There was another moment's silence. "What are you thinking about, Mike?" asked George.

"I was thinking about that barrel of bullets," said Mike.

"So was I," said George.

Hubert, who was deep in thought, knocked out his pipe. "I should very much like to see Dancey's gun," he said. "If we can get it, we can tell whose bullet was found in Klarsen's car."

"But if we can't get it?" said Mike. "If he did have anything to do with it, he'd conceal the gun or throw it away, wouldn't he?"

"I can't suspect Dancey," said Ed. "Even if he had a grudge against Klarsen. Did you get the impression that it was serious?" he asked George.

"Serious enough for Dancey to cut Klarsen dead," said George. "Evidently Dancey is very touchy and proud. But I must say that I find it hard to suspect Dancey of that job, myself, little as I know the man."

"I should say the same," said Hubert guardedly, "though I didn't get a chance to observe him much. A slightly neurotic type, I should say; inclined to moodiness. But not homicidal."

"Well," said Ed, "if Dancey chooses to say that he's lost his gun, too, it comes down to a question of veracity between him and me."

"How do you mean?" asked George. "We know that you lost your gun."

"Thanks for your confidence," said Ed gloomily, "but as a matter of fact there isn't any evidence to that effect but my own statement that I left the gun in the silo. Which I'll swear to on a stack of wheat cakes, but it might not convince a jury."

"What's the idea, Ed?" asked George. "Are you trying to make us believe that you committed this murder?"

"Believe me," said Ed gratefully, "I'll bet I'd be getting 'the heat' right now if it weren't for Gil's management."

"I guess you'll have to find those bullets in the tree," said Hubert. "I'm afraid I made a serious mistake in not keeping that barrel of bullets intact, without opening it."

"That was my fault, not yours, Gil. I had that barrel open before you could have stopped me. Yes, I guess I'll have to look for some other bullets, and it'll be a long job."

"Are you sure you got all the bullets in the barrel, Ed?" asked Hubert.

"I burned the excelsior afterward and examined the ashes."

"You say, Ed, that you and Dancey had a shooting-match. How did you keep your scores separate? Did you each shoot at a different end of the barrel?"

"That's exactly what we did."

"Did you mark initials or anything on the two ends to identify them?"

"No, I don't think we did."

"Well, Dancey won this shooting-match, didn't he?"

"He certainly did. You're right, Gil. You can tell his end of the barrel; they're nearly all bull's-eyes; mine are scattered. And if I'd only kept the barrel intact, we could have told from the lay of the bullets whose were whose."

"There's one more possibility. Do you remember whether you fired fifteen shots or twelve? If you fired fifteen, the twelve bullets are Dancey's. And vice versa."

"By golly, I don't remember. It was nearly two years ago. I'd forgotten all about it until you asked me to find some bullets."

"Well," said Hubert, "it doesn't matter. We ought to be able to tell by the number of bull's-eyes which is your end of the barrel and which Dancey's. And we'll see which end has fifteen bullet holes."

"You've got it!" said Ed admiringly. "Where is that barrel? I left it out on the driveway, by the stone wall. I'll go out and look."

Ed took the flashlight and was gone about five minutes. When he came back, it was with a woeful countenance.

"I guess that barrel's gone," he said. "It might have been thrown over the side of the ravine, but I'm afraid it's been done away with. I'll ask Jeanie."

But Jeanie, over the telephone, said that Solveig had given the barrel to the man who raked up the dead leaves, to burn with them in the ravine.

"It's not up to you to worry about that, Ed," said Hubert comfortingly. "The police know you reported your gun stolen in good faith, several hours before the murder of a man you'd never seen then. In the case of Dancey, we were inclined to suspect a motive."

"Dancey didn't do it," said Ed positively. "Assuming at the worst a bitter feud, Dancey would be more likely to slap Klarsen in the face, hand him his card, and make a date to blaze away in the ravine next day before breakfast. That would be Dancey's style. Then he'd walk into the nearest police station and give himself up."

"You may be right," said Hubert. "But we must get Dancey's gun just the same. And if Dancey knows something of Klarsen's history, I should like to question him. You think he'll be back, do you, Ed?"

"Dancey wouldn't run away," said Ed. The others looked more dubious.

"What I want to find out," said Mike, "is whether Dancey's car is in his garage or not. I think I'll just take a little sneak and a peek over there. Got a flashlight, Ed?"

"Yes," said Ed, fishing one out of a drawer, "but keep under cover, Mike. I'd hate to have Dancey's maid find out that we'd been snooping on him."

Mike left the barn and went to Dancey's garage by way of the old stone wall, which extended into Dancey's place. Hubert fidgeted a little while Mike was gone. In about fifteen minutes Mike returned. "Dancey's got a brand-new Chrysler—a beaut," he said. "With Goodyear tires." He laid a pair of license plates on the table, and threw his hat and coat on the window-seat.

"What on earth have you got there?" demanded Hubert, hopping up.

"I know what you're going to say, Mr. Hubert," said Mike apologetically. "I didn't have a search warrant, and this evidence won't be admitted. But I'll put the plates back again, and if they are evidence, you can get a search warrant and get them later."

"You newspapermen!" said Hubert, shaking his head. "How did you get in?"

"I didn't break in," said Mike. "The shed was locked, but there's a little side door that's open, and I walked in. I didn't touch the car, though as far as I can see there isn't a finger-print on it. But the license plates were covered with finger-marks. And I want to see what's on those plates. They're all that we've got of Dancey's old car."

"You're a fast thinker, Mr. Macy," said Hubert. "Well, let's see what's on them."

He got out his brushes and powders, pulled a chair up to the table, and set to work. He dusted both sides, examined them with his glass, and laid the plates down carefully.

"There are excellent finger-prints on them," he said. "On one plate are the finger-prints of two men. On the other are the finger-prints of two men—and a woman."

He went to the silo and came back with a box containing the compact and the knife blade. He examined these again and compared them with the finger-prints on the license plate.

"The same woman?" asked Mike, as Hubert turned, smiling.

"The same woman," said Hubert. "And now I think I see what she was doing with the knife blade. She used it in removing, or attempting to remove, this license plate. Being left-handed, she seized the handle of the knife in her left hand, and the point in her right hand, as a screwdriver. But the screw was tight and broke the blade."

"That looks," said Mike, "as if Dancey didn't trade in his old car. What did he do with it, then?"

"He didn't junk it," said Hubert. "Not over on the hill, anyway. But I warn you against creating fanciful pictures. We'll inquire at the Chrysler agency tomorrow."

"I wonder whether the state troopers will find that car," said Mike.

"I wonder what they'll find in it," said George hopefully.

XIV

THE CANCELLED NOTE

The next morning Ed and Hubert drove in town early to attend the inquest. George had been detailed to what he called 'k.p.' in the ravine again. And George was very wroth at himself, at the genial detective, and at all murderers who interfered with literary work. For the first time since his arrival, George felt a genuine impulse to write, and his brain, like a gas engine, was all warmed up and 'running sweet.'

Therefore, though his feet might be doing their duty, his brain was not. George walked back and forth, glancing to one side or the other, but his thoughts were on his fictional creative problems. George's novel,[1] which I read in manuscript, seemed to me, while predominantly reflecting his own idiosyncrasies, to be affected by a curious medley of influences, chiefly Sinclair Lewis, Aldous Huxley, and Wyndham Lewis (the polemical one). Instead of satirizing the babbittry or the booboisie, which point of view is intelligible enough, George had undertaken the far more difficult task of satirizing the intelligentsia. I pointed out to him the enormous difficulties inherent in the task, among them the fact that a class containing a large proportion of the people who buy

---

[1] *ernie spohr*, Braithwaite, Dolman Co. The reader may also be familiar with George's *Diamonds Are Trash*, which had a brief *réclame* for reasons utterly foreign to its intention, on which I shall not undertake to dwell here. He is also author of *Dodoism and Dadaism*, in the *Flaneur* of October, 1930, and *The Varieties of Æsthetic Experience*, in. *Walker's* of February, 1931. His detective stories are *The Sheaghan Shillelah*, and *The Murder at the Microphone*, Scaramouche Press.

and read—and review—books could not be expected to appreciate a satire directed against themselves. George replied that my statement was purely dogmatic, and that, like most dichotomies, my division of the human race into literate and illiterate was fallacious; there were others; for instance, himself. When I asked George what he called himself, he replied that he had invented the term neo-philistine to describe his type. Like most philosophers, George seemed reluctant to expound clearly his doctrine of neo-philistinism, but its aim is apparently to achieve an Oriental detachment, to emancipate one's self from mass psychology, which George declares is as potent (and as patent) among the admirers of Cézanne and Satie as the devotees of Amos and Andy. George declares that the word is a much better one than pragmatism or humanism, and ought to stir up fully as much ill-feeling.

My excuse for digressing is that George himself was at the moment digressing. George tried to change the current of his thoughts by reviewing the theories which had been considered as to the crimes. Except for the coincidence of time and the similarity of method, the murder which had dragged Clifford into publicity appeared to be another story altogether. The murder of Klarsen, despite the evidence of the footprints by the lake, would seem to have occurred in the vicinity, almost under Hubert's bedroom window. No wonder the old fellow wanted to take a hand in catching the criminal. Thus far it appeared to be either a case of robbery with a gun or murder for revenge, by their eccentric visitor of the silo, whose relationship to Klarsen remained to be discovered; or else a crime of passion, perhaps of madness, on the part of Dancey.

As for the unknown woman, George could only infer that she had been in collusion with the murderer, and had attempted to help him remove the license plates from Dancey's car preparatory to disposing of the car somewhere. That this was at least done with Dancey's knowledge and consent was indicated by the fact that he had put these plates on a new car.

As to why Dancey's car had been parked there at all that evening, how long it was there, and what gruesome purpose it might have been used for, George decided that it was useless to speculate without more abundant information. Ann Crivington, though she might be a *casus belli*, certainly had an airtight alibi unless Hugh was an accessory.

Hugh appeared to be much upset, but that could not be regarded as anything but natural under the circumstances of Klarsen's death.

George's fancy was intrigued most, at the moment, by the spade stolen from Ed's garage and left in the quarry pond. He could think of only one reason for borrowing a spade in that manner, and that was to bury something. Curiosity impelled him to explore the hilltop, though he would have preferred to have company on that quest. The spot impressed him romantically in retrospect, but less pleasantly in immediate reality. However, he figured that if the spade meant anything, it meant that the body was underground, and all that he would have to look for was the spot where it was interred.

Therefore, George unhurriedly ascended the steep and rocky road up to the quarry and stood once more in that grim theater among the pines and spruces, which he fancied might, had it been ancient enough, have been a sacred grove guarded by a priestly cutthroat; such a one as is familiar to every reader who has got as far as page 1, chapter 1, of his (abridged) 'Golden Bough.' But he averted his thoughts resolutely from such grisly pictures, and plunged into the woods.

He found that he did not have to go far in any direction to come upon the brink of a declivity, in some places just possible of descent, in others menacing to life and limb. George was of the opinion that no more ideal place could have been designed by nature for the convenience of murderers. He was disposed to doubt his theory of the spade, for no murderer, he thought, could have resisted the impulse to toss the body over the cliff into the void which seemed to yawn for corpses. Nevertheless, George paced the ground methodically looking for signs of upturned earth.

He then proceeded through the woods in the direction of the little open field to the eastward, which he had seen on his previous visit to the hill. Here it was easy. High grass, weeds, and brambles attested the fact that the ground had not been disturbed. However, he tramped through the field to the far end, turned to the right and again to the right. Here, being at the lower end of the field, he observed what appeared to be a gap in the vegetation.

I do not think I do George an injustice to say that his pulse made a swift leap toward the century mark. It was a long time since he had seen a dead Boche in the wheat, and they say one loses one's overseas aplomb quickly after doffing khaki. Common-sense told him, however, that if there were such a thing there his other senses than sight would have apprised him aforetime. So he walked thither rapidly to have the suspense over with.

There was nothing there. But something had been there, if signs meant anything; for the ground had been trodden and the grass and underbrush torn and trampled over several square yards of ground. It looked to George, offhand, as if some large animal like a horse had rolled and kicked up his heels there. But the idea of stray animals of that size on the hill George knew to be absurd. The next picture to enter his mind was of two men engaged in a death grapple.

George knelt on the ground and inspected the entire trampled area, with professional zest, looking for shells or bloodstains. He found none. But unless it were a very sanguinary encounter, he reflected, bloodstains, if any, would be pretty hard to discern on that ground; in the soil they would be lost to the naked eye. That was a job for Hubert with his magnifying-glass.

It occurred to George that someone might have planned a burial here and have been interrupted. Despite the evidence of the spade, however, George found it hard to understand so punctilious a murderer. Another theory that occurred to him was that this might have been a camping-ground. But he ascertained quickly that no tent had been pitched here; nor did the irregular shape of the patch suggest to his mind any practical method of use. But one fact was evident—there were no signs of digging.

George decided that there was nothing further for him to do about it but to report it to his superior. He betook himself down the rock road again with a leisurely sense of having filled his morning's quota. Coming to a bit of open view, he decided to sit on a rock at the top of the cliff and sun himself, smoking a cigarette the while and enjoying the view across the ravine. He saw the withered tree beneath him, but no longer did it affright him. He felt like a puny hunter perched atop a dead bull elephant.

He looked at his watch. It was only a little past ten. He could get back to his typewriter and whack out a whole chapter before lunch; it was already written, in his head. He tried to review his chapter, and found that he could not get his mind back to it. In essentials it was all there, but inert and cold.

Angrily, he gave it up. He looked idly down at the tree, studying it as a pictorial composition. One thing bothered him: there was a white object fluttering in a fork of some twigs. It made him think of Poe's 'Gold Bug.' It should be a bleached skull, indicating where to dig for treasure. It worked upon his imagination until he finally saw it as a skull, and began to wonder what it really was. As trivial things may do, it annoyed him so much that he got up and determined to get down there and see.

He peered over the cliff and saw that a narrow ledge formed by a rift in the rock led from the tree around the cliff and met what might be a track or rude footpath through the bushes. Walking down the quarry road to a point at about this level, he found the path, plunged through the bushes, and shortly came to the face of the cliff. Creeping out on the ledge and leaning on the face of the cliff, he had no trouble in reaching the tree, nor in climbing into the fork of the tree and seizing the object, which was at the end of a short bough which George would have called the middle finger of the hand.

It was a piece of paper about three by eight inches in size. George stuffed it in his pocket and climbed down. He scrambled back to safe ground and examined the paper. It was a cancelled note for seventy-five dollars. Dated 1867!

Where could that have come from? thought George. Might have blown from someone's ashbin or rubbish-heap; but surely quite recently, for the paper, though old and yellowish, was quite clean. He crumpled it up, and paused. He remembered that he had been at first of a mind to throw the knife blade away and to regard the spade as of no significance. Still, one couldn't collect all the rubbish in the ravine, on the off chance of its being a clue of some kind. Oh, well! George stuffed it into his pocket again by way of deferring decision.

He hastened back to the barn and stared futilely at his typewriter till lunchtime.

The word temperament covers a multitude of sins of which George was not guilty. However, he was subject to something like inhibition of thought at times, and he made very bad going of his chapter. Could this flat stuff be his colorful dream of this morning? Moreover, his satisfaction in his morning's discovery had now lost its glow. So when Hubert appeared, about four o'clock, George forgot for the moment what he had to tell him.

"How did the inquest go?" he asked Hubert.

"Rather disappointing, to me," said Hubert. "The ideas of your local authorities about an inquest are different from mine. I hoped to hear something from Crivington, but his testimony was quite perfunctory. I wish I'd been on that jury. I'd like to have asked several questions."

"What did they find?"

"Death by gunshot wounds at the hands of parties unknown. In both cases. They regarded the two as possibly connected. Clifford testified, and his secretary, and some of Clifford's servants. Svenhaugen, general manager of the Dynamopolis Electric Company, sketched Klarsen's history briefly, but nothing very personal. Told about his war record and his being reported killed in action, but said that he had suffered no permanent results from shell shock or gas; and testified with apparent sincerity and genuine emotion as to his excellent character. Crivington testified that Klarsen had been drinking only in extreme moderation during the evening; Ed confirmed this, and also the time Klarsen left the barn. Crivington said that Klarsen's destination was his hotel in town."

"Did they tell what Klarsen was carrying with him?"

"They explained his equipment. Said he carried a couple of hundred dollars in cash, also travelers' checks. Svenhaugen scoffed at the idea that Klarsen carried any blue-prints or data of new inventions, or anything that would be of value to any rival of the company. I'm inclined to believe it, though of course he would have denied it even if it were otherwise."

"Did the proceedings seem rather cut-and-dried to you?"

"Perhaps not," said Hubert cautiously. "Inquests are often rather formal."

"Well," said George, remembering his own duty, "I explored the top of the hill this morning, and found something that seemed peculiar to me, though it may have some perfectly natural explanation." He told Hubert what he had seen. Hubert listened attentively.

"I'll go over there now," he said, "and it would be a great help if you would go also. I want to know exactly where you looked."

They went together over onto the hill, and George showed Hubert the patch of trampled ground. Hubert examined the entire area carefully.

"Nothing that you could call footprints here," he said, "on all these dry weeds and undergrowth; and the ground's pretty hard. Now, you didn't walk around on this place yourself, did you?"

"I didn't, no. I knelt at the edges of this patch and poked around with my hands."

"Good. It appears that this ground has been trampled on rather than rolled on. The bark is bruised on these twigs and vines. That suggests a hand-to-hand fight. I see no signs of blood, but grass and small bushes have been torn up by the roots here and there, which suggests that signs of blood may have been removed. I'll look over this spot again. But it's getting too dark now."

When Ed came home, he was more outspoken than Hubert in his opinion of the inquest. He called it a farce, a frost, and a frame-up. "That coroner or whatever his official title is," said Ed, "acted toward Svenhaugen and Clifford like a nice old family doctor asking them about their symptoms. If the soft pedal wasn't put on those proceedings, the law is more of an ass than I took it for."

The conversation at dinner turned on the inquest. Jeanie was interested in hearing what Hugh Crivington said.

"Hugh never looked at me once," said Ed. "I saw him boring into you with a glance, though, Gil. Hugh's the silliest person I know in some ways—like a kid. I didn't notice any warm handclasps between Clifford and the Electric bunch, either. I'm sure Hugh must know Clifford at the Dynamopolis Club, too."

"What was the name of the lean-looking fellow with Crivington and Svenhaugen?" asked Hubert.

"Eben Clapp," said Ed. "The Company's attorney, or one of them at least. By the way, did you notice him when Svenhaugen told that about Klarsen's insurance? Clapp gave Svenhaugen a mean look when he got back."

"What was that?" asked George.

"Klarsen's life was insured for one million dollars," said Ed. "One million dollars! In favor of the Company."

"Boy!" said George. "They ought to give him a fine funeral. Looks as if he must have been a valuable man."

"Looks as if they thought his occupation was a bit hazardous, too," said Ed. "Then, when Hugh got up, he volunteered the information that the Company would spend that much and more to help convict the murderer. Or rather, he said that Borg would spend that personally."

"What sort of a man is Borg?" asked George.

"Gus Borg," said Ed, "is a human dynamo himself. I never saw a man who gave such an impression of indomitable force. Hugh has no easy job, even if he is Borg's son-in-law. From all I hear, Borg's directors all have to be yes-men. Borg pulls what seems to everyone else to be the most awful boners in policy, and yet they always turn out right. Borg doesn't reason, but either he has uncanny luck or else he has an intuitive faculty that amounts to genius. I think it's genius myself. But I'm glad he's not my boss."

"A different type from Clifford, should you say?"

"Um-m, yes. They both pack a punch. But Clifford is a fox. Borg is a bear."

"Now, Mr. Hubert," said Jeanie, as coffee was being served in the comfortable living-room of the house, "here are your photographs. I had good luck. Everyone was in, and I've marked the photographs carefully on the backs. I didn't always get the names of the maids, but where there were two maids, I got the name of at least one of them. On some of them I marked whose prints are whose; but I couldn't always remember that."

"How was the vote on the sex of the person in khaki?" asked Ed.

"It's a tie!" said Jeanie disappointedly. "Three each way, including myself. Frances Knapp agreed with me and Ann Crivington."

"Frances agreed because she's a good fellow, and Ann because she thought everyone else would say it was a man, and she wanted to be different."

"Mr. Hubert," said Jeanie, "bring your finger-print tools in here and let me see you do whatever it is that you do."

Hubert went out to the barn and returned with his brushes and boxes, and Ed unlimbered a card table. Hubert dusted all the prints, showing them to Jeanie one by one under his lens, with the compact by him for comparison.

"I guess all of Randall Green is absolved," he said. "There isn't a print here that matches."

"Can you tell the difference between those of maids and mistresses?" asked Jeanie.

"Only where you've marked them. I might guess, in some cases, but I couldn't be certain."

"Which only shows," said Ed, "that the Colonel's lady and Judy O'Grady are the same as to their skins as well as under them."

"Did you get all the employers' finger-prints?" asked George. "I don't see Mrs. Crivington's here."

"I didn't notice about the employers much," said Jeanie. "But Ann is one of those tiresomely dainty persons who pick up everything as if they were afraid of getting their fingers dirty."

"That pose is worse than dirty hands," said George. "It's démodé. All the other ladies thumbed their photographs like honest folk."

"Now, George," said Jeanie gravely, "none of your innuendoes. It's high time you were suppressed."

"Elucidate, George," insisted Ed. "You interest me."

"Well," said George, "suppose this soft pedal in evidence at the inquest is on account of a family triangle, or quadrangle, across the Green. I rather think Borg would call for *molto pianissimo* on that!"

"I'll say he would!" said Ed, laughing. "Hush, George!"

"Now, listen, George!" said Jeanie heatedly. "Ann Crivington is my *friend*—"

"I'm sorry, Jeanie," said George hastily. "I'll take it all back. I was only being literary, not literal."

But Jeanie was quite provoked.

Ed accompanied George and Hubert to the barn to 'do a whiskey peg' in the British manner before going to bed. George sat down at the big table and tilted back with his hands in his trousers pockets. He felt in his hand a piece of paper and pulled it out to see what it was. He looked at it a moment and then tossed it to Ed.

"Has that got anything to do with your finances, Ed?" he asked. "I found it in the ravine this morning."

Ed took the paper and looked at it uncomprehendingly for a moment. "Well, I'll be damned," he said, after reading it carefully. "Whereabouts in the ravine?"

"In a bough of the old tree," said George, settling forward again. "The old dead tree in the cliff. It must have blown there."

Ed handed it to Hubert. "That's from some old papers that I had out here in the barn," he said. "And the last time I saw them was when I handed them over to Hugh Crivington, the night of the party."

Hubert took the paper and scrutinized it with care on both sides, deciphering each word written on it.

"And who," he asked Ed, studying the signatures with a perplexed scowl, "are Abel—and what's this other?—and Jonas Beeson?"

XV

THE DEAD HAND OF JONAS BEESON

"Abel and Jonas Beeson," said Ed, "I believe once owned the land this house stands on; in fact, owned all of Westwood and a lot more land around here. That's about all I can tell you about them. All I know about this note is that it was among some old papers, deeds, and what not, that I've had lying around the house for years. And that last Wednesday night Hugh Crivington asked me for them, and I let him have them. Now what's he done with them, I'd like to know?"

"And how did they get out there in the ravine?" asked Hubert. "Up in a tree, on the cliff, you say?" he asked George. "Did you see any other papers lying around?"

"Not a thing," said George. "Though, to tell the truth, I didn't look further. I thought this was just something blown from some one's ash-pile."

"A thing like that could blow a long way," said Hubert. "Might have been dropped here on Ed's ground. What are these papers, Ed, and what did Crivington want them for?"

"Why, they're old stuff, Gil, that I found in a leather trunk years ago, when I first bought this house. I took out what seemed to be interesting, and left the rest in the trunk and put the trunk in the barn. I couldn't make much out of them, and I turned them over to Charley Bullivant. He was our lawyer at the time that we formed the syndicate and bought this hill. Tom Knapp was in the syndicate, and six others."

"What did Bullivant say about them?" asked Hubert. "Had they any value?"

"Not a bit. Bullivant went all through them carefully and said they didn't concern our property, and he had quitclaims and waivers from everybody concerned anyway. Charley told me to burn them, unless I wanted them as souvenirs."

"Did you burn any of them?"

"No, I didn't. I had them in the secretary here for a while, and then I chucked them in a drawer of my filing cabinet. Not long ago I took them out of there because I wanted the drawer as a transfer file. I stuck them away in a window-seat box."

"You say you didn't burn any of these, Ed. But some got burnt up in the barn?"

"Yes. I didn't burn the barn myself. I don't know who did it. Some vagabonds, I guess, camping there. But those papers were nothing but personal letters. I offered to return them to the previous owners of the property, but they said to burn them. I did open one or two, but they were hard to read, and I didn't want to pry into anybody's heart throbs anyway."

"Did you ever find out from the police how your barn happened to be burned?"

"No. We were away at the time. So far as the contents went, it was a good riddance to me."

"You bought this house with all its contents?"

"Lock, stock, and barrel. The owners lived in Ohio; didn't want any of it. I got my secretary, which isn't bad. The appraiser told me that if it had a few dinglebats here and there it would be worth four thousand dollars; lacking them, it was worth about four hundred. I never could understand the collector's point of view. I sold some of the furniture to other members of the syndicate, at the appraiser's valuations."

"Did you turn over to Crivington all of this old stuff that you saved?"

"All the legal documents. There's some other old trash still lying around here."

"Let's see it," said Hubert. Ed knelt down, under the table, and slid open a panel under the window-seat. He brought out an armful of what seemed to be old account books and loose correspondence. He dumped these on the table.

"What are these things?" asked Hubert.

"Old ledgers, bills, business correspondence, some of it quite old," said Ed. "It had to do, most of it, with the old mica quarry. They ran quite a business at one time, perhaps seventy-five years ago. You see, here they evidently ordered some machinery; had some trouble with it, from their correspondence. This is an old letter-press copy-book," he said, showing a book of bound tissue leaves, dog-eared and torn. "Ever see one of these? Horrible way to keep files."

"My grandfather had one of those," said George. "You take your letter, wet it with a brush dipped in water, put it between the leaves of this book, and then squeeze it with the letter-press. The result is an undecipherable copy and a bleary, cockled letter."

"And this," said Ed, "is a family album. This is a real antique. I wouldn't throw this away for anything. Look at that grand padded plush cover! Look at the forget-me-nots on the title-page. Here's a page for the recording of births. Mehitabel, August 17, 1853. Here's twins, Jonas and Mary. Kind of melancholy—a Spoon River anthology. Look at the exhibit of plain and fancy chin-wear. Can you beat that? I'll bet that old chap was as hard as nails; look at his mouth."

"Well, well," said Hubert, "this is interesting. And these are mechanical drawings of machinery—some kind of steam drill, perhaps. Here are some plats of property; doesn't look like yours. What was the stuff you gave Crivington?"

"A lot of old deeds and plats. I told him the papers were no good; had nothing to do with his property. Hugh bought his lot from the syndicate; he'd got married a year or so before. I believe I have some photostats of them somewhere. I had photostats made before I turned them over to Bullivant. Bullivant is one of the best title lawyers in the state, but his idea of filing stuff is to stack it up on his desk or on chairs all around his office. I never saw a lawyer yet that had any idea of system. I just thought I'd play safe."

Ed poked around under the window-seat and pulled out a roll of stiff papers tied with a string. This he handed to Hubert, who untied them and re-rolled them the other way.

"It would take a lawyer to find out the import of these things," said Hubert, sitting down to examine them, "and one familiar with real estate hereabouts. However, here's one thing I can understand. Seems to be a map or plan of the hill across the ravine. Shows the ravine, and the edge of your lot, Ed. It's a piece torn off of a bigger map."

"Yes. The syndicate thought of buying the hill, but most of them thought it was throwing away money. As a matter of fact, it wasn't offered us, though I suppose they'd have sold it quick enough."

"It still belongs to the people you bought from, then?"

"Yes. Some people named Plenty. They were descendants of the original old man Beeson, whoever he was."

"What's this thing?" asked Hubert, picking up a photostat. "There seems to be nothing on it whatever." He scrutinized it closely.

"That?" said Ed, looking at it. "Oh, that's the back of something. They always photograph the back as well as the front of things, unless you tell them not to, whether it's got anything on it or not. I suppose the idea is, you might want to prove that there was nothing on the back—no endorsement or such of some document."

"Well, I'd like to look at those again," said Hubert. "I'm glad you have the photostats."

George, who had meanwhile been sitting in an armchair under the lamp, studying a piece of paper, got up and handed it to Hubert.

"No well-planned murder is complete without a cryptogram," he said. "I am happy to say that I have found a cryptogram. What do you make of it, Mr. Hubert?"

Hubert took the scrap of paper from George and frowned at it.

"Where did you find this?" he asked George.

"It dropped out as Ed took the things out of the window-box," said George. "I looked for the rest of it, but I can't find it. It's old, and a bit brittle."

Ed leaned over and looked at it. It was written on ruled paper, in a careful Spencerian hands with a fine steel pen. The letters were faint in spots.

"Chain 10, join, 18 s.c. in ring," read Ed. "2d row, d.c. in each s.c."

"It conveys nothing to me," said Hubert. "Unless it could be instructions for assembling machinery."

"1st row. Fasten—something—between wheels," read Ed. "That's it. Some of their drilling machines."

"It's distinctly a feminine handwriting, though," objected George. "And it doesn't tie up with these drawings in any way."

Hubert handed it back to George. "You might hang on to it," he said. "In your spare time, see if you can decipher it."

George smiled, got an envelope from Ed's desk, slipped the cryptogram into it, and put it carefully into his billfold.

XVI

CRYPTOGRAMS

Hubert occupied himself the next morning in leisurely fashion by looking through the photostats that Ed had given him. Some of them were deeds of trust, indicating that large sections of land had been mortgaged at one time; and there were many photostats of cancelled notes, six or eight on a sheet, fronts and backs, showing the mortgages to have been paid off. Some of the photostats were of contracts of sale of pieces of land. Hubert tried to make out from the plats among the papers where these pieces of land lay, but his knowledge was inadequate.

He looked through all the photostats of cancelled notes until he found one of the note that George had picked up in the ravine. It was identical with the note itself, as Hubert proved by placing one over the other and holding them to a strong light.

Hubert looked through the correspondence and the book of tissue copies. The book dated before the day of typewriters, and many words were illegible. But Hubert was able to gather from this and from the ledger that a company or partnership called Beeson Brothers did a flourishing business as quarrymen for many years before the Civil War. There appeared to have been various Beesons in it, but some of them had dropped out or sold out. They also had owned a granite quarry somewhere, and another where they got feldspar.

Hubert studied the map of the quarry hill with interest and identified some of the topographical features. He looked at the perfectly blank photostats, of which there were several, and succeeded in assigning some of them to the text pages to which they belonged. One of these was the back of the map of the quarry hill, which offered no difficulty because of the torn bottom.

He took the back of the map to the sunlit window of the study to get a strong light, and with his lens examined some marks on it which had attracted his attention. His eye had caught what seemed to be writing on it. After studying this for several minutes, he got a piece of paper and a pencil and copied down what he could decipher. He got at last something like this:

```
    E  B
                P  L  B
    K  S
                N  M
                          J  B
        A  N                      J
        H  R
        Jy              ML
```

He took it in to George, who was working in the writing-room, and said to him:

"This is in your department as cryptogram expert. Let's see what you can do at decoding it."

"What is it?" asked George. "Where did you get it?"

"From the back of a map of this scene that you're looking out on now," said Hubert.

"I'd like to see the map," said George, getting up.

Hubert stepped to the table in the other room and got the front and back of the photostat of the map and gave them to George.

"I don't believe the letters have anything to do with the map," said George. "They look to me like some idle notations that someone made there because it happened to be the only blank piece of paper handy. Looks as if the lady of the house was planning to fling a dinner party and figuring out how to seat her guests. Hostesses probably had to steer clear of hot abolition arguments in those days."

"Well," said Hubert, "you stick that in your pocket and let your fertile brain play with it in unoccupied moments. I'm going over to the hill to make a more careful examination of that spot you found yesterday."

As usual in the case of requests made in that form, George stuck the cryptogram in his pocket and promptly dismissed it from his mind. He had a good morning and composed as fast as the limited skill of his fingers permitted. He yanked the last sheet of his chapter out of his typewriter and had started to read it when Hubert returned.

"No luck," said Hubert, in response to George's inquiring glance. "If that spot you found was the scene of a fight, it must have been a wrestling match and not a gun fight. If a gun had been discharged within that area, I'm certain I should have found the shell in two hours' search. Unless it was picked up and thrown away. Well, let's go in to lunch."

Jeanie asked at lunch for an accounting of their morning's work. George said that it had consisted chiefly in futile attempts to solve cryptograms.

"And what is a cryptogram?" asked Jeanie.

"Don't you know what a cryptogram is?" asked. George. He pulled out the one that he had discovered. "Here's one. It tells you how to locate the buried gold. If you can decipher it, I'll give you half."

"Where's the rest of it? How can I do anything with just a corner of a cryptogram?"

"That's Ed's carelessness. It was probably burnt up with that other stuff in the barn. Ed's thrown away a fortune without knowing it."

Jeanie put the paper beside her plate and studied it from time to time as she ate. "This has a familiar sound," she said. "'Chain 10, join, 18 s.c. in ring.'"

"How do you mean, familiar? You mean it sounds like Poe or 'Treasure Island'?"

"Well, it does sound like that. But it suggests something else to me. An old-fashioned square dance? Or a game? Cribbage? Solitaire? '2d row, d.c. in each s.c.'"

"It's a woman's handwriting," said Hubert. "Something tells me Mrs. Marsh is going to solve it."

"For some reason," said Jeanie, "it reminds me of Mother. She used to play solitaire. Oh, I know!" Jeanie burst into a peal of laughter. "George, I'm afraid your buried treasure is only a beautiful dream!"

"Shoot!" said George resignedly. "What is it? A recipe for Christmas pudding?"

"It's instructions for crocheting!" said Jeanie, and went off into another gale of laughter. "Oh, dear! Mother has a whole book of those things. They show you how to make d'oyleys and anti-macassars and things."

"Think of that," said George. "We ought to make more use of Jeanie's talents. Here's another cryptogram. I hope you can solve that with equal celerity." He handed her the paper on which Hubert had written the initials.

Jeanie took the paper, but was unsuccessful this time. "That's just nothing," she said scornfully. "It's like the kind of things people scribble on telephone pads when they're waiting."

Hubert took the train into town after lunch, on business of his own. He connected with Ed at his office at five o'clock, and rode out with him.

"Ed," said Hubert, after they had got clear of downtown traffic, "this matter of Klarsen seems to have several angles pointing in different directions. I'm interested now in those old documents that you gave Crivington. I dare say your lawyer is right in saying that they are of no value to anyone, but it's conceivable that someone might be under the illusion that some document of value exists which might have been among them. Now, I understood you to say that you did at one time keep these things in the bottom drawer of your cabinet, in the silo. When did you remove them from there?"

"Not long ago. About a week ago, I guess."

"It's possible, then, that this thief was someone who had been posted as to where you had been keeping these things, and meant to take them or look through them. It's also conceivable—even probable—that this thief was merely the agent for someone else."

"That might be. But what it's all about is beyond me, then."

"Now, when did Crivington ask you for these documents? Before he knew about the thief breaking in, or afterward?"

"Before. It was one of the first things he spoke about when he came over."

"Well, now, I've been looking over those photostats, and it's evident that these Beesons owned a lot of land around here. Do you know, by any chance, whether they ever owned the land on which the Dynamopolis Electric Company plant stands, over on the plain?"

"I'm sure I don't know," said Ed. "I only know that the Electric Company has been there on that ground ever since I was in knee pants.

Tom Knapp might know something about it. He went into all the dope about this region when we formed the syndicate. Suppose we drop over to his house when we get home and Tom will give us a cocktail."

Tom Knapp was delighted to see them. He got out his pharmaceuticals, and as he shook the cocktails, cigarette in mouth, blinking at his own smoke, he listened to Ed's questions. Tom sampled the cocktail, put out three glasses and filled them. The others reached for their cocktails and sat down again.

"Dynamopolis Electric," said Tom, seating himself with his drink, "bought that land in the eighties, from the Beeson heirs. I forget their name now, though I did know it at one time. We got our land from the next generation; I forget their name too."

"Plenty," said Ed.

"Plenty—that's right," said Tom. "Lived in Columbus, Ohio. Old man Beeson, or whoever the head of the family was, owned perhaps five or six thousand acres at one time. Let's see those photostats. You say Hugh borrowed the originals from you?"

"Yes. He hasn't returned them yet. Hugh has been acting so peculiarly the last few days that I wonder what's on his mind."

"I don't see why you wonder at that," said Tom. "This murder of Klarsen is enough to upset him. Klarsen was Hugh's guest, and I suppose Hugh feels that, if Klarsen had been somewhere else, he wouldn't have got shot."

"Could Hugh be worried about the Company's title to its land?" asked Ed.

"Oh, no," said Tom, shaking his head. "That comes up every once in a while, but it's pure stock-market fiction. Every possible heir of the Beeson family is accounted for. They did have a bad time ten or fifteen years ago. Someone discovered that old Rube Malt, who runs a filling station in the village you know him, I guess—was some relation to the Beesons, and Dynamopolis Electric approached him very gingerly. They offered him five thousand dollars to sign away his rights, if any, and I understand they had a hard time making him understand what it was all about. They set him up in business, too; got him his permit and everything; in fact, did the decent thing by him, in my opinion. They got all the history out of him that they could, and found that he was the last of his line of the family. So everybody was happy.

"There's nothing here that could worry Hugh," continued Tom, after a brief inspection of the photostats. "This is all farmland, out north; all been sold; some other emptor should caveat about that. These Plenty people must be nicely fixed now. I guess about all of that Beeson land has been sold."

"Well, much obliged, Tom," said Ed, taking the photostats. "Thanks for the dope, and for the drinks."

After dinner that evening, as they were finishing their coffee, Jeanie got a slip of paper from her desk and handed it to Ed.

"If you're interested in cryptograms, Ed, you might try to unravel this one for me."

"What's that?" asked Ed. "The telephone bill? Never. I'd rather pay it and be done with it."

"I've checked most of them," said Jeanie, "but I don't know about the calls from the barn. What's this Petunkawoc thirty-seven, at the bottom here? Twice."

"October 31?" said Ed. "Not mine, I'm sure of that. Might have been one of our guests that evening."

"Well, I'm going to find out," said Jeanie. She got the telephone book and started running a finger down the columns.

"It'll take you all night," said Ed. "I'd never work that hard for forty cents."

"Not for Petunkawoc, it won't. Here it is, right away. Gustavus Borg."

"Good work, Jeanie," said George. "I'm glad the strain is over."

"But I never called up the Borgs!" said Jeanie. "Certainly not from the barn, and not that day!"

"I'll bet it was Hugh," said Ed. "He's the only person I know who would hang up two twenty-cent calls on us without offering to pay for them. I'll collect that from him the next time I see him, if he's on speaking terms with me by then."

Jeanie and George decided to drive to the movies in Merivale Park. Hubert and Ed went out into the barn. Ed wrote a few checks, enclosed and sealed them. Hubert smoked his pipe and read 'Moby Dick.'

"I wonder," said Hubert at last to Ed, "whether we could see this Rube Malt and talk with him? It may take us off on a tangent, but it might be interesting."

"I know Rube Malt well," said Ed. "I buy my gas off of him, and tires too. We might run over there and see him."

"I'd rather get him at leisure, where he could sit comfortably and ramble on. Do you suppose you could get him over here to have a drink?"

"I might. He'd sort of wonder what was up, though. Let's see, now. I've got a flat tire to fix; it happens to be the spare, though. He'd wonder why I didn't drive over. I tell you what I'll do. I'll let the air out of one tire and tell him I've got two flats and can't get over. He can bring over a couple of tubes and put them in for me. Then I'll give him a little drink and we'll hear his life story."

"He might be suspicious when he finds the tire good," said Hubert, smiling.

"I'll run a pin into it, when he isn't looking, then. I'll have to 'phone Pepperell's drugstore. Rube hasn't a 'phone."

Ed called the drugstore. "Will you have your boy step over to Rube Malt's house," he asked, "and tell him that Mr. Marsh wants him to come to his barn right away and bring two tubes for my car? If he can't come, telephone me.

"Rube's usually there," said Ed, "smoking and reading the paper, at this hour. He's not much of a gadabout."

XVII

RUBE MALT'S STORY

Rube Malt's arrival was announced to Ed and Hubert shortly by a single loud rap on the door.

There entered a person who might well have been cast for the role of Rip Van Winkle in the movies. As young Rip, he would have had to dye his hair, which was snowy white; as old Rip, he would have needed a long false beard and some makeup, for his clean-shaven face was that of a vigorous man, and his eye was bright as a bird's. He was a powerful man, but walked with a slight limp. One would have no hesitation in saying that Rube Malt, in his picturesque way, was a handsome old fellow. His fine forehead and strong features, had they been immortalized by a sculptor, might have been taken for those of some statesman or scholar of the early Victorian era.

"Come down into the garage, Rube," said Ed, leading him thither. Ed unlocked the doors of the garage and turned on the light. Rube laid down two boxes of inner tubes.

"One's the spare and the other's the right-hand rear," said Ed. "I want to drive in in the morning, so I thought I'd get you to come over tonight."

"Glad to help you," said Rube. "Where'd this one let you down, Ed? Didn't drive fur on it, without air, did ye?"

"It let me down right here in the garage," said Ed truthfully. "The shoe's all right; it just needs a new sock."

"Heh, heh!" said Rube. "That's the way they go sometimes. I had a feller once—stopped fer gas at my place. Had no more than got his tank full when down went one of his tires. Accused me of sprinkling tacks around the place. Heh, heh! It warn't so, though. I had a hard time convincin' him that I didn't poke a knife in his tire when he wasn't lookin'. Business ain't that bad."

"Business is pretty fair with you, I guess, isn't it?" said Ed. "You've got a nice location. Ought to be pretty busy, though there isn't so much Sunday travel now."

"Well, yes," said Rube, jacking up the car. "I'm off the main high-way, but then I get more of the village business where I am. Suits me all right. It's better than blacksmithin'. Automobile can't kick you in the shin, like a horse did me once. Broke it clean in two."

"That so?" said Ed. "I didn't know you used to be a blacksmith."

"For nigh twenty year," said Malt. "Twenty year. That were better than working in the quarries, though, where I started. Lord! that were hot work in summer. Pick up a crowbar, that had been layin' out in the sun, she'd be so hot you couldn't hold it. Twistin' a drill while t'other fellers swing on it with sledgehammers. Come so near losin' both hands, that way, I quit."

"Where was that?" asked Ed. "In the mica quarry?"

"That were in the granite quarry," said Malt, pausing in his work. "I worked in the mica quarry too, when I were a youngster. Folks owned all of 'em then."

"That's right," said Ed. "I remember hearing that you were related to the Beesons. They owned all this land once, didn't they?"

"Abel Beeson were my grandfather," said Rube. "Funny thing, so many people askin' me about that lately. Was a feller askin' me about that t'other day; stopped fer gas. And another one last week. I expected they was some o' them lawyer fellers. I don't tell them nothin'."

"What lawyer fellers?" asked Ed, surprised.

Rube turned a shrewd look on Ed. "Every once in a while some fell-er drops in to see me. 'You're one o' the Beeson heirs,' he says. 'Don't you know you've got a good claim on the estate? I'll take the case,' sezee, 'and you won't have to put up a cent. All you've got to do is to sign papers.' 'Shoo!' I sez. 'I'm all through with that long ago. Signed papers and got paid for it.' 'Well,' he sez, 'you was a damn fool'; and when he starts talking that way I throw him out.

"Got well paid, too," Rube continued, with a sly look, as he tugged a tire off the rim. "I didn't have no claim on the Beeson estate. Told the

Electric people so, and they wouldn't believe me. But if a feller wants to pay me money for something I haven't got, I'm willin' to take it."

"You're dead right," said Ed. "You've got a nice business and a house over your head, and what more do you want? I'll bet you sleep better than a lot of these dealers that are selling cars."

Ed watched Rube replace the rim on the spare tire. "Tell you what, Rube," he said, "you come upstairs when you get through. I'll give you something that's good for a sore throat. I've got an old album upstairs, too, that you might like to see. It may have some of your folks in it."

"Thanks," said Rube. "I'll be up there in a couple of minutes."

Ed paid Rube, and rejoined Hubert in the living-room. He related briefly Rube's conversation up to that point.

Rube joined them in a few minutes, and sat down heavily at the table, elbows on it, and lit, with apparent pleasure, a cigar that Ed had given him. Ed set out glasses and passed the bottle and the water pitcher. He got out the album and handed it to Rube.

"Well, well," said Rube, pleased. "I remember this album. It belonged to Cousin Keziah. I saw this once when I was a kid, at her house. Only time I was ever there. She lived in your house, you know, Ed. Our folks didn't get along with Keziah. She were a hard one. Don't think I ever saw her more'n once or twice."

"Was she your first cousin?" asked Ed.

"Mother's first cousin," said Rube. "That's Keziah there," he said, turning the album around. "Kind o' flatterin', though, I'd say. Mother were Abel's daughter; Keziah were Jonas's daughter. Weren't no more alike than a weasel and a house cat. No more were Abel and Jonas, though they were brothers. Gran'ther were a big man, hearty; Great-Uncle Jonas you could a'most put your hand around, like a hoe handle. I never see him but once, either, but I remember that time. Him pointing a skinny finger at me, and sayin' to Mother, 'That your brat?' Here's Great-Uncle Jonas, like as life, though when I see him he was all shrunken up."

Ed and Hubert looked at the tight-lipped, long and full-bearded face, typical of the early pioneers of industry, and knew him at once for a hard patriarch and a harder employer.

"And there's Abel," said Rube, excitedly, turning a leaf. "That's Gran'ther. Don't look much like Jonas, does he?"

"Sort of favors you a little," observed Ed. "About the head and eyes. Fine-looking gentleman," he added. "Were they partners?"

"Yes," said Rube reflectively, "and they were heirs of all old Ezra Beeson's land. Joint heirs, they were, and partners in the quarry business. Whichever one died first, t'other one got the business and all the property. Gran'ther wanted to change that, I've heard tell, but he couldn't. Funny, I always think of Jonas as older than Gran'ther. He was really several years younger, though you wouldn't know it to see him. Wiry, too. He always figured, they say, that he'd outlive Gran'ther, and so he did. Used to cackle over it like an old hen; tell Gran'ther he was too fleshy, he'd die sudden." Rube hesitated a minute. "Old Jonas were a hard man," he continued. "Gran'ther started the business. He would have taken Father into it, but Jonas wouldn't let him. Gran'ther and Jonas quarreled a lot."

"How many children did Jonas and Abel have?" asked Ed.

"Let's see," said Rube, squinting his eyes and pulling on his cigar with relish; "Jonas had three; one died young, as a child. Gran'ther had four. My Aunt Judy died as a girl. Uncle Job and Uncle Caleb died in the war; Caleb in Andersonville Prison. Both unmarried. My mother were the eldest. Repose, her name were; and a good one, too. Jonas had Keziah, Jacob, and a boy that died young; I think his name were Jonas, too; they say he was old Jonas's favorite child. But like as not he'd have quarreled with him, too, if he'd grown up. Jake were the eldest. He run away as a lad; went West. Some say he went prospectin'. He died near fifty year ago; killed in a railroad accident. Jake were wild; fought with his father. Jonas was religious; Jake were an atheist; didn't believe in nothin', I've heard Mother tell. It was Jonas bein' so hard set Jake that way, Mother said. I never saw Jake. Wonder if his picture's here." Rube turned the leaves.

"Here's Mother," he said suddenly, and gazed at the picture earnestly.

"You can take the book home with you, Rube," said Ed impulsively. "It belongs to you by rights. If I'd known before that it was your folks, I'd have given it to you."

"No," said Rube doubtfully, after considering for a minute. "I'd like this of Mother, and one of Father, if he's there. But he wouldn't be. Cousin Keziah didn't like Father. Said he was shiftless. I won't take the album, though. Jonas's folks didn't like our folks; wouldn't have nothin' to do with them, finally. Keziah could have helped Father and Mother many a time, and never felt it; but Father wouldn't ask her. Mother spoke to Great-Uncle Jonas about money one time, and Keziah drove her out of the house; accused her of plotting, and all. Let the dead past bury its dead, I says," said Rube.

"Whom did Keziah marry?" asked Ed. "She got all the property, didn't she?"

"Yes," said Rube. "Gran'ther died ten years afore Jonas. Keziah married Joe Medro. I don't remember him much; ain't sure as I ever saw him. But he was under her thumb, they say. And he left her a widow. She kept everything in her name. And saving! You never see such a saving woman. She sold the land that the Electric Company is on now; must have got a nice piece of money for it. She had one daughter, that's all. Grace, her name was. Married a fellow named Plenty, out in Ohio."

"Grace and Thomas Plenty," said Ed. "We got our land from them."

"That's right," said Rube. "I remember signing some papers about that, too, and got some money for it. Plenty is right. I hear tell those folks are right well off. Never saw hide or hair of 'em, though. Guess they never heard of me. Don't care if they never do, either."

"Did Jake ever marry?" asked Ed.

"Jake?" said Rube. "Never heard so. Don't see how any woman would want to marry him. Jake took after his father in some ways, they said. But he and Jonas fought like wolves. They say Jake tried to get some of the money after his father died; came back and tried to wheedle or threaten Keziah, but couldn't get nothin' out of her. And they say he was so mad that he went up on the hill here and knocked over all the family gravestones and threw 'em over the cliff."

"Up on the hill where?" asked Ed.

"This hill across the gully here," said Rube. "There's the family graveyard up there. Jonas is buried there, and his wife Martha, and Gran'ther and Grandmother, and old Ezra, and some others. Not Mother or Father, though. Anyway, there ain't no gravestones up there now, whoever took 'em away."

Ed looked his astonishment at Hubert. Hubert shifted himself in his chair, took a drink from his glass, and filled his pipe.

"My gosh, that was a rough thing to do," said Ed. "Must have been a tough customer. But I've never seen any graves up there, and I've been all over the hill."

"Yes, that were their buryin' ground," said Rube, settling back in his chair with evident satisfaction in the interest shown by his audience. "There ain't anyone there 'cept only the family. And not many of them. I remember seein' the gravestones when I was a kid. Old Ezra, you know, used to live in your house, and Jonas and his wife Martha after that; and then Keziah and her husband."

"I remember the name Medro now," said Ed. "They were the last occupants."

"Yes," said Rube, "Jonas and Martha once lived there. I used to think it was gloomy there, but you've got it fixed up nice. 'Twas the only house on the hill then. Great-Aunt Martha died before I was born. They say she was a fine woman, and Jonas set great store by her. It was after she died that Jonas began to get queer. They say he thought about nothing but heaven and how he was going to get there. But he got more and more close, after his wife died. Gran'ther died the same year and Jonas got all the property. Yes, Jonas were very religious. And Keziah took after him."

"Were you an only child?" asked Ed.

Rube shook his head. "Two sisters," he said. "Died before I was born. Cholera epidemic."

"You say your cousin Jake came back to get his share of the estate," interjected Hubert. "Why didn't he bring suit? Did Jonas will all his property to Keziah?"

"I don't think so," said Rube. "I heard tell Jonas tore up a couple of wills at different times. I think he cut Jake out of one will. Then he had a fight with Keziah. Anyway, there was no will found, and Keziah claimed to be the only heir. Jake had been missing a long time, you see. Mother and Father were both dead then. I wouldn't doubt but perhaps Jake were going to bring suit, but he didn't have no money, I guess. Anyway, he was killed right after that, as I told you. In a railroad accident. There weren't no doubt about that.

"They did say," continued Rube, "that old Jonas was so queer, in his last years, and so tight, that he got the idea he wouldn't leave his money to anybody. Got the idea that he could take it to heaven with him. Anyway, he hated all his kin, and was a sore trial to them. And come to settle the estate, there weren't hardly any money found at all; nothing but the land. They knew where he banked, but they told them there that old Jonas had closed out his account and had drawn out all his money in gold pieces. Thought he was crazy, but he'd been an important customer and they humored him. They told Keziah about it, and she wanted to put the old man in a madhouse. That finished Keziah with Jonas. He put her out of the house the year he died, and she had a hard time of it."

Ed looked at Hubert, and caught a gleam in his eye.

"Never found the gold since?" asked Ed, as soon as he could regain a calm demeanor.

"Not a sign of it," said Rube, who was beginning to warm up under the influence of a second drink. "And why? Because," he said, pounding his fist on the table, "old Jonas's money was buried with him!"

"Why didn't they dig for it?" asked Ed, with bated breath.

"Dig for it?" replied Rube, with a wild look. "Who'd dig up a grave? Jonas knew his folks were too religious for that. All but Jake. Jake might 'a' done it, but he never did. He died right after he saw Keziah, and no money of his was ever found. By God, I know I wouldn't dig up old Jonas's grave for all the millions in the world!"

"Do you really think Jonas's money is in his grave?" asked Ed, who was beginning to find an element of humor in the narrative.

"From the way old Jonas talked, afore he died," said Rube. "He had a fine coffin made for himself, a couple of months afore he died, and had it set up in the best room, all ready. All white satin inside, and silver handles and all. And Jonas had the Bible put in, just where his head was to lay, and had his funeral all arranged for. None of his kin was to have anythin' to do with the buryin'. And he even had his grave already dug, and a fine headstone with his name and a verse from the Bible. Very religious, Jonas were. And they did say"—Rube paused for effect and glared at them—"they did say, them as buried him, that it was the all-firedest heavy coffin they ever hefted!"

Ed looked out of the corner of his eye at Hubert, who was looking grave as an owl.

"And Jonas Beeson," said Rube, still more emphatically, raising his hand as if he were taking an oath, "Jonas Beeson didn't die in bed. *Jonas Beeson were hanged!*"

Rube must have been gratified at the effect that he produced on his audience. Ed, who had begun to think that Rube was out of his senses, dropped his pipe and knocked an ashtray on the floor. Hubert leaned forward and gripped the arms of his chair.

Tense as they were, they were almost startled out of their wits by Rube's next act. He stared past them with a look of almost insane fear, opened his mouth, let out a piercing yell, and threw up his hands as if warding off something.

"The rope! The rope!" Rube screamed, pointing to the window in front of him. "Outside there!" And he gasped as if he were drowning.

Ed looked where he pointed, looked wildly at Hubert, then leapt up, wrenched open the front door and ran out. He ran around the corner of the house, looked at the window and at the side of the house, and then, fearing ambush, he ran around the house the other way and peered cautiously around the corner of the garage. But he saw nothing, and heard not a sound but the wind in the trees. He walked back into the living-room.

Hubert had calmed Malt somewhat and given him a nip of neat whiskey.

"You didn't see anything, Rube," said Ed, laying a hand on Rube's shoulder. "There's nobody outside. You must have seen the limb of a bush waving."

"I tell you, I saw it!" said Rube indignantly, shaking his head. "It were a noose, like a hangman's noose, swinging outside the window. And there were blood on it!"

"I'll drive back with you, Rube," said Ed. "That was an exciting story of yours all right, and mighty interesting. Next time you come we'll talk about crops and politics. You get a good sleep. That was just some fool trick someone played on us."

Ed took Rube Malt back in his car and succeeded partially in laughing him out of his fears. When Ed returned, he found George in the barn, listening in amazement to what Hubert was telling him.

"Is that any boyish prank of yours, Georgie?" asked Ed severely. "Hanging ropes outside of windows to scare people?"

"Certainly not!" said George in a manner to inspire conviction. "I may be simple, but I'm not childish. Do you think it could be our old friend, shinning up the silo again?"

Ed grunted doubtfully. "We might look outside for tracks," he said. "But it looks to me as if the two little drinks that Rube had here had acted potently on him, and he got inflammation of the imagination from his own yarn. Some story that was, too. Buried gold in coffins! Gravestones chucked over the cliff! Gran'ther hanging himself! It was well worth the two dollars it cost me for a tire."

"Where's your big flashlight, Ed?" asked Hubert. "Let's go out and look for tracks."

Hubert led the way and the others followed. They walked around to the window where Rube had thought he saw the rope, and Hubert flashed the light all over the ground. There was a bush by the window, and the earth around it was loose. Hubert examined this carefully.

"It looks to me," he said, "as if there had been footprints here, close to the wall. Now there are some marks that look as if they were made by fingers, to obliterate the footprints."

XVIII

THE GRAVES

At breakfast the next morning Rube's story furnished almost the sole topic of conversation, interrupted occasionally by the entrance of the maid, for Ed insisted that the story be kept strictly to themselves. He protested that if it got abroad, the hill would be swarming with curious-minded people, and attempts would probably be made to dig up the graves.

"And perhaps have been made," said George. "You remember that spade I found. It was very forcibly impressed on my memory."

"Also," said Hubert, "that furnishes us with an alternative explanation of the trampled spot that we thought was the scene of the murder. That may, instead, be the site of the graves. Or what someone supposed to be the site of the graves."

"You're right!" said Ed. "We'd better go over there and investigate."

"Ed!" exclaimed Jeanie. "You're not going to dig up the graves, are you?"

"No, indeed. If it were a Pharaoh or a buried Caesar, I might; but not a nineteenth-century corpse. Anyway, the money, I suppose, would have to be turned over to the heirs."

"I dare say you'd get into trouble doing that," said Hubert. "The Plenty family, who own the hill, might have something to say about it. But we might clear the ground and verify Rube's yarn."

"If you can wait till Saturday," said Ed, "I'll come with you. I can borrow a scythe, and I've got a sickle and hatchet."

"All right," said Hubert. "I'll just look over the ground there today and see if I can locate the graves. Certainly none of them has been opened recently, from the looks of the field. And I doubt that Rube's cousin Jake opened Jonas's grave, or the fact would have been discovered when the broken gravestones were found."

"'Jonas Beeson were hanged!'" said George, quoting Rube. "What I'd like to know is whether the old gentleman hanged himself or was hanged officially, perhaps for slaying his brother Abel, or was hanged by his charming daughter Keziah."

"I rather think that Rube meant that he hanged himself," said Hubert, "seeing that he had delusions in his last days, about joining his wife in heaven, and had his coffin and grave all ready."

"No doubt," said George, "and I know just where he did it. He hanged himself on that dead tree on the cliff over there, right in plain sight for the Devil to come and get him. It looks just like old Jonas's hand sticking from the grave, claiming all this land as his own."

After breakfast Hubert sat at the big table in the barn, took a piece of paper, and wrestled with the genealogy of the Beeson family from his recollection of Rube's narrative. Finally he achieved the following result:

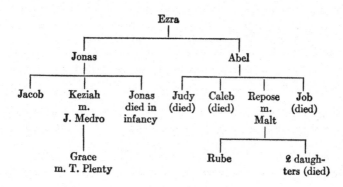

"That," he said to George, "as well as I can tell, is the Beeson family line. Now, let's look at our second cryptogram. I think we can solve it."

Hubert reached for the photostats and took out those of the back and front of the map of the hill. He took his pocket lens and examined the initials on the back of the map, going to the window to get the full sunlight. He then pinned the front of the map to the back so that the torn edges registered exactly.

"Now," he said to George, "do you see what those are?"

George took the map and looked at both sides. "No, I don't," he said, "except that those initials might be those of members of the Beeson family."

"Those initials, I think," said Hubert, "show the location, or at least the relative position, of the graves of different members of the family. After the stones were destroyed, some one of the family, probably Keziah, remembered the relative positions of the graves, and made a note of them in this fashion, perhaps with the idea of restoring the headstones. The little irregular square, marked with pen and ink on the right side of the map, shows the location of the graveyard. You see it's in the little field, and near that trampled patch of ground."

"And which are the people buried there?"

"All Beesons, I think. As I suspected just now, there are ditto marks after some of these initials. I think J. B. and M. L. are Jonas and Martha, his wife. The other J. may be the infant Jonas, and Jy may be Judy; and I think probably, A. N. and H. R. are Abel and his wife. E. B. is probably Ezra, and K. S. his wife; perhaps her name was Keziah too. P. L. B. and N. M. I give up; Rube didn't happen to mention them."

"I wonder," said George, "whether the person who climbed the silo could have known of the existence of this map with the initials on it, and whether that was what he wanted."

"It doesn't seem possible. Those marks were probably made at a time when there were only two living members of the family, Rube and Keziah. I think they were made by Keziah, and I doubt if Rube ever knew of the map or the initials. Of course, we don't know how many people have heard that yarn of Rube's, nor how far it may have traveled. The wonder is that no one has attempted this before."

Hubert got into his working clothes and went over on the hill to look for the graves. George found his own story more interesting than the Beeson saga, and settled down to a morning at the typewriter.

Hubert returned in about an hour. George at once gave him his full attention.

"I've found the graves," said Hubert, "and the fellow who was looking for them hit them pretty close. It's curious that I didn't see them when I was searching for shells yesterday; but when you're looking for something small, it's easy to overlook something big; and they're not clearly defined, either. But a further distance away I found some fragments of headstones still in the ground. Our friend Jake did a thorough job; he must have carried the gravestones, or their fragments, quite a distance to the nearest cliff, and thrown them over. I suppose we could find them if we wanted them badly enough."

"Well, then," said George, "if the fellow found the graves without the map, he probably wasn't the silo man."

"That's logical. But if he knew just where to look, without the map, I wonder who he was?"

"Now," continued Hubert, as George pondered, "I found something more relevant to our problem than that, over there. I found this." He placed a bullet on the desk in front of George.

"Ah," said George, picking it up. "Where?"

"In the brush, near the graves. Which brings us back to the theory that there may have been a scramble instead of a grave hunt. Or perhaps both. The bullet is a forty-five, metal-jacketed, from an automatic—and it's still bright."

"From Ed's gun?"

"I'm going in to Headquarters, after lunch, to find out."

When Hubert returned in the late afternoon, with Ed, from town, he reported that the bullet was from Ed's gun.

"So that's the bullet that killed Klarsen?" asked George.

"Quite possibly. At the distance at which Schlogl, the ballistics expert, says Klarsen was shot, the bullet would have spent most of its force after coming through his body. A stray bullet would either have buried itself deep in the ground or have gone well off the hill. Unless it hit a rock—which this hasn't."

"How do you figure it out now?"

Hubert shrugged his shoulders. "It's very baffling. I can't fit it in any way with the other bullet, from the same gun, found under the hood of Klarsen's car. The thing is very queer."

After dinner Mike Macy came over. He was amused at Rube Malt's story, but flatly refused to believe that it had any bearing on Klarsen's death.

"The amount of money, even in gold pieces," he maintained, "that could be tucked into a coffin, would look pretty sweet to me, I'll admit, but it wouldn't be petty cash to Dynamopolis Electric. They have more important business than digging for buried gold."

"I think you're right, Mike," said Ed. "I can't see Hugh sending Klarsen up there on the hill to loot graves. But there's no doubt that Klarsen went up there for something."

"Well, now, what about Dancey?" asked Mike. "Anything been heard of him?"

"Dancey's in Richmond," said Hubert, much to the surprise of the others, "and being watched."

"What about his old car? Did you inquire at the Chrysler agency?"

"He didn't turn in his old car," said Hubert. "He called at the agency, bought a new car, gave them a check in full, and drove it home. He said he'd sold his old car to a friend who wanted it."

"Ho, ho," said Mike. "A lady friend?"

"And he bought the new car the day after the murder?" asked George.

"Yes. But we have the factory number from the registration office, and they're on the lookout for applications for licenses for used Chrysler coupes. The police are also doing a little shopping for used Chryslers. And if the plates of the junked car are on this car, they may be spotted."

"Another man we want to hear from," said Mike aggressively, "is Crivington. That fellow ought to come across. He knows more about Klarsen than he's told. He calls up Borg twice on the night of the party, perhaps sends Klarsen on some mysterious errand, and then a document last seen in his possession is found on the scene of the crime. He can't laugh all that off."

"In other words," said Ed, "Hugh put Klarsen on the spot, and Borg gets him erased, to cash in on that million-dollar policy, maybe."

"Well, no—I hardly think they need a million that badly. But it looks mighty funny."

"What's Dynamopolis Electric doing to find the murderer?" asked Ed. "They made a great play about spending a lot of money to catch him."

Mike shook his head. "They have some 'special investigators' working on the case," he said. "And I'll bet that if Dynamopolis Electric solves it first some possibly irrelevant but interesting details will be omitted from the testimony."

XIX

THE GOLD-DOLLAR KID

Right after breakfast, Saturday morning, Ed took his car and drove to the farm of a neighbor in the well-cultivated plain to the north of Westwood, and brought back a sickle and a scythe.

"I don't know of any traveling companion for a two-seater," he said, "less agreeable than a scythe. I don't think it did the top of my rumble any good, either."

"I suppose," said Hubert, "that it would be a good deal easier to burn the dry grass than to cut it. But that might call attention to what we were doing, besides burning up possible clues that might be there. I'll handle the scythe; it won't be the first time."

The three walked with their implements across the ravine, and climbed the hill to the little field. Hubert consulted the photostat of the map.

"This corresponds with the location of the graves," he said. "We'll clear a space and see whether we can identify them."

Hubert swung the scythe like a real 'dirt farmer,' and the others hacked and hewed where bushes and vines impeded him.

"Here's a piece of headstone," he said. "And here's another," as his scythe clinked and a spark flew. "I think I begin to see the layout now."

Two or three rude low mounds appeared, barely recognizable as graves, roughly oval rather than rectilinear. "Looks as if they did their own burying," said George. "Probably got their stones from their own quarries. Tight-fisted lot."

"The rocky ground accounts for the irregular arrangement of the graves," said Hubert. "I can see what looks like four graves. Let's see the diagram.

143

"According to this," he continued, studying the diagram, "old Jonas's grave ought to be up this way. Let's clear a space here."

George took the scythe for a spell, but made such slow work of it that Ed wrested it from him. Ed was more vigorous, but hardly more effective. Hubert took the scythe and finished uncovering two more graves.

"By golly!" exclaimed Ed, who was studying the diagram. "This is Jonas's grave. And look at it, will you? It's almost a hole! The others are a little bit hollow, but not like this!"

George and Hubert stopped work to look. "Then someone did get the gold," said George. "Huh! Do you suppose those ghouls chucked the coffin over the cliff, with old Jonas in it?"

"I doubt that," said Hubert. "But they may have smashed it, and refilled the grave carelessly."

"Well, anyway, the gold's gone," said Ed. "I'm kind of sorry, though I wouldn't have disturbed old Jonas's slumbers for the world. But this didn't happen recently. There was several years' growth of brush over that grave."

"Whoever dug up the grave," said George, "evidently knew which was Jonas's. He must have had a diagram like ours, or else how could he pick out the right grave at the first try?"

"There's one other way in which the grave might have been identified," said Hubert. "There may have been a fragment of headstone left in the grave when the robber visited it. In that case, he might have gathered some of the fragments from the foot of the cliff, where Jake threw them, and fitted the right piece to the fragment."

George took a sickle and began to trim the ground around the grave. Suddenly they heard a clink of steel on something, and a yell from George, who dashed into the bushes near by.

"What's the matter, George?" asked Ed. "Cut your toe off?"

George was busy pulling aside, high grass and bushes, looking for something that he had lost. "I hit a gold piece," he said.

"Go on!" said Ed. "It was the top of an olive bottle, I'll bet." Nevertheless, he started looking too.

"Here it is!" cried George, suddenly diving after something. He held it to view. "Finders is keepers, too. See what it is?"

"A twenty-dollar gold piece!" exclaimed Ed. "Let's see it, George. By golly, we'll mow this whole field and rake it with a fine-tooth comb. Look at it, Gil."

"1879," said Hubert, taking it from Ed. "Interesting! Certainly interesting." He looked at Ed.

"1879?" said Ed. He fished in the watch-pocket of his trousers and pulled out another gold coin. "Same as mine!"

"Same as mine, too," said Hubert, smiling, as he pulled a similar coin from his own pocket.

"What the deuce!" said George, taking his coin back from Hubert. "You don't mean to say that you found some, too, and never said anything?"

"The Gold-Dollar Kid!" said Ed to Hubert.

"A curious coincidence," replied Hubert.

"What are you fellows talking about?" asked George.

"Another story altogether," said Ed. "Gil will tell you that later, over a drink. Well, what shall we do now? On with the gold rush? It's nearing lunchtime. I say we put that on the afternoon program."

"I'll quit if you'll quit," said George. "And we'll all line up at scratch this afternoon. I think you said something incautious about a drink, Ed. And I want to hear about this Gold-Dollar Kid, whoever he may be."

"When I bought this place," said Ed, as the three sat fondling tall glasses in the barn, "I found a lot of junk here, including a leather trunk full of letters, which I've already told you about; they were burned up in the barn. However, when I went through the trunk, I found in it a couple of ten-dollar gold pieces, these two that Gil and I have here. They had got underneath the lining of the trunk. Believe me, I ripped out all the lining, and I ripped up every old mattress, cushion, and chair seat, and looked in every old kettle and teapot there was in the place, but I didn't find any more.

"I used to carry these gold pieces around with me, as I do this one now, as a souvenir, and to use if I got caught short any time. Well, I was on a train, coming back from Montana—I'd been shooting wild geese with Joe Tappy, who runs a place out there—and I went into the diner and had my lunch. I happened to sit opposite Gil, whom I didn't know then, and got to talking with him. When I came to pay my check, I discovered that my last five-dollar bill had been shot to chicken-feed, so when the waiter came around I slapped a gold ten on the plate. Gil eyed it curiously, and asked me whether I'd sell it to him for paper money. I gave it to him and he passed me two fives. He looked at the date and said that it had no especial value from a collector's standpoint—it was dated 1879—and judged that I knew that also. I said that I did, for I'd asked a dealer when I found the coins. So then Gil told me a yarn about why he was interested in the coin. You remember it better than I, Gil; you tell it."

"It is a rather interesting story," said Hubert. "Well, about five years ago a friend of mine, a president of a bank in Sioux City, where I have some small dealings, slapped a coin like that on his desk while I was talking to him, and told me this yarn. A man named Sneed, Roy Sneed, who was hanging around Sioux City at the time, but came from no one knew where and had no visible occupation, had acquired there the somewhat inaccurate nickname of 'The Gold-Dollar Kid,' for this reason. He would come to the bank every once in so often, bringing with him a few ten- or twenty-dollar gold pieces, get them changed at the teller's cage, and walk off again. They held him up at first, tested the coins, and found them good money. The curious thing was, that they nearly all looked fresh from the mint, and all around 1879, 1880, and 1881. Now a man ordinarily collects few gold pieces, and for him to have a large collection of the same or nearly the same date is rather unusual. There was no question of their being counterfeit; they were absolutely good. They questioned the man about where he got them, but he got tough and practically told them it was none of their business, so long as they were good. The bank got tired of accommodating him, and he quit coming there, but no doubt went to other banks. Well, the police were of course interested in the man, and watched him, but he wasn't on their books, he behaved himself, dressed well and bothered no one, and there wasn't an excuse for pulling him in and giving him 'the heat.' The bank president, my friend, thought the fellow must have robbed the mint, but I checked up on that easily. Inquiries through banking associations failed to show that any bank had been robbed of a large number of gold pieces. I myself was very curious; but the thing remained a mystery. We did ask the banks to watch for the man; but we couldn't arrest him merely on the grounds that we were curious about him. I never knew what became of him, nor how much money he disposed of."

"Well, it's a good yarn," said George. "And it looks to me as if this fellow of yours might have something to do with the case. Except for this: that if the Gold-Dollar Kid is the chap who robbed the grave, he wouldn't come here a second time. No doubt he got all the money there was the first time."

"I don't doubt it," said Hubert. "No, I think the Gold-Dollar Kid is one person whom we can eliminate from our list of suspects in this affair."

In the afternoon George began to suffer from aches and pains from his unwonted exercise, and sloth triumphed over greed. Common-sense told him that no large number of coins could have been overlooked in that fashion by the robber, and he was content with his loot. When the others left for the hill, George picked out a Western story from Ed's library and settled down in a big chair to rest brain as well as body. The story was about Dick Warner. Dick was riding alone through a desert garnished sparingly with yucca, cholla, mesquite, chaparral, and like vegetation. He was talking to his horse, as all cowboys do, the horse having almost human intelligence as well as marvelous speed; from which conversation the reader might gather that Dick was going from somewhere to somewhere, he didn't know where, because he was 'wanted' (unjustly, it seemed) somewhere else. Dick hired himself out to a wealthy ranchman who needed a foreman in a hurry and got the impression that Dick was a bad *hombre*. The ranchman had a beautiful daughter, and as Dick could talk pure schoolbook English as well as cowboy, he made her acquaintance. She snubbed him terrifically on every possible occasion, however, especially after he had saved her from a grizzly bear, a prairie fire, and bandits in rapid succession. (The bandits, it appeared, were hired by a neighboring ranch-owner who had the most fell designs on the heroine, but whose conscience for some reason demanded a forced marriage ceremony.) The heroine's father, too, was mixed up in some kind of dirty work which George could not fathom, including rustling his own cattle and sneaking about cutting his own fences at night. George reached a point where there was so much smoke, dust, shooting, and running about that he could not make out what was happening, and had about decided to pass it up, when the telephone bell rang.

XX

THE RHESUS

Saturday afternoons at the office of the *Mirror*, to Mike Macy, always had a semi-holiday aspect during the football season. One felt cheerful in anticipation of the impending day of rest, and the football news as it filtered in enlivened the ordinary routine. One had all the advantages of sitting at a radio, and it was much more sociable and the news had a warmer, more human quality.

Mike got back from his lunch a little before one o'clock, sat back in his wobbly swivel chair and put first one number nine and a half on the corner of his desk and then the other on top of the first one. He picked the latest edition of the *Mirror* off of his desk languidly and studied it with appreciation.

"Yale plays Tennessee Aggie," he observed to another man who was tilted back in a chair near Mike's desk, equally a picture of unruffled leisure. "Ha ha. That ought to be a nice little romp for the Elis after what they did to Notre Dame last week."

The man Mike addressed evidently took no interest in the Eastern games, for he remained in his reverie.

"I see Hoke has taken that big boy Cooglefish out at left tackle and put him in at center," continued Mike. "He's been monkeying with his line all fall, and it gets worse right along."

"How he did tout Cooglefish at the beginning of the season!" said the other, grinning. "He was their big find, their all-America hope!"

"Ironpuddlers Clash with Hogskinners," read Mike. "That's the game I'd like to see."

"Harvard-Dartmouth," cried a voice across the room. "Another shake-up in the Harvard line. Lineup now stands: Bowditch, Hallowell,

149

Saltonstall, Dana, Boardman, Grew, Hemenway (A.F.), Shattuck, Sargent—"

"What are you reading, Peewee, the Boston Blue Book?" came another voice.

"Rosenblatt, and—Mulligan!" continued Peewee.

"Good! They've got a two to nine chance."

"I'll lay you a dollar bet, Wally," said Mike, "that Oklahoma doesn't touch Wisconsin's goal line. Is that a sporting proposition?"

"Even money?" said Wally. "Taken. Accidents will happen."

"Mulligan fumbles McWinkle's kick-off, and falls on the ball on Harvard's one-yard line. Time out. Mulligan replaced by Wendell."

"Guess you'd better chase this subway steal again, Wally," said Mike. "See what Alderman Swatz has to say about his real-estate investments along the projected extension. If you can't nail him, see what Kolbe has to say."

"You know what Kolbe'll have to say," protested Wally. "We've got to get some new leads, I tell you."

"Well, dig 'em up," said Mike. "Try Snudkoff and see that fellow out in Primrose. He knows something."

"Rosenblatt's kick is partially blocked. Wow!"

"I want my envelope first," said Wally. "Primrose is a long way off."

"But Wendell recovers the ball and carries it the length of the field for a—"

"Joke?"

"Touchdown! The Harvard stands are a mass of waving crimson."

"Botke's Chipmunks Picked to Rout Catamounts," read Mike, resuming his paper. "Ho, hum!"

"Cabot replaces Rosenblatt at full back."

"What's on the Yale game, Benny?" asked Mike.

"End of the first quarter," said Benny. "Yale, 33—"

"Who cares?"

"Tennessee Aggie, 38."

"Hold 'em, Yale!"

A tall and melancholy-looking man approached Mike's desk, rested the knuckles of one bony hand on it, and stuck the other arm akimbo.

"What now, Groucho?" asked Mike.

"What do you know about this cub Staver stealing my stuff?" asked Groucho indignantly. "You know that baboon stuff is my dish." He tapped himself on the chest. "I've written every line of it that's come out in this paper. That boy will ruin it. It'll be about as funny as a notice of a receiver's sale."

"What baboon stuff is this?" asked Mike.

"He got it off the Petunkawoc police station," said Groucho. "He knows a cop out there or somebody."

"What's it all about?" asked Mike.

"The baboon shot the babyroussa," said Groucho.

Mike took first one foot and then the other down from his desk, gripped the arms of his chair and stared at Groucho.

"Say that again, and say it slow," he said.

"Believe it or not," said Groucho. "The—baboon—shot—the—babyroussa!"

"With *what?*" asked Mike.

"With a gun," said Groucho. "And I want that story!"

"With *what gun?*" cried Mike.

"Ask Staver," said Groucho. "He's writing it."

"Staver!" shouted Mike across the room. "What are you writing?"

"Baboon!" shouted Staver. "I got it!"

"There you are!" said Groucho. "He calls it a baboon. It isn't a baboon. It's a pig-tailed rhesus from Borneo. Remember that raking we got from Mrs. Clifford once for calling it a baboon?"

"Is babyroussa one word or two?" asked Staver.

"Staver!" shouted Mike. "Tear that up! Where the hell's Lowry?" Mike jiggled the telephone hook frantically. "Get me Petunkawoc police station!" he cried. "That gun's got to be in Schlogl's hands for examination before the six-o'clock goes to bed. This isn't your stuff, either, Groucho! This is Rumble Murder Case!"

George had chucked his Western story on the table and was stretching himself lazily when the telephone bell rang. He got up and answered it.

"Hello? Oh, hello, Mike. What? He's over on the hill, with Ed. Sure, I'll get him. What's the excitement?"

George listened while Mike told his story.

"The baboon, eh? Well, I always did think he was a suspicious character. Who's got the gun? All right, I'll hop right over there and have him call you."

George rushed out, scrambled down into the ravine, tore his way across, pausing for breath before climbing the hill. He arrived at the little field to find that Ed and Hubert had neatly cleared the rest of the graveyard and now were exploring the woods adjacent to the field.

"Mike Macy just telephoned," said George, when he could get his breath. "It seems the baboon—you remember—in Mrs. Clifford's zoo got hold of a Colt forty-five automatic somewhere, kept it hidden, and this morning was fooling with the thing and it went off, killing the babyroussa in the next pen. Mike wants to know whether that's the gun that killed the first rumble victim, and he wants you, Mr. Hubert, to get the gun from the Petunkawoc police and take it to Major Schlogl to compare the bullets."

"How many cartridges were in it?" asked Hubert.

"Four, Mike said."

"I don't see just how Mike figures it out, then. If two shots were fired at the dead man, and one at the babyroussa, there'd be only three left. The same goes for Ed's gun. Still, that may not be conclusive. I'll come right along. You'd better come, too, Ed, and drive me."

"You bet your life," said Ed. "I don't think there are any more gold pieces, nor any shells, in this field. I want to hear what comes of this baboon business."

They all marched swiftly back to the barn. Hubert took the telephone at once and got Mike. Then he called Willoughby. Then he turned to Ed.

"Get your car out, Ed," he said. "I'll get that gun right away and we'll take it in."

The six-o'clock had the story. The keeper of the Clifford zoo had heard the shot, and had found the rhesus chattering in a corner of his hut, the babyroussa breathing his last, and the pistol, a Colt automatic, lying on the ground inside the monkey's cage. The animals all had commodious quarters, each a hut and a yard, and the rhesus had hidden the gun among some stumps and stones. The keeper had carried the bad news to Mrs. Clifford, who had called the police and turned the gun over to them. Mr. Clifford could not be reached at his office, and no one there knew anything about the incident.

But the sensational feature of the news was this. The four remaining bullets in the gun, which were fired into cakes of laundry soap for examination, did not match those found in the body of Rumble Victim No. 1. But they did match the bullet found under the hood of Klarsen's car.

"Jeanie!" cried Ed, when he and Hubert got back from town. "Have you seen anything of a little red book that had a lot of addresses in it? The last I saw of it, it was in a little drawer of the secretary, but I've looked in every drawer and pigeon-hole and I can't find it."

"I remember it," said Jeanie, "but I haven't seen it for a long time. The addresses in it were all out of date, and you never used the book."

"I hope to heaven it hasn't been thrown out," said Ed. "It had the number of my automatic on the back fly-leaf."

"Well, sit down to dinner now," said Jeanie, "and I'll help you look for it after dinner."

"Oh, it must be my gun, I suppose," said Ed, "that this monkey had. But how could it ever get there? Talk about Hallowe'en pranks! If this business isn't the work of witches and pixies, I don't know what!"

"The Mirror doesn't say it was your gun, Ed," said Jeanie. "I hope you didn't tell the police so."

"Well, it was exactly like my gun," said Ed. "And it matches up with the bullet in Klarsen's car and the one found over on the hill. And my gun was stolen. It certainly looks as if the two murders were connected."

"Surely the monkey couldn't have killed a man, could he?" asked Jeanie, bewildered.

"And driven him into Putnam Lake?" asked Ed. "No, but the gun must have been dropped or thrown by someone, near the monkey's cage."

"Are you sure the pistol expert hasn't got those bullets mixed up?" asked George of Hubert. "It's easy enough to see how this might be the gun that shot the other fellow."

"If he got the bullets mixed," said Hubert, "he ought to be fired in disgrace. As a matter of fact, I'm sure he didn't, because Willoughby and I were both present when he made the examination, both this and the other time, and I watched closely to make sure that didn't happen. But what puzzles me most is why this gun still had four cartridges in it. A Colt holds a magazine of six. We found one bullet from this gun in Klarsen's car and another bullet from it on the hill near the graves. A third bullet hit the babyroussa. That should leave only three still in the gun, unless I've forgotten my arithmetic. It looks as if the man with the gun must have fired a lot of shots and refilled."

"He must have refilled it," said Ed. "It must have been a noisy night on the eastern front."

"I suppose it must be your gun, Ed," said Jeanie hopelessly, "if it matches your bullets."

"No," said Hubert, "because there are bullets of Dancey's also that came from the barrel of excelsior, and we don't know which are whose."

"Oh, dear!" said Jeanie reproachfully. "Was that barrel important? Solveig asked me about the barrel, and I saw that it was all smashed and dirty, and couldn't be used again. I'm terribly sorry. But how could the barrel help you?"

"Well," said Ed, "if I had the barrel heads I could tell whether I fired twelve or fifteen shots into it, and identify my own bullets. But we may find the little red book. Bring on your dessert, and we'll go at it again."

After hastily gulped coffee Ed went at the secretary again. He took out all the drawers and opened up all the parcels contained therein. Jeanie helped him.

"Here you are," said Jeanie calmly, showing a packet of old insurance policies that she had untied. "Tucked right up in the midst of these. It must have been in this pigeon-hole."

"Good!" said Ed cheerfully, putting back the drawer. He took a look at the back fly-leaf of the book, and showed the number marked therein to Hubert.

"*Not* my gun!" he remarked.

"That's good!" said Jeanie. Then a look of perplexity came over her face. "Why! Then it must be Arthur Dancey's!"

XXI

DANCEY GETS 'THE WORKS'

Sunday morning, right after breakfast, Mike Macy came over, and found Jeanie and the men discussing the newspapers.

"Well, Mike," asked Ed, "who committed these murders?"

Mike shook his head. "It gets worse and worse," he said. "You notice we didn't say anything in the *Mirror* about its being your pistol. You can thank me for that. But I see the morning papers got it all right."

"The joke's on them," said Ed. "Because it isn't my pistol."

"What!" exclaimed Mike. "I thought you were sure it was your pistol."

"Just because my pistol was stolen," said Ed, "doesn't make it my pistol. It's Art Dancey's pistol."

"Oh, Lord!" said Mike. "Why didn't you tell me last night? Is this gratitude?"

"I didn't know till I got home," said Ed. "I found my pistol number, and that is not my gun. And as it matches some bullets that were found in the barrel, it must be Dancey's."

"Hoity-toity!" said Mike. "Aren't you going to put Dancey under arrest now, Mr. Hubert?"

"Dancey will be back here today," said Hubert. "Unless he tries to escape—which he won't succeed in doing. He reserved a berth on the Pickaninny Flyer for last night. A plain-clothes man has the berth opposite him. All of which is an excellent reason for not publishing the fact that his gun has been found."

"What on earth," asked Ed, "would Dancey be doing in Clifford's zoological garden, at the witching hour of midnight, Hallowe'en?"

"He could have been there," said Mike. "He left the barn about nine o'clock, and none of us has seen him since. He had the opportunity, and we suspect he had the motive. We know this was his gun, and we know it was the gun that killed Klarsen. That'll take explaining."

"Just the same," said Ed, "I don't believe Dancey did it. I'll bet his gun was stolen, same as mine."

"The thief must have a hobby of collecting Colt forty-five's, then," said George. "Well, we'll soon know."

The telephone bell rang, and Ed answered it.

"It's Dancey," said Ed, hand over the mouthpiece. "He wants to see you and me, Gil, over at his house this afternoon right after dinner."

"Tell him we'll be over," said Hubert. "And let Dancey tell his story first, Ed. Don't tell him what we know—till he's through."

Arthur Dancey met Ed and Hubert at the door, on their arrival, with a pleasing manner combining formality with cordiality. His face was drawn, a bit pale, and he looked very tired. He took them into a large living-room, which had been remodeled in the Southern Colonial style, and whose furniture had evidently been brought there from some statelier mansion. Hubert got a swift impression of white paneling, tall windows, shining old mahogany, and family portraits.

"You are a detective, sir," Dancey said to Hubert, with a noticeably Southern inflection, "and also a friend of Mr. Marsh's. I have no doubt that you will try to help me out all you can, as I am also a friend of Mr. Marsh's."

"Indeed I will, if I can," said Hubert. "I will say that both Ed and I find it hard to believe that you are seriously implicated in this matter."

Dancey looked at Hubert with evident surprise. "Just what matter do you mean, sir? I haven't told you my story yet?"

It was Hubert's turn to show surprise. "The matter of Mr. Klarsen's death," he said. "Isn't that what you have in mind?"

"Mr. Klarsen!" exclaimed Dancey in amazement. "Do you mean Mr. Klarsen who was out here ten days ago, as a guest of Crivington?"

"Certainly. Haven't you seen in the papers that Klarsen was murdered?"

"Murdered, sir? By whom?"

"That is what the police want to know. All we know is that he was probably shot over here on the hill."

"On the hill!" Dancey stopped abruptly, as the maid brought in a silver tray of old crystal glasses, a silver pitcher of plain water, a decanter, and some White Rock. He waited till the maid had retired, then got up and closed both doors.

"You must excuse me," he said faintly. "Will you help yourselves?" He waved for them to partake. "I hadn't heard that news. There was nothing in the papers about it Friday, when I left for Richmond. There was something about a body found in a car belonging to Mr. Clifford, and they were pursuing a car which had gone north. But the Richmond papers had nothing about it. How and when was Klarsen killed?"

Hubert gave Dancey the principal facts of the case, omitting, however, all reference to Ed's gun or Dancey's.

"You knew Mr. Klarsen?" Hubert asked casually.

"Slightly," said Dancey, darting a look at Hubert. "But this has nothing to do with what I have to say. My story begins under the bridge—the Monument Avenue Bridge."

"What!" exclaimed Ed and Hubert together.

"It has to do with the other murder," said Dancey, "of which I know equally little. But I fear I have played an imprudent part in it. This happened Thursday, the day after I met you at Ed's barn. I drove into town Thursday morning, as usual, in my car, which I parked under the approach to the bridge. You know the place? I spent most of the morning at my office, which is in the Engineers' Building, across the street from Ed's building. I went early to lunch and to do some errands. I got tickets for myself and my mother for the five-o'clock train Friday to Richmond. Mother has a strong feeling, whenever she feels ill, that she wants to get back to her old home, and the doctor advised it. I did some other errands, took my packages under the bridge, about four o'clock, to get my car and go home." Dancey took a long drink from his glass. "I opened my rumble to put my things in, and there I found the body of a man."

Hubert leaned forward, but said nothing.

"The body," continued Dancey, with a long breath, "was in underclothing, and the head was bound up in rags. The man appeared to be a workingman. I was astounded, and did not know what to do. I saw that a murder had been committed, perhaps while I was shopping, and

I knew that I ought to report it to the police. But I closed the rumble again, and got to thinking. I was to go to Richmond the next day with Mother, and did not want to disappoint her. I dreaded the explanation I should have to give her, for putting off the journey. It would have been a serious shock to her. I should have been detained as a witness; my name would have been in the papers, and it would have been impossible to keep it from her. It was evident to me that the murderer had picked out my car purely by chance. And I thought, why shouldn't it have been some other car? What difference would it make in tracing the criminal whether it was my car or the next one?" Dancey paused for breath.

"I can understand that logic," said Ed, smiling.

"So I decided to transfer the body. There wasn't a soul under the bridge, and I was in a dark recess. My car had a side door in the rumble, and that made it easier to get the body out. I looked around and saw another car with a similar rumble, opened it, slid the body in, and closed the rumble. I had first to take something out of the other car; a bag, I believe, which I put into the rumble of another car. I think my only regret at the time was that I had lost someone's bag for him."

"Did this body, Mr. Dancey," asked Hubert, "leave some blood in your car?"

"It did. But I had a rubber mat in the bottom of my rumble, which took most of it. I washed the mat after I got home, and the inside of the rumble, too, for some blood got into one corner."

"And what did you do then?"

"Then," said Dancey, "I decided to dispose of my car. I had intended to get a new car, and had thought of trading in my old one. But the superintendent of our building, who is very friendly with me, had several times made me an offer for my old car, whenever I should want to sell it, and, as it was not much under what I should have got in trade, I let him have it.

"I drove the car in Friday morning and left it at a downtown garage for him. Then I thought I would look at a new car, and went to the Chrysler agency. They had one in demonstration use that was just the color and model that I wanted, so I gave them a check on the spot and drove the car home."

"After attaching your old license plates, which you had removed from the old car?"

"Yes, sir. I had them taken off at the garage where I left the car, and carried them with me, wrapped in a newspaper."

"Now, Mr. Dancey, did you happen to notice whether either of your license plates was loose when you took them from the old car?"

"Loose, sir? How did you know that? The rear one was loose all day Thursday, but I didn't discover the source of the rattling till Friday."

"Your car was parked on Ed's ground, wasn't it, while you were at the barn Wednesday evening?"

"Yes, it was. I had driven to the village drugstore for a prescription for Mother, after dinner, and instead of putting up my car I drove to Ed's and parked. And when I came out, I forgot that my car was there and walked back to the house. I did not remember it till nearly midnight, after the doctor had gone."

"Had you left your keys in your car, by any chance?"

"I had. I did not expect to be at Ed's more than ten or fifteen minutes. I had to get back to Mother."

"When you went to get your car, Mr. Dancey, about midnight, did you notice whether the engine was warm, or whether the car was in a different position from that in which you left it?"

"I didn't notice anything like that. I think the engine was cold, though. You don't think"—Dancey looked aghast—"that the body was put in out here?"

"I don't know, Mr. Dancey. But it would have been quite easy, apparently, for anyone to have stolen your car. Much easier than Klarsen's," he added, to Ed.

"I do not believe, sir," said Dancey stubbornly, "that either of those murders was committed out here!"

"Now, Mr. Dancey," said Hubert, "I am anxious to find out anything that I can of Mr. Klarsen's history. You say you knew him slightly. I believe you spoke to him Wednesday night."

Dancey looked startled. "I—I did, sir. Or rather, I did not, I am sorry, now, to say. I have never been on terms of close friendship with Mr. Klarsen. I have not seen him for many years."

"You had had a quarrel with him?"

"A difference of opinion," said Dancey stiffly. "I don't believe you would consider it important."

"Perhaps not, Mr. Dancey. But since you have told us about finding the body, you will, I fear, be called before a less sympathetic audience than Ed and myself, and I think in your own interest you should tell us all that you can."

"I can only assure you, Mr. Hubert, that the incident had no bearing at all on the matter of Klarsen's death."

"Very well, then. But can you tell us, Mr. Dancey, whether Klarsen was ever married?"

"I can tell you very little about Mr. Klarsen," said Dancey, a trifle excitedly. "The only time I knew him was in training camp, in 1917. I knew him only as an excellent officer and fellow soldier. He served with distinction overseas, was reported killed in action in the last offensive before the Armistice, but was later found to have been sent from hospital to some friends in Denmark, and he returned to this country in 1920. I know nothing of him since then except that he has been with the Electric Company."

"You don't know," insisted Hubert, "whether Klarsen was ever married, or whether any woman has figured importantly in his life?"

"I cannot tell you any more about Klarsen than what I have said. As I say, I was not in any way in his confidence at any time."

"One more thing, Mr. Dancey. You have a pistol. Would you mind letting me take a look at that pistol?"

"Certainly not," said Dancey, with mild surprise. "I have a number of pistols. I have made rather a hobby of firearms."

Dancey led the way into a small room with a little alcove, very cozy with open fireplace, easy-chair and bookshelves, topped by a bust of Dante. The tooled bindings suggested the bibliophile, but a collection of books on the Civil War suggested the student of history. Dancey unlocked by a single lock a half-dozen shallow drawers in a mahogany chest evidently built for the purpose, and pulled open one of the drawers. Hubert, who had followed him closely into the room, laid a hand gently on his arm.

"This is rather a careful operation that I am going to perform," he said, "and I shall have to ask you to let me open the drawers. In a moment you will understand why. May I clear off this table by the window?"

Dancey assented with polite alacrity. "All the drawers contain pistols," he said. "Those that you see now are Revolutionary types. In other drawers are earlier types; in others, Civil War. The upper ones contain examples of the types used by the different armies in the last war."

"A most interesting hobby," said Hubert, opening the bottom drawer first. It was full of flintlock pistols, so he closed it again. "I have quite a number of pistols myself, but nothing like your collection." He continued opening and shutting the drawers again until he came to the top one. Ed recognized in it a Luger, a Browning, and in a corner a Colt automatic.

Hubert lifted the drawer carefully and set it on the table by the window. He ran his eye over all the pistols, and then took from his pocket a case from which he extracted a most scientific-looking field microscope with a German name. Setting this over the Colt automatic, he examined the surface of the pistol, then lifted the pistol gently and examined the surface of the drawer where the pistol had lain. Then he turned the gun over in his fingers and looked at the number.

"What was the number of your gun, Ed?" he asked. Ed took out his little red book, read the number, then bent over, and looked at the pistol.

"My gun!" he exclaimed. Dancey looked astonished.

Ed burst into a hearty laugh and clapped Dancey on the shoulder. "Shake, old topper!" he exclaimed, and chuckled again.

"That is your gun?" asked Dancey, bewildered. "Then where is mine?"

"At police headquarters," said Ed. "Do you remember the time a couple of years ago when we had a contest and shot at a barrel in my yard? We cleaned our guns in the barn and laid them on the table. You must have taken away my gun and I took yours."

It took considerable explanation to make Dancey understand the point of the matter. Apparently he was inclined to regard the whole thing as a minor mishap. Hubert took the pistol, still carrying it gently, and they went back into the living-room.

"I think this clears you of a serious charge, Mr. Dancey," said Hubert. "And I am very glad indeed of it. But there is another charge, serious enough, that you will have to face. It is that of being an accessory after the fact and of obstructing justice, though perhaps ignorantly.

In view of the circumstances the court may be lenient; however, it is a legal offense. Now, Mr. Dancey, I am an officer of the law, with authority from Dynamopolis Headquarters. It is strictly my duty to put you under arrest; but I am going to stretch my authority as far as possible for a period. I shall have to leave an officer with you, and you will actually be a prisoner. But meanwhile I urge you to get into immediate touch with your lawyer and see if it will be possible for you to get bail. If you have no lawyer, I'm sure Ed can tell you of a good one from among his friends. But you must act at once."

Dancey looked like a spook. "I shall not attempt to escape, sir," he said, his eyes glittering. "I—my grandfather, sir, was once a prisoner of war. He gave his word—and kept it. He was allowed his liberty, within bounds."

"I am sorry, Mr. Dancey," said Hubert, glancing for a moment at the portrait of the bearded soldier in gray over the mantel, "but the law knows nothing of chivalry. It is not that I don't trust you; it is that the law doesn't trust me to that extent. I have no choice. Now, have you a lawyer?"

"Call Walter Knapp, in Sunset Hills, Art," said Ed. "He's Tom Knapp's brother, and a leading lawyer. He's handled some criminal cases, and he lectures on criminal law at the University. He plays golf with some of the big judges, too. You'll have no trouble."

"Thank you, Ed," said Dancey. "I think—I have a lawyer, but this may be better—" He took the memorandum that Ed handed him. "Thank you, Ed—and Mr. Hubert." Hubert shook hands with him heartily. They left him staring with bent head absently at the memorandum.

As they walked to the barn, Ed saw that a strange car was parked near by. Hubert stopped a moment and spoke to a man who was sitting idly at the wheel. The man nodded, alighted, and walked toward Dancey's house.

"Today," observed Ed meditatively, as they entered the barn, "is Armistice Day."

XXII

WHAT JEANIE KNEW

As Ed and Hubert entered the barn, George leapt up to meet them.

"What have you got there?" he asked on seeing the Colt automatic which Hubert was carrying between thumb and forefinger.

"First, I want a box for this," said Hubert. "Can you find me an old shoe box?" he asked Ed. He laid the gun on the mantel.

"That," he said to George, "is Ed's gun. He swapped guns with Dancey and didn't know it."

"By cracky!" exclaimed George. "Why didn't we think of that? So the bee is on Ed again after all. Well, what did Dancey have to tell you?"

"Let's get Macy over here," said Hubert. "No use going all over it twice. Will you give him a ring, Ed?"

Ed did so. In a few minutes Mike's car snorted outside.

"Been hanging around the 'phone all afternoon since dinner," said Mike. "Amy's sore because I wouldn't go over to the Bells' and play tennis. Now shoot it! What's Dancey got to say?"

Hubert gave a fairly detailed account of the conversation at Dancey's house, and told about his collection of guns.

"So Dancey put the body in Clifford's car!" said Mike. "What a simpleton he must be. He'll be lucky if he gets off with a fat fine and some hot shot from the bench. I'm surprised that he shouldn't know better."

"Well, it looks foolish to us now," said Ed, "but I can see how a man in a hurry and in a quandary might do it without due thought. Dancey is a curiously unworldly person in some ways. I don't doubt for a minute that he always intended to report it later."

"Well, I hope he gets out on bail," said George. "The poor fellow would think he was branded for life if he had to spend a minute behind the bars."

163

"That ought to prove to you," said Hubert, smiling, "that the law is no snob."

"You make me laugh, George," said Mike. "It was only a day or two ago that you were nearly convinced that Dancey's hands were red with the blood of two victims."

"Well," said George, "let's figure it out all over again now. So you think the body of this other fellow could have been put in Dancey's car out here? What were the circumstances of that murder, Mike?"

"That fellow," said Mike, considering carefully, "was shot in the top of the head, also in the abdomen. That abdomen shot was a puzzler; must have been fired from a distance of over a hundred yards, they said. Both bullets from the same gun, but they've never found the gun. The fellow's head was all tied up but whether that was first aid or to keep the blood from the rumble, no one knows."

"I think that man," said Ed, "is the man who climbed my silo. He seems to have been looking for Klarsen and he evidently found him. I think this man stepped aboard Klarsen's car as soon as Klarsen got in, on the running-board, and held a pistol—Dancey's pistol—to Klarsen's head and made him coast his car out quietly and drive around into the ravine. Gil showed us a place where the car ran off the old road into the ditch. I think Klarsen deliberately drove off the road so as to throw the fellow off the car—that's the kind of a bird Klarsen was—and whipped out his gun and shot the fellow in the head as he fell on the ground."

"And then," suggested George, "Klarsen walked away a couple of hundred yards and shot another bullet into the man's abdomen. At night, too. Good shooting, that."

"Oh, hell," said Ed. "You figure it out then."

"Well," said George, "here's how I dope it. In the first place, here come two people out of the West, a man and a woman. On the same day, here comes Klarsen from out West; he arrives in Westwood, stops at Crivington's house, apparently for a purpose. Klarsen reports to Crivington that these people have arrived and are on the hill, lying doggo. Crivington reports this to his boss, Borg, by telephone. He suspects what these people are after. Now, in the evening, Ed flings a party. Crivington isn't invited, but he muscles himself and Klarsen in on it. What for? We shall see.

"When Crivington gets to the party, the first thing he does is to wangle these mysterious papers out of Ed, which the thief wants and Dynamopolis Electric doesn't want him to have. Crivington calls up Borg and asks him what to do with them. Borg says, 'Send them by Klarsen over to me.' And Borg adds, 'We've got the papers; *now get the man!*'"

"Too hot, George, too hot," commented Ed.

"All right," said George. "Now, who is this man? Why, none other than the missing heir to the Beeson acres! Klarsen's found that out in his travels. Crivington gives Klarsen Borg's orders, Klarsen sticks his gun in his pocket, and drives off quietly to the quarry. Klarsen parks his car, takes his gun in his hand, sneaks stealthily up the hill. Peering through the bushes, he sees the man and the woman sitting by their camp-fire. He takes good aim and pots the man in the abdomen."

Mike and Ed looked at Hubert inquiringly.

"Then," said George, "the woman screams and runs away, and Klarsen comes up and finishes the man off with one in the head. But as he turns to leave, the woman, concealed in the bushes, pots Klarsen in the back."

"And then," said Ed, "the woman walks over to Klarsen's car and fires a bullet into the engine through the footboard."

"It's Mike's turn now," said George, discouraged. "Let's see what he can do, and then Mr. Hubert can tell us the truth."

"I'd like to know first," said Mike, "whether Mr. Hubert and Ed are convinced that Dancey was telling the truth."

"I believe that Dancey was telling the truth when he said he had not heard of Klarsen's death," said Hubert. "His surprise seemed to me quite genuine. But after that, I don't know. I don't think Dancey is guilty of either murder, but I think he suspects someone whom he is attempting to shield."

"Dancey is no liar," said Ed, "but I think there are circumstances in which he might consider a lie more honorable than the truth."

"To shield a woman, for instance?" suggested Mike.

"I agree with you," said Hubert. "I doubt if a woman committed these murders, but she might be the cause of them."

"I distinctly got the impression," said Ed, "from Dancey's attitude, that Klarsen had been married and Dancey perfectly well knew it."

"I think you are correct there," said Hubert.

"Mr. Hubert," said Mike deliberately, taking a fresh cigarette from his pocket, "I suppose you, like most detectives of standing and repute, know a good many secrets that would blow up homes if you told them, and are pretty expert in keeping them to yourself."

Hubert smiled. "I know some secrets that might, I think, blow up nations. I might add that it takes a bit of skill as an actor, at times, to keep a secret. Mere silence is often as bad as shouting."

"I've kept a lot of good stuff from my paper," said Mike, lighting his cigarette and waving the match out, "in the understanding that our conferences here were confidential. Now I want the rest of you to understand that I have something confidential to tell which I want you to pledge me solemnly to keep secret. Otherwise I shan't tell it."

"I'll give you my pledge, Mike," said Ed, "provided you will assure me that it has nothing to do with my own concerns, as I don't suppose it has."

"I never have kept a secret," said George, "but I'll try anything once."

"There's absolutely nothing doing on this, George," said Mike sternly, "unless you pledge your word of honor and realize that it means just that, that you're a dog if you don't keep it. It might cost me my job, and it might bring great misfortune down on innocent people. The only reason I'm willing to tell it is because it may be important for Mr. Hubert to know it."

"That's different," said George. "Pledge or no pledge, I wouldn't spill a secret like that. But I'll pledge, absolutely."

"Well, then," said Mike gravely, looking at each of the others in turn, "Anna Borg and Harold M. Klarsen were married at Bascom's Point in August, 1917, just before he embarked for France. And that marriage has never been annulled."

Ed stared at Hubert.

"That's what Dancey knew!" he exclaimed.

"Ah," said George, "that's what Jeanie knew, too!"

XXIII

THE SPENT BULLET

The four looked grimly at one another.

"There you have a motive," said George, "for at least four people—Crivington, his wife, her father, and Dancey."

"Why Dancey?" asked Ed.

"Didn't you intimate that he was in love with Ann Crivington?" asked George. "He's exactly that idealistic type of sentimentalist that loves self-immolation."

"It certainly created an intolerable situation for the Crivingtons," said Ed. "They have three children. A divorce wouldn't have been near as bad. That would be much more conventional."

"There's enough motive," said Hubert, "for all these four people, but the evidence so far seems to point to one man, the man who got Ed's pistol from the silo. We find one bullet from that gun under the hood of Klarsen's car, and another up on the hill, which would appear to have gone through his body."

"That seems conclusive," said Ed. "He's the man who did it."

"And yet," said Hubert, shaking his head, "I'm not satisfied with that evidence. I can't understand those two bullets being found in just those two places. Nor can I understand how that gun could get into the hands of a monkey six or seven miles away, nor how, when the monkey fired one shot more, there should be four cartridges left in the gun. You've got to have one bullet for Klarsen's car, one for his body, and one for the babyroussa. Unless someone refilled the gun, which I can't believe, I can't account for five additional shots fired."

"The monkey might have emptied the gun," said George gravely, "but I doubt exceedingly that he refilled it."

"Maybe there was just one cartridge in the gun when you left it in the silo, Ed?" asked Mike.

"If you'll believe me under oath," said Ed, "I emptied that gun and cleaned it before putting it there."

"Ha!" exclaimed Hubert, slapping his knee. "Ed, will you come out on the driveway with me a minute?"

"Private confab?" asked George, surprised.

"No, no," said Hubert. "All come, if you want to. Ed, show me the tree you shot at when you emptied your gun a week or so ago."

They walked out hatless and coatless onto the drive. Ed led them several paces and stopped, looked around, and scratched his chin.

"It was about here," he said, "and I'm pretty sure it was at that biggest tree there. You see, from here, that tree stands out a little separated from the others. If you move to the right or left, the other trees get into your line of fire."

Hubert stood where Ed had stood, and squinted in the direction of the tree indicated. "And you hit the tree?" he asked, looking at Ed slyly. "Both times?"

"I couldn't swear to that," said Ed. "But I saw the bark fly, the first shot, and I fired the second right after it."

"Well, Ed," said Hubert, smiling, "I guess you're not such a dead shot as you thought. How far do you think the quarry is from here?"

"I should guess three or four hundred yards. More or less."

"I'd say about the same. And I guess that bullet that I found on the hill is one of those you fired at the tree."

Ed seemed doubtful. "A spent bullet would go farther than that, Gil."

"It might not, if it grazed the tree or hit a twig. And while it seems a strange coincidence, I think it's more reasonable than the theory that Klarsen was killed there with your gun, the one from the silo, I mean. We can check up by examining the tree, later."

They hastened back to the barn, feeling the chill.

"I think that's it," said Hubert, filling his pipe. "Now, whose gun killed Klarsen? Our silo friend is exonerated—we've accounted for the other two bullets from his gun."

"It might have been any automatic," said George. "And Dancey has all the kinds there are."

"Every one of those guns in his cabinet," said Hubert, "was covered with a thick layer of fine dust. Of course he may have had others. But I still don't believe Dancey killed either man."

"The silo man may have been Klarsen's pal," suggested George, "and someone else may have killed them both."

"I think," said Ed, "that Dancey suspects someone. And I think it's either Crivington, or Borg, or both."

When they went in to Sunday supper, Jeanie owned up. She was painfully distressed.

"I thought I was the only person who knew that," she said. "Ann told me herself; she said she had to tell somebody, and she pledged me to absolute secrecy. She was very happy about it then, but I was sorry. It wouldn't have been a good match; their tastes were utterly different. Her parents opposed it. It was all war hysteria, reckless romance, and all that. It was an awful mistake for her not to tell Hugh. And yet you can't blame her; Klarsen was reported dead. Surely it won't have to come out now, will it, Mr. Hubert?"

"Unless we get a lot more proof," said Hubert, "I shouldn't worry. Motive alone won't convict anyone."

"Do you think, Mr. Hubert, that I should have told you before?"

"Most certainly not, Mrs. Marsh," said Hubert heartily. "You did quite right."

"I did another thing, Mr. Hubert. I erased her finger-prints from the photograph."

"I observed that," said Hubert, with a smile, "but I hadn't asked you to get them. I shouldn't think of asking you to finger-print your friends for me. I wanted the finger-prints of maids—particularly of one whom I thought might have been planted in some household as a spy."

"A spy?" asked George. "A specific woman?"

"A hypothetical woman," said Hubert. "Occasionally hypotheses come to life in our business."

Supper had progressed to dessert when the maid entered to say that Hubert was wanted at the telephone. The announcement seemed to cause him little surprise. He returned in a few minutes.

"It was Mr. Hugh Crivington," Hubert informed them on his return. "He is coming over after dinner to see me, in the barn, with his lawyer, Mr. Clapp. Inasmuch as he is bringing Mr. Clapp, I requested, Ed, that you also be included in the conference."

"Coming voluntarily?" asked Ed. "Good Lord! This looks like a showdown!"

XXIV

CRIVINGTON 'COMES CLEAN'

Hugh Crivington entered the barn with somewhat the air of a princeling accompanied by his Minister of State. Eben Clapp, the Company's attorney, also looked his part. A lean, bald, hatchet-faced man, he gave at the same time, with his rather fine features, long nervous hands, and careful yet casual tailoring, the impression of a cultural background to his alert, keen efficiency. His firm, cordial grasp of Hubert's hand conveyed the flattering courtesy of a foeman; the sword, flourished in salute, then *en garde!*

"I am glad of this chance to meet you, Mr. Hubert," said Clapp. "Unfortunately, I had not placed you until your friend Chief of Detectives Willoughby posted me on your distinguished services. You have, I understand, been entrusted with great responsibility in the handling of many delicate and important matters."

"A compliment from Willoughby is worth having," said Hubert. "He is the most competent police official I know in any of our large cities."

"We have come to consult you," said Clapp, "on what is to us a delicate and important matter, and one that we can broach only to persons who recognize fully its confidential nature." He shot a flickering glance at Ed.

"Mr. Marsh has been in my entire confidence during my investigations out here," said Hubert, "which is only right, since he himself is more or less circumstantially involved in the matter."

"Mr. Marsh's help will be of value to us," said Clapp. "To come to the point: Mr. Crivington, about a week ago, borrowed some old documents from Mr. Marsh. These documents, I regret to say, were stolen before Mr. Crivington had an opportunity to examine them. Now we should like you, Mr. Marsh, if you can, to tell us what these documents were."

Ed reached over to the table, took from it the roll of photostats, and handed them to Hubert, who passed them at once on to Clapp.

"Those," said Hubert, "are photostats of all the documents, which Ed, fortunately, happened to have made at one time. You are welcome to look through them and see whether they are of any importance."

"Thank God for that," said Hugh. "I've had infernal worry over those since that night."

Clapp unrolled them and pulled his chair closer to the lamp. He glanced through them with rapid efficiency and passed them on to Hugh, who examined them.

"These are of little value to anyone," said Clapp. "Certainly not to us. They don't concern any of the Electric Company's property."

"Are you sure, Ed," asked Hugh, "that you have here copies of everything you gave me? Was there, for instance, anything that looked like a will?"

"That's all the documents," said Ed. "And I'm sure there was no will. I'm no lawyer, but I think I can tell a will when I see it."

"A will," said Clapp, "especially a death-bed will, might be quite informal in appearance. It might even be written on a piece of wrapping-paper, and be good, if properly witnessed and the signatures could be proved. But I am not much concerned about the existence of a will."

"Have you ever had any reason to think there was a missing will?" asked Hubert.

"We had an anonymous letter," said Hugh, "which mentioned a will."

"And I might say," added Clapp hastily, "that we have received, in the past twenty years or so, at least twenty such letters, all of which have turned out to be spurious. We have also defended several groundless suits which have been thrown out of court. We have ceased getting into a flutter over every cock-and-bull story of a will."

"This anonymous letter, however," said Hubert, "might have a certain importance as evidence, coming just at this time. Can you tell me who received it, and when?"

"Mr. Borg received it," said Clapp, with a disapproving tightening of his lips. "I did not see it. Most such letters are addressed to Mr. Borg personally."

"What did Mr. Borg do with it? Do you know, Mr. Crivington?"

"He threw it into the waste-basket," said Hugh. Hubert's slight shift of position in his chair was eloquent of his disgust.

"Mr. Borg undoubtedly took it to be simply another frivolous threat," said Clapp.

"Did you tell Mr. Willoughby about this letter?" asked Hubert.

"We didn't think it of importance at the time," said Hugh. "It was received before we knew of Klarsen's death."

"On what day, Mr. Crivington?"

"Mr. Borg received it on Thursday forenoon, the day following our evening out here at Ed's. It was postmarked Phoebus, 7 A.M., which I suppose is the first morning collection. Phoebus is a small town just outside the city limits, on the west side."

"Yes, I know Phoebus," said Hubert. "To detectives it is as well known as Dynamopolis. Do you remember what that letter said?"

"It said, as nearly as I can remember, 'Throw parcel containing fifty thousand dollars into open window of vacant building at Third and Derry Streets, Phoebus, at 3 A.M. sharp Friday morning. Will throw out will and other papers. Can get that much from others. Send only one man.'"

"Mr. Borg sent no one?"

"No. Mr. Borg absolutely refuses to pay blackmail under any circumstances. We got another letter next morning at the same hour, from Phoebus. It read, 'Will give you one more chance. Seventy-five thousand this time.' Then Mr. Borg sent five men there to raid the place. They found no one there."

"Has Mr. Borg that letter?"

"I think one of his investigators has it."

"Now, Mr. Crivington, you have said that the papers you got from Ed were lost. How were they lost?"

"I gave them to Klarsen."

"At what time, and where?"

"I gave them to him a few minutes after I got them from Ed. I was standing in the silo at the time, with Klarsen."

"And what did you say to Klarsen when you gave them to him?"

Hugh looked at Clapp, and inferred approval from his impassive countenance. "I told him he was to deliver the papers to Mr. Borg, that they were for Mr. Clapp to look over, to see whether they had any bearing on our property. Klarsen asked, 'Is that all of them?' And I said, 'Ed says so.'"

"It was common knowledge that Ed had some old documents of the kind?"

"It ought to have been," said Ed. "I never made a secret of it. Knapp and Dobert knew it, anyway; they were in the syndicate."

"And then you telephoned Mr. Borg?" Hubert asked Hugh.

"I did," said Hugh, looking at Hubert curiously. "I telephoned him first, to say that I had borrowed the papers from Ed and to ask him whether I should send them to his house that evening. Borg said yes. Then, as we remained longer than I expected, I telephoned Mr. Borg again to ask him whether Klarsen could not bring them to the office tomorrow instead. Mr. Borg said no, send Klarsen over with them."

"And then?"

"Then I told Klarsen to hurry over to Mr. Borg's house and deliver the papers on his way into town."

Hubert paused a moment. "If I remember rightly, Mr. Crivington," he said, "you testified at the inquest that Mr. Klarsen left Westwood to go into town."

Hugh was piqued at this. "If you'll wait till I get to that point, Mr. Hubert, you'll understand me better. When I got home after the party, I received a telephone call from Mr. Borg, who was very angry that Klarsen hadn't arrived. I told Mr. Borg that I thought Klarsen must have misunderstood me, and that he had probably gone on into town and expected to bring the papers to him at the office next morning."

"I beg your pardon, Mr. Crivington," said Hubert. "But there is another point that I don't quite understand. Mr. Borg, it seems, was aware, first, that documents had been given Mr. Klarsen by you, which might, possibly, include a will. Secondly, he was aware, certainly by Friday morning, that Mr. Klarsen had not been heard from. Thirdly, he had received two anonymous letters from Phoebus offering him a will—"

"Mr. Hubert," interrupted Clapp, with a trace of hostility, "you are not investigating Mr. Borg or Mr. Crivington or me. However, I will say, on that point, that the first letter was received by Mr. Borg before he had knowledge of Klarsen's disappearance. The second letter was received by him Friday morning, before he knew of Klarsen's death. These letters were postmarked in Phoebus, a notorious nest of crooks of all kinds. Mr. Borg absolutely did not connect the letters with the papers that Klarsen had; he had received many such letters. Moreover, it seems hardly likely that anyone could possibly have known that Klarsen had these papers on him at the time."

"You didn't know, then—you or Mr. Crivington—that the thief who took Ed's gun was in the silo upstairs, during the earlier part of the evening, and possibly at the precise moment when you were handing the papers to Mr. Klarsen?"

"I did not," said Hugh, astonished. He looked at Clapp inquiringly. "It is possible, then, that that man may have been the murderer!"

"Yet so far as we can judge from the evidence," said Hubert, "that man was not the murderer of Klarsen. We have accounted otherwise for the only two bullets, apparently, that were fired from that gun."

Clapp looked intensely interested. "That was the gun," he asked, "that was found in Mr. Clifford's gardens, wasn't it?"

"It was," said Hubert. "Have you, or anyone in the Company, any idea who this man was?"

"Not the slightest," said Clapp. "But does it seem a possible theory to you, Mr. Hubert, that this man held up Klarsen in the ravine, and then that a third man shot both him and Klarsen and made off with the papers?"

"A hi-jacking operation?" asked Hubert. "And why such a fierce contest for such papers?"

"I can only say," said Clapp, "that if such persons wanted these documents, they were probably the agents for someone else who knew how to use them."

"Such as who?"

"Any blackmailer," said Clapp, elevating his eyebrows.

"You said, Mr. Crivington," said Hubert, "in quoting the blackmailing letter that Mr. Borg received, that the writer said that he could get fifty thousand dollars from another party. Have you any idea what party he may have meant?"

"Not the slightest," interjected Clapp promptly. "Not the slightest."

XXV

THE TRAIL OF THE FOX

"Now, Mr. Crivington," continued Hubert, "to digress for a moment, we have gathered some evidence that seems to indicate that a woman was concerned in one or both of these murders. We found, for instance, this—" He took the little compact from a drawer of the table, where it lay enclosed in a box of cotton. He held it toward Hugh. "I shall ask you not to handle it. It bears feminine finger-prints, and it is a feminine article. We found it at the foot of the cliff, out here."

Hugh looked at it indifferently. "I don't see how that can have the slightest bearing on the case," he said. "It's the kind of article any woman might have thrown away or lost. Sunday strollers go over on that hill, you know."

"There is no woman involved in this business," said Clapp impatiently. "I think you can throw that thing away."

"I rather imagined," said Hubert, "that some woman might have figured in Klarsen's life. Do you know, Mr. Crivington, whether he was ever married?"

"Klarsen?" said Hugh. "Never. I've asked him half a dozen times why on earth he's never got married, and he always said that he led too busy and active a life. It's too bad, too. I suppose it's partly the Company's fault," he added with a smile.

"Well, we'll dismiss that then," said Hubert calmly, putting the box back in the drawer. "Now, let us indulge in a little conjecture as to how Klarsen met his death. In the first place, there are two minor circumstances which seem to me important. It seems, in the first place, that Klarsen's departure from the party was a little abrupt; at least Mrs. Marsh says that he dashed out to his car without having said good-night to either her or Ed. She says that he seemed suddenly to discover that he had left something in his car. Now, did Mr. Klarsen carry a gun?"

"I think he did," said Hugh; "at least it was his custom when traveling out West, and he had a permit."

"Well, then, it may be that what he remembered was that he had left his gun in his car, perhaps in the door pocket. Now, there is the second circumstance that no one heard the noise of his car starting. Now, the ground where his car stood slopes so that it would have been possible for him to start his car easily enough with no noise at all, simply by unlocking his brake and coasting out into the Green and perhaps even down into the ravine. It looks either as if he had a reason for departing quietly, or as if he were held up by someone who put a pistol to his head and compelled him to start in this manner."

Clapp and Crivington listened attentively and glanced at one another.

"I understand, Mr. Crivington, that Mr. Klarsen had no orders from you to stop in the ravine. Was there any reason of his own for stopping in the ravine?"

"I can't think of any possible reason," said Hugh.

"You have heard from Rube Malt, I dare say, his story about the gold that was buried with old Jonas's body?"

"I see," said Clapp, with evident annoyance, "that your investigations have taken you far afield. But I don't suppose you took any stock in that fanciful tale."

"We discovered some evidence of truth in it. We examined the graves and found that Jonas's showed signs of having been looted several years ago. And we found a twenty-dollar gold piece there of the coinage of 1879."

"You don't say!" exclaimed Clapp, his indifference dispelled. "How did you know which was Jonas's grave?"

Hubert handed him the photostats of the map, back and front, and showed him the diagram of the graves. "Moreover," said Hubert, "we suspect that someone has recently contemplated digging up the grave again." He told of the discovery of the spade in the pond.

Clapp's attitude became thoroughly serious. "This may be important, Mr. Hubert," he said. "It would seem to indicate the existence of

some person who knows more about those graves than either Rube
Malt or Mrs. Thomas Plenty. Neither of those persons had any knowledge of the locations of the respective graves nor of any paper showing
their locations. It is difficult to believe that such a person can be anyone but a descendant of Jonas Beeson. You heard from Malt, I suppose,
about a son of Jonas's, named Jacob, who went out West and was killed
in a railway accident?"

"We did. And as you say, it's possible that he married and had children. But the interesting point is this: if Jacob had such a son, and that
son looted the grave and got the gold some years ago, he would be the
least likely person in the world to want to reopen the grave. He would
know for certain that the money was all gone."

"Unless he had left some there, which is not probable," said Clapp.
"And this apparently determined search for a will or other documents
can only mean that someone is convinced that there is another heir
living, or at least a plausible pretender. You understand, of course, Mr.
Hubert, that it makes not a particle of difference whether Jonas made
a will or not, unless there is another valid claimant. And that even then
the will would be of additional importance only if it gave that claimant
more than would have been his by the law of descent."

"I do understand that much of the law. Even without a will, a co-
heir with Keziah would, I suppose, be entitled to half the estate. And
we know that Jonas threw Keziah out of the house just before he died,
and may have made a will cutting her out, and leaving all to Jacob. He
disliked Jacob, but his quarrel with him was older. And suppose that
a son was born to Jacob just before Old Jonas died. That might have
caused a change of heart. Jonas might even have passed over Jake and
made his grandson sole heir."

"We have considered such possibilities," said Clapp, "and they are
what have given a tinge of plausibility to every yarn of a missing heir
that we have heard."

"Now, Mr. Clapp, I need not tell you, as a lawyer, that the problem
of such a claimant would not be so much to obtain a will in his favor,
as to obtain evidence with which to identify himself, supposing him to
have nothing of the kind already."

"You are right. Identification would be pretty difficult."

"Old letters might be good evidence," said Hubert. "Ed had a trunk-ful of old letters in his barn at one time, but unfortunately for our re-searches, those letters were all burnt up in his barn while Ed was away some years ago. That may be what the search is for."

Clapp merely nodded absently. Hubert got up, apparently looking for a match. He accepted one from Ed, and, as he bent over, put a finger on his lips meaningly.

"Now I have a bare suspicion," continued Hubert, seating himself again and drawing at his pipe, "that someone may have intended to un-cover the grave again for something that was left in it when the money was taken."

"Not old Jonas's bones!" said Clapp, with a piercing glance at Hubert.

"No," said Hubert. "A family Bible."

"Bible?" asked Hugh, surprised.

"Do you remember, Ed," asked Hubert, "Rube Malt saying that Jonas was buried with the old Bible under his head? The family Bible, in pioneer families, usually contains on the fly-leaf a record of births."

Clapp and Crivington looked fixedly at Hubert. "The Bible," contin-ued Hubert, "would prove, if entry had been made, the birth of a son to Jacob Beeson. It might be helpful evidence in a court of law."

"Such evidence," said Clapp, "would make a colorable case, but one that could be well contested and probably compromised. I doubt if such an heir would have the money to sustain long litigation. It seems to me more likely that such evidence would be sought for blackmailing purposes, with the object of selling it, not to the heirs, but to our Com-pany, or any other interested party."

"What would be the effect, Mr. Clapp, of a cloud of that kind being cast on the Company's title to their land?"

"The land is an extensive property," said Clapp. "It is covered by the Company's plants, laboratories, and yards, and I need not say is worth many millions more than when they bought it in the eighties. This property is part of the security behind our first refunding mort-gage bonds, a hundred-million-dollar issue. I need not say that the consequences would be unpleasant not only to us, but to a good many people, and to several banks."

"The effect on the stock would be still more pronounced, I suppose," said Hubert. "Who, Mr. Clapp, if I may ask, are the principal stockholders of the Company?"

Clapp shifted his position and turned toward Hubert. "Mr. Borg, of course, is a very large stockholder. The stock, as you perhaps know, is selling, in the current depression, at a price much lower than either its book value or the Company's prospects warrant. Mr. Borg has added to his holdings for that reason, as have many far-sighted investors, including several of us on the directorate."

"Is Mr. Clopendyke Clifford, by any chance, a stockholder?" asked Hubert.

"We have no means of knowing what stock is held in brokers' names," said Clapp. "But Mr. Clifford's name does not appear on our books. I have heard, however, through sources whose reliability I cannot vouch for, that Mr. Clifford has been selling the stock."

"Short?"

"Short. Of course, that may be mere rumor. Several years ago, however, Mr. Clifford was a considerable stockholder, and actively sought a place on the board of directors. I may say, also, that we did not want him to have it. We did not feel that his interests coincided wholly with ours."

"By depressing the price of the stock, I suppose, Mr. Clifford could of course make a profit on covering. But as I understand it, he is not a mere trader. The fall in price of the stock, however, might enable him to acquire large blocks cheaply, and the possession of a claim to land might enable him to exert a good deal of pressure through his banking and other connections."

"It would enable him to do a good many things that can be imagined. But I should not think of bringing any such accusation against Mr. Clifford. Please do not understand me as voicing any suspicion of that kind."

"I mention these possibilities, or improbabilities, we may call them," said Hubert, "only because they might occur to blackmailers who had something they wanted to sell."

"Well, Mr. Hubert," said Clapp, rising abruptly, "I thank you on behalf of the Company and Mr. Borg for your intelligent cooperation and able efforts. If we had been so fortunate as to know you earlier, we should have saved ourselves a lot of trouble. Your counsel has been invaluable."

"I will give you two more pieces of counsel, if I may," said Hubert. "First, I suggest that you induce Mrs. Thomas Plenty, whose interests are identical with yours in this matter, to remove all her dead to a safer resting-place. It will save you and her worry. Second, I suggest, in your own interests, that you dismiss your own special investigators, as they call themselves, and in future investigate your investigators more carefully. The ones that your Company has selected have no standing in official circles or in the courts. Some of them are themselves reformed petty criminals. They will eventually get your Company into serious trouble."

"I thank you for your advice," said Clapp, "and I may say that your second suggestion has already been acted upon, at the instance of myself and Mr. Crivington. Good-night, Mr. Hubert, and Mr. Marsh."

At the door Clapp turned as if something had suddenly occurred to him. "I believe, Mr. Hubert, that it was here, in Mr. Marsh's car, that Mr. Clifford's suitcase was found. I have forgotten—can you tell me whether anything was found in the suitcase?"

"Nothing, Mr. Clapp," said Hubert, covering up a smile. "Not a scrap."

"Crafty lot, these lawyers," said Hubert, as the door closed. "It's evident enough what Clapp wants us to think. Well, he may be right, at that."

"What was the high sign you gave me, Gil?" asked Ed. "I didn't know what it was for, but I kept my mouth shut anyway."

"When I mentioned that the letters were burned in your barn, I didn't want you to pipe up and offer them the album. I want to take another look at that myself. Did you notice Clapp's expression, or lack of it, when I mentioned the Bible? He knew about that already, and he could tell us, I think, something about this silly business of scaring off Rube Malt with a rope in the window. I rather think that it's Borg who is responsible for those roughneck detectives. The roughest thing that they did, however, was to burn your barn several years ago."

"They did, eh? By golly, I'll sue the Company if I can prove it!"

"I don't think it would be worth your while. It would be hard to get the evidence of it. But one of Willoughby's men said that the fellow who did it spilled the beans to him once. And he was one of Borg's so-called detectives."

"Well," said Ed, "I think Hugh is clear of the murder of Klarsen. It's evident that he knows nothing about that secret marriage. Unless he's a lot better actor than I give him credit for."

"I agree with you there. Of course, as to Borg, never having seen the man, I can't judge."

XXVI

THE FAMILY ALBUM

Hubert seemed thoughtful and taciturn the next morning, and took little part in breakfast discussion. When Ed drove off for town, Hubert gave him a large envelope for air mail. Ed glanced at the address.

"A new line of attack," said Hubert, by way of explanation. "I'm going to try investigating the dead instead of the living. Perhaps it's just a 'hunch,' as Mike would say."

George decided to ride in with Ed, spend the day in town, and lunch with Ed at the club. Hubert retired to the complete solitude of the barn. He stretched himself in the biggest easy-chair and gave himself up to pipe and 'Moby Dick.'

After half an hour's meditation, Hubert got up and went to the silo and got out from the cabinet the old Beeson family album. He carried it back to the living-room, pulled up a chair to the table, and began looking carefully through the album.

He paused, relit his pipe, and smoked for a few minutes. Then he began again at the beginning of the album, taking each photograph out of the top of its slip pocket and examining the back of it. Whenever the photographer's name and address was printed on the back, he made a careful note of it in his little blank-book.

On one he found written, 'Uncle Jonas and Aunt Martha, from Judy.' Rube's aunt; a sweet-faced girl of about twenty. One was of a man in uniform, a non-commissioned officer, who might be Job or Caleb. Another, resembling it but for a mustache, might be the other of the two sons of Abel. Or Jacob? Hardly, from the character given of Jake. Hubert compared that and several others with the picture of Jonas; there was little family resemblance between the two branches.

Jake probably wasn't there, and no wonder, with the family feeling toward him. Besides, Hubert reflected, if there had been a picture of Jake there, Rube would have identified it, for Rube had looked for it. Hubert knew Keziah's picture; Rube had shown him that. He wished now that he had had Rube identify them all, and wondered if it might be possible to get Rube to come over again. Hubert knew Abel, and assumed that the elderly woman in a cap, on the same page, was his wife. Some of the people, he reflected, might be merely family friends.

Hubert laid down the photographs he was holding, and went to the silo again. He took from the cabinet the envelope containing the photographs of the dead man found in Clifford's rumble, of which he had given Ed duplicates to mail that morning. He took out the photographs and examined them closely.

He turned to the photograph of Jonas Beeson and compared the two pictures detail by detail. The same type of high forehead, and the same kind of nose. Hubert regretted Jonas's tonsorial vanities, for the dead man had rather a characteristic mouth and chin. The mouth looked as if the man were about to say something amusing but caustic. The man's ear, too, was distinctive; large, and with almost no lobe. Ears were useful in identification. But Jonas's picture was full face.

Hubert pondered over these photographs, and shook his head. If he only had a photograph of the man while living, it would have been easier. But a man shot through the head? No, you couldn't tell; it was possible, that was all you could say.

Finally Hubert put away the dead man's photographs in their envelope, and began putting back in their pockets, in the album, the photographs which he had withdrawn. One of them stuck; something inside was impeding it.

Hubert took the photograph out again, peeked inside the pocket, and pulled out a crumpled old envelope. It was addressed to Mrs. Joseph Medro, and was postmarked Septimus, Nevada, 1886.

Hubert looked inside and pulled out an unmounted photograph, of the kind once known as a solio print, reddish-brown, dog-eared, and stained. It looked like an early attempt of a youthful photographer. It was a picture of a boy astride a pony; a boy about seven years old.

Hubert got out the photograph of the dead man again, and compared it with that of the boy. A likeness, surely; forehead and nose, mouth and chin. What was a cynical quirk on the dead man's face was a mischievous smile on the boy's. If only the boy's ears had shown; ears don't change; but this was full-face. Hubert compared the photograph with that of Jonas; yes, a family resemblance, indefinable but strong. Suddenly Hubert turned the picture over. On the back was written, in a childish scrawl:

> Dear Aunt Keziah
> This is me an
> Buck. I have a
> new camara.
> I hope you are
> well.
> Jonas Beeson.

Hubert put the photograph back in its envelope, laid it between the leaves of the album, and sat back in his chair, smoking. His face showed elation, but not triumph.

Jonas Beeson, Jr. No doubt of it. 1886. The boy had perhaps written to his Aunt Keziah, to make peace. At his father's urging? Or after his father's death? Hubert visualized the boy of seven, alone in the world. Had he written letters? Had Keziah burned them? Had she rejected his appeal? 'Keziah were hard.' Had she left the boy to the mercy of the world? Some impulse of affection must have prompted her to preserve the photograph, to put it with the others in the album. Perhaps she had relented too late, and had been unable to find the boy. Perhaps her greed was great enough to cause her to abandon him.

Hubert looked at the photograph of the boy again. Obviously it had been developed and printed by the boy himself. It was stained, spotted, and covered with thumb-prints, ineradicable, on its once sensitive surface.

Thumb-prints! Thumb-prints don't change!

Hubert shook the photographs of the dead man's finger-prints out of their envelope, and looked at the prints of his thumbs. He laid the two photographs side by side, took out his lens, and compared them. Smaller, of course. But identical! Tented arches on both. Broken in the same places everywhere. Could experts refute him? Hubert thought not. He looked at his watch. He would not go in to Headquarters yet. He should get a telegram by five o'clock at latest; he would wait.

He looked at the ghastly photograph of the dead man, and glanced again at the boyish scrawl.

'Dear Aunt Keziah. This is me—'

When Ed and George returned in the late afternoon, they found Hubert sitting just as they had left him, in the armchair, with 'Moby Dick' turned down upon his knee.

"Well, Gil," said Ed, "looks as if you'd been having a quiet day. Anything new?"

"I have always despised armchair detectives as much as anyone," said Hubert, "but the fact remains that I've accomplished more sitting right here all day than I have in all our tramping around."

"We'll have a drink on that," said Ed, "and hear about it."

After Ed had shaken up a couple of rounds, Hubert spread the photographs on the table: old Jonas; Jonas, Jr., dead; and Jonas, Jr., as a boy.

"I'm willing to stake my reputation," said Hubert, "that these are the same finger-prints, man and boy."

George was impressed. "So this is Jonas, the last of the Beesons! I dare say that will bring cheer to some people in the Dynamopolis Electric Company. I suppose, then, that he was the man who broke into the silo, and that this photograph, or something of the kind, was what he was after?"

"We can only infer that," said Hubert. "But this I know." He spread before them a telegram dated that afternoon at Sioux City.

THREE TELLERS IDENTIFY PHOTOGRAPH POS-
ITIVELY AS SNEED STOP HAVE NOT TRACED
SNEED'S MOVEMENTS BUT GUARDIAN BANK RENO
REPORTED LAST YEAR TWELVE THOUSAND GOLD
EIGHTEEN SEVENTY NINE AND EIGHTY DEPOS-
ITED TO ACCOUNT OF FRANK MYERS STOP HAVE
WIRED GUARDIAN FOR SUBSEQUENT DETAILS

"That is from my friend in the Drovers' Bank," said Hubert. "Here is a later telegram from him."

GUARDIAN ADVISES MYERS OPENED ACCOUNT LAST YEAR INTRODUCED BY D. Y. WEBBER STOP HAS PAID SUMS AGGREGATING TEN THOUSAND DOLLARS TO WEBBER WHO ALSO BANKS AT GUARDIAN STOP MYERS LAST CHECK DATED NOVEMBER THIRD WAS FOR EIGHT THOUSAND DOLLARS TO ORDER OF WEBBER AND DEPOSITED BY WEBBER AT COMMONWEALTH BANK DYNAMOPOLIS STOP MYERS AND WEBBER OUT OF TOWN STOP MAY BE IN DYNAMOPOLIS

"Who are Myers and Webber?" asked Ed.

"Wisey Webber," said Hubert, smiling, "is an old acquaintance of mine. So far I think he has kept out of jail, though I've done what I could to send him there. Myers, I suspect, is Jonas Beeson, Jr., and if so, I think we can hold Mr. Webber on a little matter of forgery. We have apparently discovered an exposed flank of Webber's which he thinks is quite protected. My friend of the Drovers' Bank has accomplished more for me than the police could have in this instance.

"Unless Mr. Webber has left town," continued Hubert, "I think Willoughby will find him before morning. I'd like to have a look at him again."

Mike came over in the evening. He declared it to be the most sensational identification, without exception, that he had ever heard of.

"But why should a fellow like that commit robbery to get things to identify himself with?" asked Ed. "If he'd blown in here and told me he was Jonas Beeson, Jr., I'd probably have turned over the album and everything to him, just as I offered it to Malt."

"Would you?" asked Hubert. "Think a minute. This man was heir to the property your house and barn are on, as well as to all the land the syndicate disposed of. What would you say to a man you had never seen before—and remember, Malt had never seen him—who came to you and said, 'I am Jonas Beeson, Jr. Give me a batch of evidence so that I can throw you out of house and home.' Do you think you'd hand it to him? Maybe you would, but most people wouldn't. And Beeson probably figured you were like anybody else."

"Great Scott!" said Ed. "You're right. I'll swear I never thought of my being in the same boat with Dynamopolis Electric. I suppose—humph!"

He checked himself, but he was thinking that if Borg had caused the burning of his barn, Borg could excuse himself on the ground that he was protecting Ed's interest as well as his own.

"Well, Mr. Hubert," said Mike cheerfully. "This runs tomorrow, doesn't it?"

"By no means," said Hubert. "At least, not until I give the word. I must get a confirmation on those finger-prints, and we must have our hands on Webber first. Otherwise the whole case may be lost. And we may hear of a third murder—the murder of a witness."

XXVII

THE VOICE ON THE TELEPHONE

In the morning Ed drove Hubert in extra early, to Headquarters, and left him there. Then he drove to the Spindler Building, where he arrived about ten minutes to nine, parked his car, and stepped into the offices of E. & O. E. Pettimyer, members of the New York Stock Exchange, the Dynamopolis Stock Exchange, the Board of Trade, and what not.

The customers' room, with its deep leather lounges and its new-fangled quotation board—the kind that automatically dispenses with boys who jump around and make illegible marks with pieces of chalk and get in the way just when you want to read something—was deserted, but Mr. Pettimyer, who was rambling around back in the auditing department, came out and greeted Ed cheerily.

"What do you think of this market, Ed?" he asked. "It's hell, ain't it?"

"It certainly is," said Ed. "What was the closing on DYL last night, Ted?"

"DYL?" said Pettimyer. "It's over there in the corner, last column on the board. Closed at 137 1/8; 136 bid, 137 1/4 asked. You never played with that stock much, did you, Ed?"

"Not me," said Ed. "It's a little too much of a mystery stock. I like to know more about 'em. What do you think of DYL, Ted?"

"We-l-l," said Pettimyer sagely, "I don't know." (The mark of a successful broker is the ability to say "I don't know," and to sound profoundly wise when saying it.) "It's been slipping off for more'n a month now. It was pretty heavy yesterday. A lot of it's long stock coming out, too. They call it good selling by insiders. Just steady liquidation. No news to account for it."

"Much of a short interest in it?" asked Ed.

"I think some of it's short selling now," said Pettimyer. "They say Henry F. Fogarty's gone short of it. He's a wise bird."

"Well," said Ed decisively, "it looks low enough to me. I think I'll take a couple o' hundred. At the market."

"Better wait and see how she opens, hadn't you?" asked Pettimyer. "It'll only be a couple of minutes now."

"No," said Ed. "Let her shoot. I want to get up to my office."

"All right," said Pettimyer, scribbling on a pad. There was a bare suggestion in his tone as of one who should add, "Don't say I didn't warn you."

At ten minutes past eleven a telephone call came to Ed from Pettimyer's office.

"DYL is up seven points and still jumping," said Pettimyer. "Now you tell me, Ed."

"Go buy a copy of the *Mirror*," said Ed, and hung up.

At Headquarters, Hubert went directly to Willoughby's office, where he sat and waited till Willoughby got through with two subordinates who were at his desk. Willoughby then greeted Hubert tersely and turned to his telephone.

"Ask Dr. Flemingen if he'll come in now," said Willoughby.

A lean, scholarly-looking little man, with a pointed beard, came in, and, after being introduced to Hubert, looked carefully with a hand glass at the finger-prints of Jonas, Jr., and those of the dead man, as shown on the photographs handed him by Hubert.

"There's no doubt about it," said Flemingen. "They're the same. That's very interesting, too. We don't often get a chance to compare finger-prints of the same person taken at such an interval of years. I'd like Priedieu to see these, too. Don't tell him my conclusions. I think his will be the same."

"Have enlargements made right away, then," said Willoughby. "Now, Gil, we've picked up this bird for you. We'd better talk to him right away." Willoughby telephoned again.

"This fellow," said Willoughby, "is a smooth baby, but I can't see much wrong with him. We got him easily enough, through the bank; he's stopping at a good hotel, under his own name; says he's a criminal lawyer from Reno, and the Reno police confirm it; at least there is such a man. Made no fuss about coming, offered to be finger-printed voluntarily, and simply said that if any undesirable publicity was given him about it he'd file charges against us. We've treated him real nice. I'm doing this on your say-so, but I don't see how I can hold him long, if he hasn't got a record."

"If he makes a fuss," said Hubert, "I can give you plenty of dope to show that his reputation isn't one to suffer from a little detention. And I think we can hold him for forgery, if I know anything about this matter."

A policeman brought in the man, and then left the room. The man was dark, sleek, smartly dressed, and about thirty years of age. A typical young shyster lawyer of the kind that possesses considerable shrewdness, usually has profitable connections with some political ring, and prospers. He evidently had plenty of nerve and was very sure of himself. The air of mild impatience which he affected gave way to surprise when he saw Hubert.

"How are you, Gil?" he said breezily, offering his hand as an equal. "What's on your mind? You didn't chase all the way out here to look for me, did you?"

"Just a little worried for fear you might get into trouble so far from home, Wisey," said Hubert, lighting a cigar that Willoughby had given him. "Attending to a little law business in town, are you?"

"Matter of getting together some witnesses for a case I'm handling," said Webber affably. "And don't you kid yourself that I'm going to tell you anything about it, either. You're probably working on the other side."

"No," said Hubert. "I don't work on fictitious cases, only real ones. I'm interested now in locating a friend of yours by the name of Frank Myers. Also in knowing what he paid you ten thousand dollars for. Pretty nice fee, that; must be big business."

"I'll tell you this much," snapped the lawyer. "Myers is my client, and he's deposited the money with me for safe-keeping. And, by God, I'll make it hot for that banker that's spilling my affairs. Where Myers is I can tell you, but I won't; that's his business and mine. He's no criminal."

"I guess we know pretty well where Myers is," said Hubert. "Have you seen his latest picture?" He suddenly flashed on Webber a photograph of the dead man.

"What's this?" asked Webber, shrinking a little. "Don't try to frame me, Gil. I never saw that man."

"Here's another friend of yours," said Hubert. He showed the man one of the enlarged photographs of the figure in khaki.

"Never saw her either," said Webber sharply, and then scowled.

"Her?" said Hubert, with a grim smile at Willoughby. "I guess you know the lady, all right. She's no friend to you, though—I'll take that much back."

"You must think I don't read the papers," said Webber, recovering his poise. "I see now that you're trying to connect me up with this Rumble Murder Case. Well, you'll be the prize fool if you pull that. I'm no gun guy, and you know it better than anyone."

"One thing leads to another," said Hubert blandly. "And if you'll read the papers this afternoon, you'll read how Roy Sneed, *alias* the Gold-Dollar Kid, *alias* Frank Myers, but whose real name is Jonas Beeson, is none other than the dead man whose picture I've just shown you. And you might run down to the Morgue and put a lily into the hand of your client, whose check you cashed and which was dated three days after his death. Bert, I hope you've got a nice front room with a view for Mr. Webber."

Willoughby swung around and stared at Hubert with the nearest similitude to astonishment which he ever permitted himself.

"Just my little joke, Bert," said Hubert, chuckling silently. "I neglected to give you another telegram that I received this morning." He handed it to Willoughby. It was dated at Reno, and read:

MYERS IDENTIFIED AS DEAD MAN FROM PHOTO-
GRAPHS STOP SENDING YOU PHOTOSTAT CAN-
CELLED CHECK AND SIGNATURE CARDS TODAY
PER YOUR INSTRUCTIONS

When Hubert got back, just before lunch, he found George in a state of frenzied impatience.

"A woman called you up, Mr. Hubert, half an hour ago. Wants to talk to you and no one else. I got it traced back to a booth at the Brooks Street El station."

"Quick enough!" said Hubert, surprised and pleased. "Did she say anything?"

"Just asked when you'd be back," said George. "She's going to call up again. You'd better stick around."

The call came again just as Hubert finished lunch. It was brief, and the woman hung up before Hubert could reply. All she said was:

"You've got the right bird. I'll be out to see you at the barn about five o'clock."

Ed came out early in response to this news, telephoned him by Hubert. Mike, who called up during the afternoon and was told, came out at once and reached the barn a little before five. "Sounds as if things were cracking open," he said. "Do you think we ought to have cops here?"

"I'm a cop," said Hubert, smiling. "But if I could have prevented her coming here, I'd have done so. I'd rather see her at Headquarters. But I guess the only thing we can do is to wait for her. I hope she's prompt."

But dinner-time drew on, and no visitor arrived. Hubert began to look worried, and insisted on staying in the barn until Ed and George could finish their dinner and release him. Jeanie was quite alarmed, and would have sent the children across the Green to a neighbor's but for Ed's promise to remain in the house while the others were in the barn.

"I'm not worried about anyone troubling us," said Hubert, to George and Mike, when they assembled again in the barn, "but I'm afraid something's happened to that woman. If not, why hasn't she telephoned?"

"It's a lady's privilege to be late," said George, "but in the present circumstances it's particularly harassing. She's certainly spoiling my evening."

"I don't think—" began Mike, and suddenly stood rigid. "Someone is coming to the door," he said softly.

Hubert stood up calmly, but George noticed that his hand was in his coat pocket. There was a noise that sounded like someone kicking against the door rather than knocking. Hubert opened the door gently. A woman almost fell forward into his arms.

She was dressed in khaki trousers and sweater, the latter almost falling off of her in shreds. Her sweater was covered with blood, and her face bled from cuts. One of the puttees which covered her legs was trailing on the ground. She was clutching a bundle, which she dropped to the floor.

"There's the gun!" she said, looking around with glassy eyes. She swayed a moment and fell, Hubert darting forward just in time to prevent her head striking on the arm of a heavy chair.

XXVIII

THE WOMAN

Hubert and Mike together lifted the woman gently and laid her on the window-seat. Hubert gave her a couple of fingers of straight whiskey.

"Is there a doctor in the neighborhood?" he asked Mike.

"Pritchard, across the Green," said Mike. "I'll call him up."

"Let Ed do it," said Hubert. "George, will you run into the house and tell Ed?"

George dashed out of the door and in a moment was back again with Ed.

"Pritchard will be over in a minute," said Ed. He bent over the prostrate woman for an instant. "What happened to her?" he asked. "And what's this stuff she brought?"

Hubert was already examining it. It was a bundle of clothing, and a moment's examination of the contents of its pockets was sufficient to show that it was Klarsen's. As Hubert disentangled the garments a pistol dropped to the floor. He picked it up carefully and laid it on the table. A Colt automatic, forty-five.

"Klarsen's, no doubt," he said, removing the magazine. It held four cartridges.

He was interrupted by the arrival of the doctor, whose friendly greeting of Ed was at once succeeded by a more professional manner. His first office was to cut away the woman's sweater and swab the blood from her face. He was about to begin a preliminary survey for broken bones when the woman roused herself.

"Cut all that!" she said. "I guess I'd never have got over here if I had any broken bones. Prop me up with those pillows and fix my face."

Ed tossed the doctor some sofa cushions.

"Jesus!" she cried, "but I've got a few bruises. Give me a cigarette now."

Ed handed her a cigarette and lit a match.

"My God!" he exclaimed, turning suddenly to the others. "It's Laura! The children's governess!"

"More correctly addressed, I think," said Hubert, smiling, "as Mrs. Jonas Beeson."

The woman violently refused first aid other than treatment of the open cut on her forehead, but agreed to be taken to the hospital in an ambulance, for which Hubert had telephoned. She proved her assertion about broken bones by sitting up, though not without much facial contortion. "It takes more than that to kill me," she said. "I was in a mill riot once and got beaten up worse than this. I was reporting for a Labor paper." She smiled, blew out a cloud of thin smoke, and glanced at the four with cool appraisal.

"She was your children's governess?" George asked Ed, as if he had not heard him aright.

"She was," replied Ed, grinning. "But she didn't have that snappy haircut then."

George looked at her with interest. In that light, he hesitated whether to call her a girl or a woman; he might have called her good-looking, but hardly pretty. Her face had character, George decided, and a hint, strangely, of something aristocratic. She was not unfeminine, but nevertheless somewhat youthful-masculine. Or perhaps it was merely her atrocious shingle-bob, and her air of despising feminine charm and rejecting masculine gallantry.

"What happened to you?" Hubert asked her.

"You people are clever," said the woman, "but you're lazy. You looked all over the top of the cliff and you looked all around the foot of the cliff, but you didn't look halfway down the cliff. And that's where these clothes and the gun were."

Hubert made an apologetic gesture. "We were expecting you to telephone us that information," he said. "We didn't expect you to do the work for us."

"You couldn't have found them, anyway," said the woman. "But I was a fool to try it. I slid more than halfway down that cliff. And if I hadn't landed in a patch of bush, I'd be there still—damned still! God knows how I ever got here; it was near dark when I came to. But I think you'll find Webber's fingerprints on that gun."

"I presume, Mrs. Beeson," said Hubert, "that you intend to testify for the State. Also that you have sufficient documentary evidence of your marriage, and that you intend to present your claims as an heir."

"Right you are. But I'll not bother you Randall Green folks," she said to Ed. "And I'll be reasonable if the Electric Company will."

"It's only proper to warn you," said Hubert, "that you yourself will be suspect in this case, and that you are entitled to consult a lawyer before talking to anyone."

"To hell with that!" she said, striving to sit up higher. "I'm going to make a statement, and what I say I'll stick to. Webber shot Klarsen, with Klarsen's gun."

"And who killed your husband?"

"Klarsen. Frank never killed a man in his life. But it was Frank got into your silo, and he saw the other chap giving Klarsen the documents he was after. So Frank hopped Klarsen's car and made him drive around into the ravine. Klarsen threw him off the car, and shot Frank in the head. Frank never knew what hit him, poor guy!"

"Frank took a shot at Klarsen, though. One of his bullets was found in Klarsen's car."

"Maybe so. Or maybe it was accidental."

"Well, then, who shot Frank Myers, or Beeson, from a distance of over a hundred yards?"

"No one. Frank died on the spot."

"Humph," said Hubert. "You say Webber shot Klarsen with Klarsen's gun. How did he get it away from him?"

"Klarsen started to pick up Frank. He tore off Frank's shirt and tied up his head. He laid his gun on the running-board of the car. Webber came out of the bushes and picked up Klarsen's gun. And shot Klarsen in the back—that's Webber for you!"

"Ah," said Hubert, turning to Mike, "there's your abdominal bullet. It went clear through Klarsen and into Beeson's body." Mike grinned and slapped his knee.

"You were watching all this from near by?" Hubert asked the woman.

"I was standing near, in the brush," she said, "waiting to help Frank if I could."

"Then," asked Hubert, "what did you do with the bodies?"

"Well, I was for putting Frank's body in our car—Webber's car, which was up by the quarry—and skipping out. But Webber said nothing doing on carrying a body in an open car. So I junked Webber's car over the cliff. Then I found that Webber had put Klarsen's body into Klarsen's rumble—he put on Klarsen's overcoat and gloves so's not to get any blood on himself—and I asked him, what the hell about poor Frank's body, for the rumble wouldn't hold two. Webber said there was a car parked by the barn here for the night that would be a cinch to steal. So we carried Frank's body up and put it in the rumble, and I tried to loosen the license plates, because Webber said I'd better change them along the road somewhere, because as soon as the owner missed his car he'd give the police the number and they'd radio it out. While I was doing that, my God! if the owner didn't come and take his car, and Frank's body with it!

"Well, Webber saw he'd messed the job, and he blames me for chucking the clothes over the cliff, and I said, why on earth did you strip the bodies, and then he blames it all on Frank. He picked up all the shells and dusted over the blood spots. He said he had a plan of some kind, but I think myself he was cuckoo.

"Well, if I'd got away with that other car I'd have headed due West, and I'd have given Frank a decent burial if I'd had to do it with my own hands. I never did have any use for Webber. I knew he was in it to trim us, and I was pretty sure he'd double-cross me the first chance he got. He had the papers he'd taken from Klarsen, and he said he was going to try to dispose of them quick, because it would be hard for us to use them unless we could explain how we got them. He said that if he did he would put me in touch with the parties and I could work with them, whatever that meant. Well, that didn't sound straight to me, but I thought I'd stick around and see what came of it. We were to separate and I was to 'phone him at his hotel when I found a place to stay.

"He was going to drop me at an inter-urban station, but we nearly ran down a cop, and Webber got scared and stepped on the gas. That was after he'd changed the license plates. But Webber said we'd better ditch the car at the first chance, so he drove hell-bent looking for a good place."

"Just a minute," said Hubert. "Did you stop at a big house in Petunkawoc?"

"Petunkawoc?" she asked. "That's the swell town, with the lawns and gates, isn't it?"

"Yes."

"No. We didn't stop till we got to Dugan's Grove."

"Your pistol was found in the Clifford place, in the zoo."

"Oh, that," said she, laughing. "I got quite a kick out of that when I read it in the papers. I had Frank's gun, and I thought if we were stopped they might frisk us. So I threw it out as we were going around a curve, where there were thick woods, and it went a long way. I suppose I threw it into the zoo."

Mike looked at George and grinned. "Clifford's out," he commented.

"Well," continued the woman, "we got to Dugan's Grove, and passed the roadhouse. Webber stopped by the roadside and said he was going to see if a man he knew was there, and if not, to telephone, and he parked in a dark place and told me to wait for him. I was nervous as hell waiting, and I got out. Well, a fella bumps my fender, and begins to bawl out. When he went away, I got into the car and stepped on it. I came to the lake and drove the car into it; tried to get the top down and couldn't. I put on Klarsen's shoes, found a canoe, and shoved off. There was no paddle, but I got a pole, and there was a stiff wind offshore that blew me across the lake. Then I poled my way along the shore, chucked the canoe in the woods, and legged it to a railroad and rode a box car into town. That's old stuff to me." She grinned at their astonishment.

"Where did you first meet Myers, or Beeson?" asked Hubert.

"Out West. I've been all over the country. Frank used to be top hand on a big ranch. First-class puncher. Got out of a job, tried rodeos, but was getting too old. Frank was a good guy and a square shooter. No ambition, though. He might have been rich. It was me put him up to claim his estate. We were married five years ago. Then this crook Webber got hold of Frank. A hot lawyer he is! I was the one who had the idea for getting the stuff to identify Frank. I found out where it was, but it was always locked up. But Frank said that wouldn't stop him. Then it seems the stuff has been put somewhere else. But you've done the job for me, better than I could; and, gentlemen, I thank you!"

"Well, Mrs. Beeson," said Hubert, filling his pipe, "we thank you in return. I'm certain we should never have got to the bottom of this without your assistance. And if the gun you brought bears Webber's finger-prints, that will help considerably. But he's a sharp chap, and he'll no doubt make countercharges against you. So look out for yourself."

"One thing I yearn to know," said Ed caustically, "is where you got those references you gave us. They were swell, and Mrs. Marsh looked up every one of them."

"Don't get snooty, you big yap!" cried the woman furiously. "My folks owned niggers when yours were hoeing potatoes!"

XXIX

THE MICA

Mike Macy accepted with equanimity the fact that the morning papers got the break on the story of Mrs. Jonas Beeson, Jr., *alias* Laura Brayman (a friend whose name as well as whose references she had borrowed) and *née* Crystal Verree, of an old Virginia family, as officially recorded on a wedding certificate which she produced. Mike's story was much fuller than the others and contained several columns of exclusive matter.

Ed also accepted philosophically the fact that DYL opened ten points down from its previous close, for he had taken his twelve points profit the day before. He had hoped to sell it short in the morning, but prudently refrained.

The case for the State received a setback in the morning when Hubert discovered that, either because Webber had wiped them off or because they had become obliterated by the rough handling they had received from the woman, the hoped-for finger-prints were not on Klarsen's gun. There was therefore no evidence, aside from Mrs. Beeson's, that Webber had ever set foot within twenty miles of Westwood, although admittedly he was the Beesons' attorney. Naturally he denied vigorously having been there, and pointed out the likely motive that Mrs. Beeson had for killing the man who had shot her husband.

George and Hubert went over to the hill again in the afternoon, this time with a long stout rope. With one end of this tied around him, and the other tied around a big tree, George climbed down the cliff on all sides and explored it, bringing up the remainder of Beeson's and Klarsen's clothes, and armfuls of price books, data in binders, and other paraphernalia belonging to Klarsen and taken from his car; but nothing, not even Klarsen's watch and cigarette lighter, bore Webber's finger-prints.

Then it was that George had the brilliant idea that saved the case from collapse.

"The mica!" he exclaimed to Hubert.

Hubert looked at George steadily for a minute.

"My boy," he said, "you'd make a first-class detective. We'll examine every piece of mica there is on the hill!"

They took two hatfuls of pieces of mica over to the barn, and Hubert spent an hour and a half dusting them for finger-prints. It appeared that the bits of mica—particularly the black mica—were irresistible to the idle curiosity of visitors to the hill. Moreover, the chips had a tendency to flake, thus exposing a fresh and highly polished surface to each impression. Among the many unknown finger-prints that they revealed, they found several of Beeson's, one of the woman's, and two of Webber's, including one fine piece bearing the prints of all three!

This evidence, however, proved only that Webber had lied, and had in fact been on the scene. It came down ultimately to pretty much a question of veracity between Webber and the woman; and the jury believed the woman. She let her hair grow, put on a smart tailored suit at the trial, and made a good impression. The jury gave Webber first-degree murder, but he at once appealed. The judge who tried him for forgery and grand larceny, however, gave him the limit, and he had to take it.

Crystal Verree Beeson was hot stuff for the tabloids, and she fed them all they would take. She was featured as the heiress of the Beeson acres, and Randall Green shivered for a couple of months. But things looked bad for her at one point of the trial, and the Electric Company attorneys got very busy and slapped down fifty thousand dollars, and she took it, after signing all kinds of documents renouncing all rights whatever, which she did have or might or may have had, in every way, shape, or manner, to everything that old Jonas Beeson had ever owned, including Randall Green; Hugh saw to that. She talked demurely to reporters and signed a fat contract for the serial rights of her story—and it wasn't ghost writing, either. She had offers from movie producers, talked for the newsreels on what life meant to her, and had hundreds of letters from unknown men offering her their hearts and hands in the holy bonds of matrimony.

Ed tried to make Hubert take a fifty-fifty split on his profits in DYL, but the old gentleman's notions of professional etiquette were shocked at the suggestion. He agreed, however, to take a long hunting trip later at Ed's expense. They did this, and Ed brought home some trophies for the barn.

It was on this trip that Ed visited Hubert for several days. He told George about it. Amelia, South Dakota, according to Ed's estimate, was a town of about two hundred population, and Hubert owned the town. Hubert was sheriff for life, and knew every man, woman, and child by first name.

"How the folks been behaving?" Hubert asked the station-master as Hubert and Ed got off the train on their return from the trip.

"Fine, Gil, fine," said the station-master. "Ain't been a shootin', or no drunks, or scandal, sence you bin away." He gave Ed a large wink.

A neighbor of Hubert's drove them in his car to Hubert's house, a stout little bungalow on a wooded hill, with a magnificent view. Hubert had a man about the house who served good hearty meals, his idea of breakfast being fruit, oatmeal, ham and eggs, flapjacks, coffee, and enough pie, doughnuts, and bread and jam to fill in any chinks that might be left.

What impressed Ed most was Hubert's medals and diplomas and letters from people in *Who's Who*. "Some boy, he is," said Ed to George. "Gifts from crowned heads, signed photographs, fancy saddles, decorated guns, gold-plated pistols, and no end of junk. Medals from Congress and foreign nations. But the thing that interested me most," declared Ed, "was an old sheepskin of resolutions of thanks for something, all in French. I found it rolled up in a bottom drawer, all dusty. It was addressed to Hippolyte Achille Guillaumin-Hubert, Chevalier de What's This and Who's That. Gil looked kind of foolish when I pulled it out."

"For Heaven's sake!" Ed had exclaimed. "Is all that you?"

"My father was a Frenchman," said Hubert. "My mother was a German. They came from Alsace."

"Were you born there?" asked Ed.

"No," said Hubert. "I was born in Switzerland."

"Well, well," said Ed. "What nationality are you, then?"

"American," said Hubert, a bit curtly.

"Right-o," said Ed, rolling up the sheepskin. "And so was Klarsen," he added meditatively.

George asked Ed whether Klarsen had left anything to relatives.

"No," said Ed. "Hugh said all Klarsen left was forty-seven thousand dollars on salary account that was standing to his credit on the Company's books when he died. He left that to be divided between two buddies of his, disabled vets."

"A man's man," commented George.

"A man," was Ed's epitaph.

AFTERWORD

AFTERWORD

David Chinitz

THE POP ADVENTURES OF
HENRY WARE ELIOT, JR.'S
FAMOUS YOUNGER BROTHER

"For what is the sensibility of our age?" asked the influential literary critic Cleanth Brooks in 1947. "Is there any one sensibility? Do we respond to T. S. Eliot, Dashiell Hammett, Mary Roberts Rinehart, or Tiffany Thayer?"[1] To Brooks, Henry Ware Eliot's brother stood at one cultural pole, while Hammett, Rinehart—sometimes called "the American Agatha Christie"—and romance author Thayer stood at the other. Brooks was hardly alone. The art critic Clement Greenberg began his important 1946 essay "Avant-Garde and Kitsch" by noting the seeming paradox that "One and the same civilization produces simultaneously two such different things as a poem by T. S. Eliot and a Tin Pan Alley song."[2] Mystery novels and popular songs—these were cultural trash, catering to the vulgarity and mental laziness of twentieth-century audiences. T. S. Eliot, in contrast, was a shining symbol of the opposite of "kitsch": he stood for the pure high art that critics feared was threatened by the overwhelming popularity of mass culture. How ironic, then, that early jazz had been one of the crucial early influences

---

[1] Cleanth Brooks, *The Well Wrought Urn: Studies in the Structure of Poetry* (New York: Harcourt, 1947), 232.

[2] Clement Greenberg, "Avant-Garde and Kitsch," *Partisan Review* 6 (1939), 34.

on Eliot's poetic style, and that Eliot himself loved the same detective fiction whose implacable enemy he was supposed to be!

Eliot had never hidden his keen interest in mysteries, both classical (Edgar Allan Poe, Wilkie Collins) and contemporary (Raymond Chandler, Peter Cheyney). His friends regarded his devotion to the genre as an almost comical personal oddity; serious-minded cultural critics preferred to ignore it. But Eliot was proud of his encyclopedic mastery of Sherlockiana and was not ashamed to declare in the 25th-anniversary report of his Harvard graduating class, "I like detective stories but especially the adventures of Arsène Lupin"—the gentleman-burglar of Maurice Leblanc's French detective novels.[3] Nor was he a latecomer to the genre, for Eliot had publically declared his enthusiasm as early as 1927. In an article in the *Criterion,* the literary quarterly he founded and edited, he appeared to sense that detective fiction was in the midst of a "Golden Age." Normally a pessimist who was always prepared to notice signs of cultural decline, Eliot here was pleased to see that the expanding market for "thrillers" was "producing a different, and as I think a superior type of detective story."[4] He personally reviewed twenty-four mysteries and two nonfiction works on the subject of murder in the 1927 *Criterion,* and in one review he attempted to set down some "general rules of detective technique" to which the best fiction adhered. Although many similar sets of rules would be published, including the well-known "Ten Commandments" of Ronald Knox (1929), Eliot's list may be the earliest of them all as well as the only one not contributed by a professional novelist:[5]

> The story must not rely upon elaborate and incredible disguises. . . . Disguises must be only occasional and incidental.

---

[3] "Autobiographical Note: *Harvard College Class of 1910,*" in *The Complete Prose of T. S. Eliot,* ed. Ronald Schuchard et al., 8 vols. (Baltimore: Johns Hopkins University Press, 2014–forthcoming), vol. 5.

[4] "Homage to Wilkie Collins," in *Complete Prose,* 4:14.

[5] Michele Tepper, "T. S. Eliot and the Modernism of Detective Fiction," American Literature Association Conference (Baltimore, 23 May 1997), 10–11.

The character and motives of the criminal should be normal. In the ideal detective story we should feel that we have a sporting chance to solve the mystery ourselves; if the criminal is highly abnormal an irrational element is introduced which offends us.

The story must not rely either upon occult phenomena or, which comes to the same thing, upon mysterious and preposterous discoveries made by lonely scientists.

Elaborate and bizarre machinery is an irrelevance. . . . Writers who delight in treasures hid in strange places, ciphers and codes, runes and rituals, should not be encouraged.

The detective should be highly intelligent, but not superhuman. We should be able to follow his inferences and almost, but not quite, make them with him.[6]

Each of these principles is elaborated in a short paragraph. As Curtis Evans observes:

Eliot's strictures emphasize the importance of maintaining "fair play" ("we should feel that we have a sporting chance of solving the mystery ourselves"). To do this, Eliot advocates a prohibition on outré devices. . . . Testing the nine mystery works in his review essay against these rules, Eliot concluded that of them R. Austin Freeman's *The D'Arblay Mystery* was "the most perfect in form" (despite one violation).[7]

Though the literary critics who campaigned for Eliot's experimental and intellectually challenging poetry made little of his occasional writings on detective fiction, other fans of the mystery genre took note

---

[6] Eliot, "Homage to Wilkie Collins," 15–16.

[7] Curtis Evans, "Murder in *The Criterion*: T. S. Eliot on Detective Fiction," in *Mysteries Unlocked: Essays in Honor of Douglas G. Greene*, ed. Curtis Evans (Jefferson, NC: McFarland, 2014), 173.

of "the considerable cachet of his intellectual blessing," as Evans puts it.[8] Indeed, Eliot's name was often invoked alongside those of Franklin Roosevelt, Woodrow Wilson, and André Gide by educated fans of detective fiction seeking to legitimize their own taste.

Eliot's writings on high art and popular culture show that he—unlike many of those who revered his poetry—regarded their relations as friendly. "[F]ine art," he wrote in 1923, "is the *refinement*, not the antithesis, of popular art," adding that to treat them as antagonists had "dangerous consequences" for culture.[9] The hazard he foresees becomes clear in a 1927 essay titled "Wilkie Collins and Dickens." Here, amid serious discussion of *The Moonstone*, which he calls "the first and greatest of English detective novels,"[10] Eliot argues that readers should not have to choose between well-crafted, intelligent fiction on the one hand, and exciting action, high drama, and strong emotion on the other. When he refers to these last qualities as "melodrama," he means no disrespect to them. Far from being inimical to great art, melodrama is a vital constituent of it, and for the "serious" novelists of his time to dismiss this element is a grave mistake. Looking back to the 19th century—which, in 1927, was not so very far in the past—Eliot observes that "such terms as 'high-brow fiction,' 'thrillers' and 'detective fiction'" had yet to be "invented." In the age of Collins and Dickens, neither readers nor writers perceived any opposition between "literature" and "thrillers"; in fact, "there was no such distinction":

> The best novels *were* thrilling; the distinction of genre between such-and-such a profound "psychological" novel of today and such-and-such a masterly "detective" novel of today is greater than the distinction of genre between *Wuthering Heights*, or even *The Mill on the Floss*, and *East Lynne*.[11]

---

[8] Ibid., 172.

[9] "Marianne Moore," in *Complete Prose*, 2:495–96.

[10] Eliot would write the introduction to a new edition of *The Moonstone* the following year; see *Complete Prose* 3:356–63.

[11] "Wilkie Collins and Dickens," in *Complete Prose*, 3:164. In other words, 19th-century works that we now regard as literary classics were relatively close cousins of "sensation novels" like Ellen Wood's *East Lynne*. The gap between serious fiction

The literary fiction of his own time risks being "dull," Eliot charges, as it abandons melodrama to the commercial novel. And he predicts, "If we cannot get this satisfaction out of what the publishers present as 'literature,' then we will read—with less and less pretense of concealment—what we call 'thrillers.'"[12] Thirty-five years later Eliot would confess, or perhaps boast, that he had read no "'serious' prose fiction" since around the time of this essay. What he *did* read, with little pretense of concealment, we have already seen. It was at just this moment that he began to review detective fiction in the *Criterion*.[13]

To be sure, Eliot's interest in popular art extended beyond detective fiction. His attraction to American vaudeville, English music-hall comedy, popular song, comic strips, and even crossword puzzles had an essential influence on his creativity and his career. None of this is to deny that his poetry, especially early on, was dense, allusive, intellectual, and, in a word he himself used, "difficult." Even so, his art was productively engaged with popular culture in some form at every stage of his life. Only with this recognition can we account for the fact that Eliot devoted almost the entire creative effort of his last 30 years to an effort to develop a popular verse drama. The attempt was an embarrassment to his supporters, who were never more uncomfortable than when Eliot appeared to be succeeding, and particularly in 1950, when *The Cocktail Party*, starring Alec Guinness on Broadway and Rex Harrison in London, became one of the year's hit plays. It was as a critic and as a poet, in the traditional sense, that Eliot had made his considerable reputation; why did he not simply remain, in that same sense, a poet? Just as the "serious" novel appeared moribund to Eliot if it could not close the gap with popular fiction, he thought that poetry, too, needed to take a form that could speak to and entertain a "large and miscellaneous" (i.e., diverse) audience. The theater, he imagined, might be "the best place in which to do this." By working in a popular

---

and popular fiction had widened considerably by Eliot's day. To take another example, Dickens is now treated as an English classic, but in his own time he was an extraordinary popular author. The same, of course, may be said of Shakespeare, the most popular playwright of his era.

[12] Ibid., 170, 164.

[13] Igor Stravinsky, "Memories of T. S. Eliot. *Esquire* (Aug. 1965), 92.

genre, Eliot speculated, the poet might win the opportunity to engage
with a substantial public, and, in this way, claim "some direct social
utility."[14]

Maybe it should not surprise us, then, to find Eliot incorporating
popular elements even in such high-flown work as his poetic drama
about the martyrdom of the twelfth-century prelate St. Thomas Becket.
Written in 1935 and still generally regarded as Eliot's best play, *Murder
in the Cathedral* nods more than once at detective fiction, beginning
with its title, which won out over such contenders as "The Archbishop
Murder Case" and "Fear in the Way." Late in the action, one of the
four knights who have stabbed Becket to death attempts to recast the
assassination as a murder mystery: "What I have to say may be put in
the form of a question: *Who killed the Archbishop?*"[15] Deploying facts
and deduction like a skilled detective, he builds his case that the crime
he and his accomplices just committed in full view of the audience was
actually perpetrated by their victim: what appears to have been a homicide was really a suicide. Eliot even interpolated several lines from
Conan Doyle's "The Musgrave Ritual" into the dialogue, where they
passed unnoticed for years. In spite of these detective-fiction elements,
the play's overall effect is far more liturgical than melodramatic. Lit-
urgy, however, is not necessarily highbrow: Eliot recognized religious
ritual as a communal activity and thus as a form of popular culture. In
its language and rhythms, and arguably even in its structure, the play
approaches the poetry of the church service, a cultural form no less
familiar to contemporary audiences than, say, jazz or "thrillers."

The influence of detective fiction remains visible in Eliot's plays
after *Murder in the Cathedral*. Wishwood, the isolated old country
house in *The Family Reunion*, furnishes just the proper scene for a
murder mystery, and it is peopled, as the biographer Lyndall Gordon
points out, by "aunts and uncles . . . out of English detective fiction
from Conan Doyle to Agatha Christie: the old buffer of the club, the retired Indian army officer, the spinster of the vicar's teas."[16] Although,

---

[14] *The Use of Poetry and the Use of Criticism*, in *Complete Prose*, 4:690–91.

[15] Eliot, *Complete Poems and Plays, 1909–1950* (New York: Harcourt, 1980), 218.

[16] *T. S. Eliot: An Imperfect Life* (New York: Norton, 1999), 326.

when the play opens, the protagonist Harry's murder of his wife has already occurred—if (for that is part of the mystery) it occurred at all—Eliot is still clearly drawing on the traditions of crime fiction. His most popular play, *The Cocktail Party*, begins with two mysteries: Edward's wife, Lavinia, has inexplicably disappeared just before a party they had planned together, leaving him to host it alone and to make awkward excuses for her absence; and one of the guests is a complete and rather enigmatic stranger. This "Unidentified Guest" later turns out to be something of a psychologist, something of a priest, and something of a private investigator. (Two of the other guests, who had appeared to be merely friends of the central couple, are actually, in a way, his snoops.) The detective element persists in Eliot's final plays as well. *The Confidential Clerk* features multiple puzzles of parental identity and a twisting series of Poirotian revelations in the final scene, while *The Elder Statesman* gradually exposes the dark secrets of a prominent man's checkered past. These deployments of mystery conventions perhaps do not run very deep, but it seems clear that Eliot saw them as a way of maintaining the necessary melodrama or thriller interest in his plays, as his essay on Wilkie Collins and Dickens had advocated years before.

In 1957, at age 69, Eliot married his second wife, Valerie, who was only 30. I was fortunate to meet her once, in 2004, for about three minutes at a reception. This was not the appropriate occasion for an interview, but, since I knew I'd probably never get another chance, there was one question I wanted to be sure to ask her. "Mrs. Eliot," I said, "I've heard that your husband wrote a mystery novel and published it under another name. Is that true?" For a few seconds she looked flustered, and I wondered whether it was because this rumor was completely implausible to her or because the secret had been found out. But in a moment she rallied and replied, with a smile, "I suppose that will have to remain a mystery, won't it?" For me it remains a mystery to this day.

COACHWHIP PUBLICATIONS
COACHWHIPBOOKS.COM

COACHWHIP PUBLICATIONS
COACHWHIPBOOKS.COM

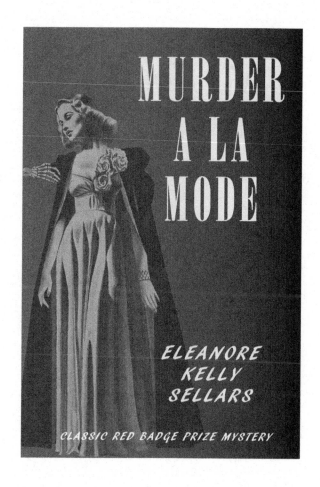

COACHWHIP PUBLICATIONS
COACHWHIPBOOKS.COM

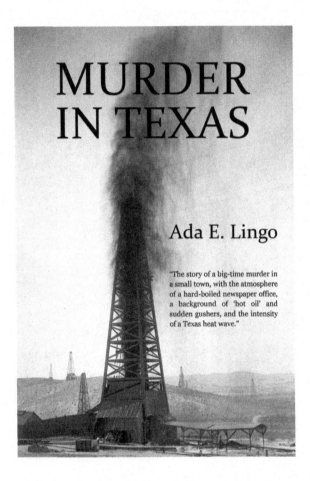

MURDER
IN TEXAS

Ada E. Lingo

"The story of a big-time murder in
a small town, with the atmosphere
of a hard-boiled newspaper office,
a background of 'hot oil' and
sudden gushers, and the intensity
of a Texas heat wave."

COACHWHIP PUBLICATIONS
COACHWHIPBOOKS.COM

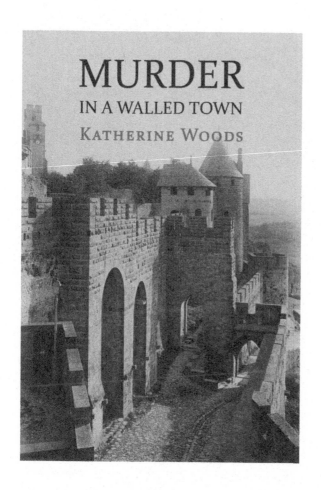

MURDER

IN A WALLED TOWN

KATHERINE WOODS

COACHWHIP PUBLICATIONS
COACHWHIPBOOKS.COM

ANITA BOUTELL

DEATH BRINGS
A STORKE

CRADLED
IN FEAR

COACHWHIP PUBLICATIONS
COACHWHIPBOOKS.COM

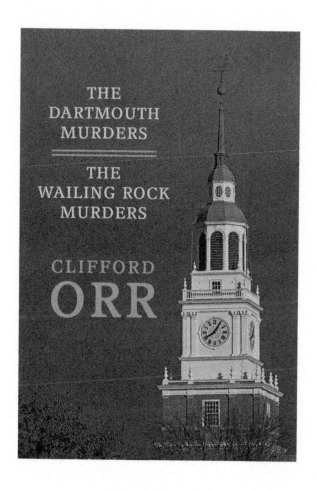

THE
DARTMOUTH
MURDERS

THE
WAILING ROCK
MURDERS

CLIFFORD
ORR

COACHWHIP PUBLICATIONS
COACHWHIPBOOKS.COM

LOUIS F. BOOTH

THE BANK VAULT MYSTERY

BROKERS' END

COACHWHIP PUBLICATIONS
COACHWHIPBOOKS.COM

VULTURES
IN THE SKY
A HUGH RENNERT MYSTERY

TODD DOWNING

CPSIA information can be obtained
at www.ICGtesting.com
Printed in the USA
BVOW04s1051300417
482749BV00001B/181/P